Taboo

FORBIDDEN FANTASIES FOR COUPLES

Taboo

Forbidden Fantasies for Couples

Edited by

Violet Blue

CLEIS
PRESS

Published in the United States by Cleis Press Inc., P.O. Box 14684, San Francisco, California 94114.

Printed in the United States.
Cover design: Scott Idleman
Cover photograph: Thinkstock
Text design: Frank Wiedemann
Logo art: Juana Alicia
First Edition.
10 9 8 7 6 5 4 3 2

Acknowledgments

Taboos are wonderful for so many reasons. I had no idea when I began this project that all the really important people in my life are dedicated to exploring (and sometimes exploding) sexual and cultural taboos. I am very lucky, and grateful to be surrounded by so many inquisitive, fearless, and loving people. Thank you, friends and colleagues.

Cleis Press knows a good taboo worth breaking when they see it. Huge thanks to Felice Newman and Frédérique Delacoste. The fun has only begun.

Survival Research Laboratories is my family. Love and thanks to my closest family member, Mark Pauline.

My dearest friends: Thomas Roche and Alison Tyler. Thank you for everything.

There is a man who loves me. Courtney, thank you for everything you do, *Uz jzme doma.*

Contents

Introduction: Delirium, Danger, and Connoisseurs of Desire

The human mind is an incredible thing. We still barely understand how sight really works, let alone how an image or idea can instantly blossom into arousal, desire, need—especially when that idea courts the forbidden. When what we desire is taboo.

Whole libraries have been filled with books attempting to explain the psychological basis of our attraction to sexual taboos. But not this one. *Taboo* will feed you erotic stories of forbidden desire like fingerfuls of warm chocolate, dripping onto your tongue, and coaxing from your lips words of sexual delirium, erotic danger, and sweetly explicit detail.

Here are twenty-two superbly written, brand-new short stories featuring couples who want it so bad they can taste it—and they do, over and over again. Old pros, such as M. Christian, Thomas S. Roche, and Alison Tyler, rub elbows with highly talented newcomers, such as Donna George Storey, P.

S. Haven, Saskia Walker, and many others, to present stories of couples who make their most taboo erotic fantasies come true. I've worked closely with each of these authors to ensure that every detail is realistic, each taboo is stunningly wicked (yet entirely possible to re-create in real life), and to guarantee the sex you'll read about here offers some of the hottest encounters you'll find in print.

These stories are intended not only for the sublime satisfaction of solitary reading. They follow in the tradition of *Sweet Life 1* and *Sweet Life 2*, anthologies of erotic fantasies for couples that encourage readers to "try *this* at home." *Taboo* takes the fantasies even further, into the realm of the forbidden, an oft-voiced request from readers who regularly deluge my inbox with email. Everyone wants more fantasies, yes, but with more daring, more edginess, a bit more danger mixed with desire, though still safe enough to try at home—and in an assortment of other creative settings. (In fact, *The Ultimate Guide to Sexual Fantasies,* my next effort in Cleis' *Ultimate Guides* series, was written just to help readers make those fantasies come true with wet, sweet, and sticky success .)

Take for example Alison Tyler's "You Can't Always Get What You Want," in which a couple's long-distance separation brings their kinky fantasies to the boiling point, culminating in a public encounter sure to shock and arouse.

Dexter Cunningham's "Old Friends" turns a common fantasy on its head: a husband hopes to join his wife and her visiting schoolmate in a threesome, but what the women have in mind goes far beyond his expectations. In Ayre Riley's "The Fifth Day," a sexy housewife has her husband's blessing to seduce a handsome housepainter, but then is dealt a surprise that gives her—and our—fantasies a very postmodern twist.

Some fantasies of sexual taboo are not for the faint of heart; they are carefully laid traps that slam our forbidden fantasies up against pure, unfettered lust. In Erica Dumas' "Dress Me Up," a woman in an elegant restaurant is compelled to enter a situation rife with rough sex and public humiliation. Skye Black's "Medical Attention" goes far beyond feet-in-the-stirrups doctor's office fantasies (and even the doctor-nurse story "After Hours," by Dante Davidson, twists the rules of medical ethics in a fresh new way). In Thomas S. Roche's "Cocked and Loaded," what begins with a day at the shooting range climaxes at home when dominance and submission become the target for a couple who get off on intense edge play.

Welcome to *Taboo*. The couples whose deepest, darkest, sweetest, and naughtiest fantasies are played out within these pages are committed to each other without question. They push the limits of sex, lust, and fantasy as far as they can to please each other and get off together. I find each of these stories to be remarkable. They offer hot and very explicit sex, loving couples, realistic details, distinctive and unforgettable writing, and a full menu of taboos where no one is hurt, exploited, or in danger, and everyone gets off. These stories have become a personal source of prime fantasy material for me. I hope *Taboo* inspires you, too.

Violet Blue
San Francisco
February 2004

You Can't Always Get What You Want
Alison Tyler

Trust me. You can't. At least, not when what you want is a firm and powerful over-the-knee spanking from your deliciously strict boyfriend, and he's half a world away from you in a place you'd never heard of before he announced he was about to leave.

"Georgia," you said when he broke the news. "That's not so bad. I can visit."

"No, not *Georgia*—Georgia," he told you, smiling without being condescending in the least, without saying, "What the *fuck*, baby? Did you sleep through geography class?" Instead, he petted your dark hair and kissed your soft lips and said, "Not Georgia-Georgia, but Tbilisi. Kazakhstan. Azerbaijan. Turkmenistan. Former Soviet Union. *That* Georgia."

And you blushed a rosy pink and tossed your glossy dark hair and said, "Oh, right. *That* Georgia." As if you knew all along—but you didn't. (Though suddenly that line about

Georgia from "Back in the USSR" made sense.)

So no, you can't always get what you want. Because when your man is somewhere you've never heard of, and you're all by yourself in an apartment that seems much too large, what you want seems as far away as he is. Add in the fact that all you can get is phone sex disturbed by constant static and an air of confusion between the two of you because what's "night" to you is "day" to him, and vice versa.

"Come on," you said, yearning for release, "please Sam, please tell me what you'd do if I were there."

"Baby, I'm at work. You have to call me later. Call me tonight and I promise I'll take care of you."

"It is tonight," you insisted. "It is very tonight, Sam." The sky was dark outside your window. You tried to imagine him beneath a sunlit blue sky.

"Then call me tomorrow—"

Sometimes, you can't even get what you need, when what you need and what you want vie for attention in your head until you are nearly crazy with desire, constantly shifting, moving your body to find a comfortable position that has eluded you for the four months, three weeks, and six days since he left. Nothing is comfortable, because your ass isn't freshly spanked and your pussy hasn't been sweetly fucked, and you haven't given a blow job that lasted until your jaw ached. Comfortable is no longer comfortable.

With your eyes shut, you fiercely tried to get yourself off.

Christ, kid, you knew how to masturbate before you met him. Why couldn't you do it now? There should be no difference. Your fingers still made those lulling circles. Your vibrator still used two C batteries. Your stash of porn rested in its special place, in a floral hatbox under your bed. What was the problem?

You needed him.

You wanted him.

You craved him.

But phone calls to Tbilisi cost more than twelve dollars a minute, and you agreed that you would only talk occasionally, using email the rest of the time. When you made that plan, you didn't know that email hadn't come to his job site. So you broke down and made a few phone calls, and those became marathon sessions in which you confessed that you might actually be losing it here.

Because here's the thing—when it costs twelve dollars a minute to talk, it's difficult to relax enough to get off. And when you *can* forget the cost, crashed out on your bed after several stiff drinks, touching yourself as you beg him to tell you what he so desperately wants to do to you when he gets back in town, well, it's lunchtime for him—so you can see how that might pose a problem.

"Please," you begged. "Christ, Sam, tell me—"

"You know, baby. I'd give you the spanking of your life."

"Tell me more."

"Your red ass growing redder by the second."

"Oh, yes—"

"And…. Oh, shit, baby. The other line is beeping."

"Ignore it."

"Could be work."

But it never is. The other line is always for his roommate, whose name is something like Zeno or Zero or Zorro, and whenever *he* gets on the phone, he refuses to get off. So you can't get what you want—which is uninterrupted phone sex.

3

And your man can't get what he *needs*, which is uninterrupted sleep, because bands of starving dogs roam the streets, and thugs with machine guns find it amusing to demolish Pepsi cans with their ammo, and happy drunks—after running out of friends and family to toast—noisily exit the bars to toast the local trees.

By the time Sam arrived back in the states, he'd lost fifteen pounds, a bit of his sanity, and every last ounce of willpower. He'd promised you from a pay phone during a stopover at the airport in New York City that he was going to do two things before you even left the airport: fuck your ass, and spank your bottom until it was raw and red and cherry-perfect. You couldn't have been more excited to have both of those things happen.

Finally, you were going to get what you wanted! He was going to quick-step you back to the truck and take care of you in the way you'd been dreaming of for months now. But when Sam walked up the ramp, everything changed. He didn't smile. He didn't kiss you. He grabbed your hand and dragged you outside, into the muggy Los Angeles air. He chose a spot behind a pillar, where a concrete planter was half-filled with dying flowers. He set down his huge camping-style backpack filled with all of his possessions from his trip, filled with everything he hadn't given away to people who needed things more than he did, if you want to talk just a little bit about "need"—and he sat down on the edge of the planter, hauled you over his lap and lifted your silly little Catholic schoolgirl skirt that you'd thought he'd find so sexy. While taxis vied for curb space, he pulled your white panties down your thighs and began to punish your ass for you right there, on the cigarette butt-littered sidewalk of LAX. And you thought for about half a second that you were in public with your bare-naked ass showing, and you thought for another half a second that someone was going to call the police or that people were going to complain.

And then Sam wrapped his hand in your hair and pushed your head down and continued to spank your ass in rapid, smarting strokes until you forgot to think about anything except the pain flaring through you and the fact that you'd been longing for a real spanking, not a pat-a-cake spanking, but a real, serious spanking for what felt like ever.

Still, you had some sense of decorum left in you, and you said, "Sam, the truck's just over—"

"Bad girls get punished in public all the time," Sam hissed, interrupting you. "Nobody says anything about it. Why should anyone say anything about you? Besides, people see worse every day in Los Angeles."

And you supposed he was right, because nobody did anything. Yes, you were behind a pillar, but only barely. Anyone could see if they thought to look. People walked right on by as his hand continued to spank you, over and over again, marking you, bruising your pale skin, and somehow you just forgot about yourself, about your need to be refined and present a certain appearance to the world. You'd wanted this feeling of surrender for months, and you gave in to the sensation, so that you actually came when his fingers spanked between your cheeks to touch your pussy. And then, after letting you vibrate for several seconds with the climax, Sam thrust you off his lap, grabbed his overstuffed backpack and said, "Where's the truck?"

You tried to pull up your panties, but Sam shook his head.

"Leave them."

"What?"

"Step out of them and leave them."

And despite thoughts of littering and being disrespectful to the earth, you still couldn't be disrespectful to Sam, so you stepped out of your panties and looked down at the shiny blue silk you were about to discard as Sam repeated, "Where's the truck?"

You were turned around, your head all happily hazy, and you had to think for a moment before nodding toward the structure across the street. Sam led, even though he didn't know where you'd parked, but in moments you'd found the red truck, all shiny from a recent detail job, and the two of you got in the back, where you'd put a blanket out, thinking that this might actually happen.

Now that he'd spanked you while pedestrians and commuters could see, you felt much less worried as he pushed your skirt up to your hips, reached for the lube you'd also put out in the truck bed, and began oiling up your asshole for you. His pants were open and his cock was out, and you watched over your shoulder as he jacked himself with another handful of the lube.

"Take your skirt all the way off."

With fumbling fingers you searched for the zip, then heard a rip as Sam "took" the skirt off for you. Then his weight was on top of you, pushing you down, and you felt his firm hands parting your asscheeks, felt his cock press forward and then thrust in. You screamed, but the sound was muffled by the blanket. You thought of the fact that you'd circled for half an hour before finding this out-of-the-way corner of the parking structure, but, still, anyone walking back here would see you rutting together—and that maybe that was something that you both wanted and needed to know.

He fucked your ass the way he always did, with his fingers gripping your waist and his mouth finding the ridge of your shoulder through your sheer white top, biting you hard as he fucked you harder. You sensed when he was going to come, and you slid your own hand down under your body and thought about all the times you'd tried to get off while he was gone, unable to talk him to orgasm, unable to reach one yourself. You thought about wants and needs and desires. Your finger tricked over your pulsing, swollen clit, and you thought about the thugs with machine guns still roaming the streets and you wondered if anyone was ever able to come in Tbilisi. But that didn't matter, right? All that mattered was that you and Sam were about to come, right now, in the back of your 4X4, and that he was going to fill your asshole with his seed so that it would slowly seep out of you over the next few hours, and that when you got back to the privacy of your apartment, much kinkier things were going to happen to you. That was for sure.

And then he came, and you came, and you rolled over and looked at him, love in your eyes, before you each wiped off on the blanket and you did your best to put your skirt back together, but failed.

In order to leave the parking lot, you had to hand over your ticket and pay for the time spent. The man in the tiny booth looked at the two of you. Sam had been up for more than twenty-six hours. You no longer had on a skirt or panties.

"Pleasant trip?" he asked.

Pleasant trip. The words echoed in your head. He'd

been gone too long. That's what had happened. That's what had gotten you to this point. A crazy, uncaring point. He'd gone to a place where drunken men toasted trees, where his roommate—Zero? Zorro? Zeno?—barked at you when you called too late, where email didn't exist, where neither of you could come.

Pleasant trip.

You couldn't hold up the line in traffic explaining to this man that *pleasant* wasn't quite the right word, but Sam just laughed. "Not this time," he said.

And the ticket taker laughed back and said, "Well, you can't always get what you want."

You couldn't believe it, couldn't believe he was so accurately putting into words what you'd thought about for months, but Sam just nodded as you pulled the truck out onto the busy L.A. thoroughfare, as if he couldn't agree more.

"But if you try sometimes—" you started to say.

Sam finished it up for you with his standard, trademark sinful smile: "You just might get what you need."

Richard's Secret

SASKIA WALKER

"A gimp?" Richard was a sex slave? Could it be possible? I swallowed, breathed deep and tried to make sense of what Tom had just told me. "But what does it mean…?" I looked up at him, spluttering the words out. "I mean, I know what it means…I just don't know what he means by it, by approaching us."

Tom rested his hand reassuringly on my shoulder. There was a look of deep concern in his eyes and he was watching me carefully for my reactions. Oh, how I loved this man; when he had said he had something "a bit heavy" to talk to me about, I thought the worst was about to happen, that he was going to say there was another woman, that he was leaving me. The last thing I expected was for him to reveal this, Richard's secret. Richard's darkest secret.

I had actually known Richard longer than I had Tom. He had been working in the international trade department when

I was transferred to the London branch, about six years earlier. Admittedly he was the dark horse in the department, and the office gossips plagued him with questions about his private life, all of which he managed to avoid and dismiss without being in the least bit offensive.

To me Richard was just a shy, reclusive guy; a small man, and very attractive in an understated way—nicely packaged, dark hair and vivid blue eyes. I just assumed he was comfortable around me because I was the only one who didn't quiz him about his private life. That was also how I had learned more about him than the tenacious office gossips. He lived alone in an apartment overlooking the Thames and enjoyed a number of extreme sports, like acute and prolonged bouts of mountain biking, martial arts and kick boxing. I supposed that was what gave him his good packaging—the guy worked out, you know—but none of that seemed to go with his shy, understated image. Neither did this fetishistic sexuality that I had just learned about, but then...maybe it did kind of make sense?

I had kept the personal information he gave me to myself, which is why he liked me, I assumed; he appreciated that kind of respect. Now that I reflected on it, I guessed he had been even friendlier to me since Tom had arrived on the work scene and moved in with me two years ago; but shy single men often feel more comfortable around women who are attached. Little did I know he was observing Tom and me with this kind of proposal in mind. He wanted to be our sex slave, our gimp. My heart rate went up several notches and my body was hot, almost uncomfortably hot. I fanned myself with a magazine while trying to come to terms with the conundrum, and the rather extreme affect it was having on me—I had to admit it, the idea made me horny as hell.

"Suzie, I can see you are interested, my love." Tom folded his arms. He was standing in front of me and nodded down at my breasts, where my nipples were swollen and crushed beneath the surface of my silk blouse. There was no hiding it. My sex was clenching, my body was on fire.

"Yes, I can't deny it...the idea of it makes me hot, but you know...I want *us* to be okay." I eyed his long, lean body, the fall of his dark blond hair on his neck. I couldn't bear to lose this man...hell, I could hardly get through a day without wanting us to meld our bodies together and fuck each other senseless.

"It won't affect anything between us, it's just an adventure." He began to stroke my face, pushing back my hair where it was sticking to the damp heat of my neck. "He said he will be transferring soon, so there wouldn't be any awkwardness at work, it would just be a one-off." My, he had thought of everything, and he'd obviously been planning the whole thing for quite a while, too. Tom lifted my chin with one finger, his thumb stroking gently over my lower lip. "He said it would be up to us, he said we could do what we wanted with him." There was a dark, suggestive look in Tom's eyes.

"I see..." I mumbled, not sure if I did.

"One thing I'd like to see..." His voice was hoarse. He ran a finger down the collar of my blouse and into my cleavage. He slipped one finger inside, pulling the blouse open, looking at the shadow between my breasts. His other hand lifted mine and led it to his groin, where his cock was already hard inside his jeans.

"What...?" I wanted to know. The blood was rushing in my ears; the magazine in my hand fell to the floor.

"I'd like to watch him going down on you." His eyes were filled with lust. I groaned, my hips beginning to shift as I rocked back and forth on the hard kitchen stool, my sex hungry for action. He leaned forward and kissed me, his tongue plunging into my mouth. My fingers fumbled with his fly buttons, and then I was bringing his heavy cock out and stroking it with my whole hand. He pushed me back, over the breakfast bar. He was going to fuck me, right there and then, and I was ready; sweet Jesus was I ready. I hoisted my skirt up around my hips. He dragged my knickers off and pushed my thighs apart with rough, demanding movements. He stroked my inflamed clit, growling when he saw the juices dribbling from my blushing slit. Then he fucked me while I perched on the kitchen stool, pivoting on its hard surface with everything on display.

"Get your tits out," he whispered as he thrust his cock deep inside me, his body crouched over me. I pulled my blouse open, my hands shaking as they shoved my breasts together, kneading them and tweaking the nipples, sending vibrant shivers through my core. I was whimpering, jamming myself down on his thrusting cock as hard as I could. Tom watched with hungry eyes as my hands crushed my breasts. I suddenly remembered Richard blushing when I had caught him looking at me over his monitor, just the other day. Was he aroused then? Had his cock gotten hard as he thought about me and Tom? He had glanced away, furtively, his color high. Dear God, the man had been thinking about us doing this; maybe even thinking about doing this *with* us. He had told Tom his dark secret, and Tom was now rutting in me like a wild man.

I was on fire. I whimpered, my hands suddenly clutching at Tom's shoulders. I was about to come. I had never come so bloody fast in my entire life.

"You look very beautiful, Suzie," Richard said. My fingers fidgeted with my neckline, nervously. "I always thought you looked like Audrey Hepburn with your hair up like that." He smiled; he seemed quite calm now, and he was leading the situation even though he was going to be the slave. We were nervous, but then we were the novices; presumably he had done this many times before. I glanced at Tom. He had chatted happily about work while we made our way through several glasses of wine, until now—until Richard had moved the conversation on to a personal note. Now Tom had grown silent and watchful.

"Thank you," I replied, swigging another mouthful of wine. Both men were staring at me; the sexual tension had risen dramatically. "It's the little black dress," I added, with a smile. That morning I had told myself that I wasn't dressed any differently; I always wore stockings, garters and high heels to the office. The little black dress underneath my jacket was the new addition. It was very soft and clingy, and now that I had abandoned the jacket I felt good in it. Besides, what does one wear when one is about to take on a sex slave?

"You want to know what I've got in the briefcase, don't you?" He'd seen me looking at his black leather briefcase when we left the office that evening, the three of us headed to Tom's and my place for drinks. Yes, I had been curious. I nodded. "I like to wear a mask," he said. "I've brought it with me and I'd like you to put it on for me."

My sex twitched. The combination of power and deviance he had suggested in that simple comment hit my libido like a narcotic entering the bloodstream.

"Okay, I'll do it," I replied, as nonchalantly as I could manage.

Richard stood up, taking off his immaculate suit jacket as he did so, and placing it over the arm of the sofa. He picked up the briefcase and carried it over to the breakfast bar, where he set it down, flicked the combination lock and opened it. Tom and I both watched with bated breath. Richard undid his tie, rolling it slowly and tucking it into a section in the top of the briefcase. Then he lifted something out of the case and turned back to us, leaving the briefcase sitting open on the breakfast bar. As he walked back to me, I stood up.

"It's perfectly safe," he said, allaying any concerns we might have in advance. "It was handmade, for me." He passed the soft, black leather mask into my hand. I turned it, feeling it with my fingers. It was cool to the touch and incredibly soft, molded, with laces down the back and breathing holes for the nose, a closed zip over the mouth. A powerful jolt went through me when I realized that there were no eye holes; Richard would not be able to see what we were doing once he had the mask on. My eyes flitted quickly to Tom and I saw that he had noticed that too. Richard undid his shirt, revealing well-muscled shoulders and torso. He dropped it on the sofa and stood in his black pants, looking from one to the other of us, for our consent.

"Turn around, and I'll put it on." Even as I heard my own voice another wave of empowerment roared over me. Richard smiled slightly and inclined his head.

Tom suddenly stood up. "I think you should take that dress off, first," he instructed. The mask dangled from my hand. Richards's eyelids fell as he looked at the floor, hanging his head, but I could see that he was smiling to himself. The atmosphere positively hummed with sexual tension. Tom's instruction had completed the dynamics of the triangle. This was it; the scene was set for action.

I put the mask down on the coffee table and pulled the soft jersey dress up and over my head.

"You can take one look at her, before she puts your mask on." Tom's eyes glittered. Richard's head moved as he looked back over to my stiletto-heeled shoes, up to my stockings and the scrap of fine French lace barely covering my crotch, then up and on to the matching balconette bra that confined my breasts. I knew I looked statuesque and glamorous in this, my most expensive underwear, and I could see that he approved.

"Thank you," he said, his gaze sinking to the floor again. Before he turned his back he passed something else into Tom's hands. It was a set of intricately carved manacles. As Tom looked down at the object, Richard turned his back, bent his head and put his wrists behind his back—awaiting both the mask and the manacles. Not only would he not be able to see, he wouldn't be able to touch. Tom looked at me, his eyebrows lifting, a wicked smile teasing the corners of his mouth.

Tom came forward and enclosed Richard's strong wrists in the manacles. Then it was my turn to take action and I moved over, heart pounding, and began to ease the mask over his head. It pulled easily into place and I gently tightened the laces, gauging my way until the mask was molded tight and secure over his face. When the knot was done Richard slowly descended to the floor and squatted down on his knees, eyes unseeing, his head cocked, as if awaiting instructions.

We circled him, taking in the look of this creature, as he had now become, kneeling between us in the center of our personal space. I had prepared the room well, with the furniture pushed back and subdued lighting. He knelt between us with his masked head lifted up and back, his strong arms manacled behind him, his cock a discernible hard outline in his pants. With Tom towering over him, Richard presented an image I would never forget.

Tom nodded at me, pushed an armchair forward and indicated that I sit down.

"Do you remember what I said?" He kissed me, then pulled my knickers down the length of my legs and up, over my heels, stroking my ankles as he did so. I nodded. "Good." He smiled—it was devastating, wicked—and then he grabbed our slave around the back of the neck and urged him forward. "Your mistress is one horny bitch. I want you to go down on her, and make sure you do the job properly. I'll be watching." With that, he unzipped the mouth on the mask and slowly lowered Richard's head into the heat between my thighs.

I couldn't believe this was happening—Tom was so dominant, so strong and commanding. I was getting wetter by the second. I couldn't look down at the man between my thighs; I felt a sudden rush of embarrassment and strangeness as he crouched there, unseeing and yet so sexual. My eyes followed Tom as he moved away. He was looking into the briefcase that had been left open on the breakfast bar. What was in the briefcase? I wondered, again. Then I felt the surface of the mask, cold against my thighs as Richard moved his head along them, feeling his way toward the hot niche at their juncture. The tip of his tongue stuck out and I felt its blissful touch in the sticky, cloying heat of my slit. He used his tongue like a digit, exploring the territory of my sex, before he began mouthing me, his tongue lapping against my swollen lips and over the jutting flesh of my clit. It felt so good; my embarrassment was quickly replaced by something else: sheer rampant lust. I tried to stay calm and take my time; I had to resist the urge to gyrate on the edge of the seat and push myself into his obedient face.

After a moment I became aware of Tom's presence again and looked up, gasping for breath. He had stripped off his shirt, his leanly muscled chest bared for my eager eyes. I purred; he blew me a kiss, and then grinned.

"Stop now." At the sound of the order Richard's head lifted, cocking to one side again. "I've found some of your other toys and I intend to use them. Do you understand?" Richard nodded. My fingers clutched at my clit, replacing the tongue, keeping myself on the edge while I tried to see what Tom was holding in his hands.

He pocketed a shiny blue condom packet, and gestured at Richard with a stiff leather cock harness. Tom looked dangerous now. He always had a certain edginess about him during sex, but I'd never seen him quite this intense before.

"You really are a deviant one, aren't you?" He gave a deep chuckle. Richard hung his head in shame. "Oh, but there's no need to be so embarrassed, we can both see you've got a stiffy, Richard." With that he crouched down on the floor and grabbed at Richard's belt. He opened the buckle, the button and zipper in the blink of eye and, yes, Richard did have a stiffy—a major stiffy.

"You are a bad boy, and did you get hard when you had a taste of Suzie?" Richard nodded. "Right, I'm going to have to take care of this. No one said you were allowed to get a hard-on did they?" He pulled Richard forward so he was kneeling straight up, his pants falling down around his knees. He wasn't wearing underwear and my eyes roved over him in appreciation. Tom pushed Richard's head to one side and bent down, his hand measuring the other man's cock in a hard vigorous fist. God, what a sight! I shot two fingers inside my slit, probing myself while I watched Tom handle Richard's cock.

With some effort, he pushed the cock harness over Richard's erection and secured it with the stud fastener around his balls. He was almost entirely covered. I could just see his balls squeezed up inside the circles of leather, and the very head of his cock pushing out of its containment. The harness was extremely tight and I could see the effect it was having on Richard, his whole body growing more rigid by the second, as if he was being gripped in a hard heavy hand, his blood-filled cock bursting for release.

"Get back to work on Suzie, right now." Tom pushed him back between my thighs. By then I was on the very edge of the chair, my legs spread wide to get more of him. Tom walked behind him and pulled the condom out of his pocket, turning it over in his hands. He looked at me; his green eyes glittered like gemstones. His eyebrows lifted imperceptibly and his mouth was fixed in a devilish smile. He wanted my approval. I whimpered, my head barely nodding, but I really wanted to see him doing it. Tom opened his fly and got out his rock-hard cock. He pumped it in his hands for a moment, his eyes on mine. This was one of my favorite sights; I couldn't get enough of seeing him with his hands on his cock, and he knew it. He looked down at my chest, growling. I followed his gaze and saw that my nut-hard nipples were jutting up from the edges of my bra, my breasts oozing out of the restraining fabric.

Tom eased the condom on and then knelt down behind Richard. When Richard felt his legs being pushed apart his mouth stopped moving and clamped over my sex. His body was rigid between us, his buttocks on display to Tom, his face pushing in against my sex, his muscled arms bound tightly behind his back. If I rolled my head to one side I could see his harnessed cock.

He remained quite still, his tongue in my hole, when Tom began to probe him from behind. Tom's face contorted and I felt Richard's head thrust in against me as he was entered from behind. My hips were moving fast on the chair, moving my desperate sex flesh up and down against the leather mask, his mouth and the rough edges of the zipper. I couldn't help it, I was gone on this.

Richard's cock looked fit to burst. Tom pulled out and ploughed in deeper, his teeth bared with effort and restraint. He must have hit the spot, because Richards's body tensed and arched, his tongue going soft and limp against my clit. I glanced down and saw his cock riding high and tight in its harness, then it spurted up under his arched body, which was convulsing.

"You made him come," I cried accusingly, but with delight, and a dark laugh choked in my throat. Tom grinned at me and then jammed into him hard again.

"Suck her good, Richard; I want Suzie to come next."

Our obedient slave began to tongue me again. I gasped my

pleasure aloud for Tom—Tom, my gorgeous lover, watching me. It was just like our sessions of mutual masturbation, but with Richard's darkest secret filling the void between us; tonight he was the gap across which we watched each other's deepest pleasures rising up and taking us over.

Tom's lean body was taut, his hands gripping on to Richard's hips, the sinuous muscles in his arms turning to rope. His eyes were locked on mine, urging me on as he sent Richard's tongue lashing my clit again and again with each deep thrust. I began to buck, wildly out of control, shock waves going right through the core of my body and under the skin of my scalp as wave after wave of relief flooded over me, and then Tom threw back his head, roaring his release as his hips jerked repeatedly and he shot his load.

Tom sat across the breakfast bar from me. He sipped the rich black Colombian coffee I had made us, his fingertips running against mine as he eyed me over his cup. He smiled as he put the cup down and lifted my fingers to his lips.

"You looked incredible," he whispered, kissing my fingertips. It was an extremely intimate moment; he was looking at me with possessiveness and something akin to awe.

"So did you," I replied and I meant it; I was overwhelmed by my lover. Richard had long since left us, but the images he had given us of each other would be with us for a very long time.

"Do you think we'll ever see him again?"

"Maybe," he replied. "Maybe not. Would it bother you if we did?"

I gave it some thought. I pictured us casually speaking to

him in the office, the way we used to, but this time the three of us would be looking at each other and knowing what had gone on. The idea of it made my pulse quicken again.

"No, not in the least." I liked the idea. I smiled at Tom. Not only had we seen each other anew, but Tom and I had become part of Richard's secret, part of Richard's darkest secret.

In the Back of Raquel

P. S. HAVEN

It was after midnight when I arrived. I checked the name Trinh
had scrawled on the napkin against the sign on the façade and
then parked Raquel under a streetlight and joined the steady
stream disappearing into the club. The music was loud and
hypnotic and I had to ask twice of the girl behind the ticket
counter what the cover was.

"Thirteen," she yelled, and I peeled the bills from my
money clip and stepped into the smoky neon haze, surrounded
suddenly by the flash of naked skin as skirts fluttered and
raised, revealing sweaty thongs and hips gyrating to the
relentless electronic grind of the music. I moved quickly,
hugging the wall as I avoided the dancing, surging throng,
navigated the rows of tables along the outskirts of the dance
floor and finally slipped behind the railing that separated the
liquor bar from the rest of the club.

I saw Elisa, standing at the bar and sipping something blue, obviously alone despite the fact that she was surrounded. She was wearing the dress, despite her protestation that it fit better last year. It was black, of course, satin, no larger than a pillowcase, baring her entire back, her skin as pale as moths' wings. It was short, sheer and sleek, the hem floating about her thighs, the banded tops of her coffee-colored nylons just visible. Elisa saw me in the mirror over the bar and watched me as I made my way toward her, a slow smile creeping across her face as she smoothed the satin to her body with her palms, her hips swaying, her legs long and slender in five-inch patent spikes. Perfect. She returned to her drink as I approached.

"Sorry I'm late."

"You're not," Elisa said. "Late, that is."

"How long have you been here?"

"Not long," she lied. Elisa sipped from her drink and then leaned into me, kissing me softly, leaving behind an intoxicating scent of alcohol and perfume. She gestured with her drink toward the crowd outside the bar. "They have a table. Let's go."

Elisa and I made our way around the dance floor, one of her hands tucked into my arm, the other holding her drink carefully away from stray dancers. Trinh and Trey were seated at a small table near the DJ's booth and Trinh spotted us and waved with a flick of her tiny wrist. Trey rose as we approached, extending his hand. "Good to see you again," he said, a little louder than he had to.

"You remember Trey," Trinh told me. I nodded and smiled, and took Trey's hand and shook it.

"Hope I haven't kept you waiting," I said to Trey.

"Not at all," Trey smiled and everything about him seemed to almost shine; his blond hair, his golden skin, his silk shirt, even his fucking teeth. We sat and a girl with pink hair instantly appeared to take our drink order. Elisa showed the girl her blue drink and I ordered a beer, as did Trey. Trinh told the girl she wanted a Cosmo and got only a confused look.

"A Cosmo*politan*," Trinh snarled, leaving the girl to walk away muttering "cunt" to herself, not quite loud enough for Trinh to hear her over the music's incessant throb. Trinh lit a thin, exotic-looking cigarette and smiled, either unaware or unconcerned she had just been insulted.

Our drinks arrived mercifully fast and after tasting hers, Trinh let out a little laugh and said to Trey and me, "Maybe you two should get to know each other." I drank my beer and listened to him convincingly enough, nodding and responding when appropriate, and based on very little conversation, I decided that we had absolutely nothing in common except Elisa. Trey began to tell me how lucky I was to be married to such a beautiful, intelligent woman and I could see Elisa blush.

"Let's dance," Elisa abruptly interjected. She was up and ready, pulling me by my wrist, tugging at me like a child, her voice insistent. I pantomimed my protest, exaggerating my reluctance as I held fast in my chair until Elisa took Trey by the hand, and said, smiling, "You, then." Trey needed no encouragement and Elisa led him onto the floor, checking over her shoulder as the pulsing crowd absorbed them, making sure I was watching. I was.

As Trinh and I watched, Elisa and Trey began to dance, their bodies pressing into each other as they moved to the music, Elisa's little dress twitching about her thighs. Watching them dance, it would've been easy to mistake them for lovers, Trey's hands gliding onto Elisa's naked back. But they weren't lovers. Not yet, anyhow. I watched his hands slowly move around her waist before sliding down onto the swaying curves of her hips, clutching at the smooth fabric of her dress, pulling it taut across her ass. Her buttocks were soft and full, and for just an instant Trey's hands seem to hold them before moving quickly up her back, letting her dress fall free. For a moment, the bodies surrounding them parted and Elisa's eyes met mine. In them I could see that she knew I was right, that what I had been telling her all along was true: she was still sexy. She was still desirable. And Trey knew it, too. And there was suddenly an unfamiliar fluttering in my stomach and for a moment I thought it was jealousy.

"So," Trinh said abruptly, starting one of her sentences that come out of nowhere and disappear just as fast. I waited as she drained her Cosmopolitan before gesturing toward Elisa and Trey with her emptied glass. "What do you think?" I looked back at Elisa, watched her smiling up at Trey, her arms slung around his neck, causing her dress to rise on her hips. Trinh stabbed her cigarette into the glass ashtray on the table, the butt rimmed with her maroon lipstick, and before I realized it, she had slipped silently into Elisa's vacant seat next to me. "Is he attractive? Do you like him?"

"All I want is to see her fuck him. Then I can get on with my life."

"He's only twenty-two," Trinh said, almost whispering, as if trying to keep it a secret. "And he's hung like a fucking *horse*." The pink-haired girl had lit at the table behind us and Trinh turned to show the girl her empty glass and I took a good look at Trinh for the first time since I'd arrived. She was Vietnamese, I finally decided, pretty and quite young, even more so than I had originally thought. Her hand was on my leg and I looked down at it and beyond to her crossed legs, long and bronze, naked almost to her waist, her tiny black skirt stretched across her lap, and she tugged at it once to let me know she knew I was looking. Then she said, "Are you sure you want to go through with this?"

I looked at Trinh and for a moment I was tempted to tell her everything. For a moment I wanted to tell her how Elisa and I used to be when we were first married, when we couldn't get enough of each other, before we became distracted by our careers, our schedules, our money. I wanted to tell her how mortgages, a kid, and fourteen years had all conspired to somehow, inexplicably, turn us into old married people. But only for a moment.

Before I had to give Trinh an answer the drink girl came back and dropped off Trinh's Cosmopolitan as well as another blue drink for Elisa and two more beers. I looked again for Elisa, and for a moment couldn't find her, then she and Trey suddenly appeared at the table and sat in the two seats across from Trinh and me. Elisa smiled at me and I could see her chest rising, her skin glistening with sweat. They began their fresh drinks in unison.

"You two look good together," Trinh said to them, and then to me, "Didn't they?" She was right, but I couldn't answer before she said to Trey, "He likes to watch."

"Really?" Trey said, almost laughing.

"What about you, Trey?" Trinh went on. "You like watching?"

"I like *doing*."

"Sounds like you two are perfect for each other," Trinh laughed, pointing at me with her glass and at Trey with her finger. Trey suddenly stood and announced to the table (and anyone else within earshot) that he had to take a piss, then disappeared into the darkness as Elisa watched.

When he was out of sight, Elisa turned to me and said, simply, "Well?"

And then Trinh: "What are you afraid of?"

It was a challenge, not a question. I understood this, but I had an answer nonetheless. More than anything, I was afraid of regret. Regretting doing this. Regretting *not* doing this. What if Elisa hated herself for doing this? What if she hated *me* for letting her? What do you do when fantasy and reality lie too far apart? I looked at my wife, looked for the answers, and in her eyes I could see that it was now or never, too close to the latter. I could see that she was ready, for the first and only time, maybe, to let this happen, and I knew that I had only that moment to make my decision.

"Do you want to or not?" Elisa asked me.

Of course I wanted to. For as long as I had been married to Elisa this had been my deepest desire, my most pervasive fantasy. But it had always been just that: *a fantasy*, things said in the heat of the moment, with the understanding that we never really intended to act upon them. Until now. I had no way of knowing what would happen if I said yes—I hadn't even known Trey before tonight—and somehow that excited me even more.

Before I could say anything, Elisa saw Trey returning. "Do you love me?" she said quickly.

"Yes."

"Do you trust me?"

"Of course," I said.

"Then trust me, you'll love this."

"1967 Shelby Mustang GT500," Trinh suddenly began to recite as we approached Raquel. "428-cubic-inch engine, two Holley 600 cfm four-barrel carburetors. 355 horsepower." Trinh ran her fingers down Raquel's fender and across the chrome Cobra badge. "Only two-thousand-forty-seven ever made."

"Two-thousand-forty-eight," I said.

As I produced the keys from my front pocket Trinh asked, "May I?" She was smiling, her hand outstretched. Trinh could sense my hesitation and said, "Not a scratch. I promise."

Any other night, any other circumstances, I wouldn't have even considered it, and I think Elisa was as surprised as I was when I handed over the keys and turned to quietly ask her, "Are you sure you're okay with this?" She nodded, but it wasn't enough for me. "You don't have to do this," I said.

"Do you want me to?" Elisa said.

"I...yes."

"Then I have to," Elisa said, and then, as Trinh watched and waited, kissed me. It was a perfunctory, almost calculated kiss. Almost like the kiss she gave me when we got married, the "you-may-now-kiss-the-bride" kiss. The kind of kiss that was meant more for the people watching than the person receiving it. And I thought, then, of the vows we'd made before giving each other that kiss. Vows to love, cherish, and obey. And how, in some strange way, by letting happen what was surely about to, Elisa was honoring those vows.

Trinh told Elisa she would be riding in the back and Elisa obediently climbed in, followed immediately by Trey, his distended cock straining conspicuously against the front of his pants as if following Elisa of its own free will. Trinh slid behind the wheel, tugging at her skirt as she sat and I walked around Raquel to the passenger side, Elisa watching me through the back glass, her eyes bright, childlike with anticipation.

I got in and Trinh hit the starter, Raquel rumbling to life, and we moved through the maze of one-way downtown streets, starting and stopping at traffic lights until the road opened up. Trinh wound her way through the gears, redlining every one as we got out on the highway, and I realized as I watched her that I had never been in Raquel's passenger seat before, had never let anyone else drive her. And I started to notice things that I could only see from this point of view: the green glow the gauges cast on the driver's face; the relative positions of the clutch and accelerator, the gearshift and the wheel; and how Trinh was almost too slight to use all four at the same time.

Trinh adjusted the rearview mirror until she and I could see Elisa and Trey in the blue shadows of the backseat, intermittent bands of light sweeping across their faces as we passed under streetlights. Trinh lit a cigarette, its red glow dancing across the interior of the car, and she almost sighed as she exhaled the thick smoke. "Do you like sucking cock, Elisa?" she said suddenly as I watched the speedometer creep past eighty.

"What?" Elisa said, her voice barely loud enough to hear.

"You heard me," Trinh told her. "Simple question, yes or no?"

"I..." Elisa began tentatively. "Yes."

Trinh turned to look at Elisa over her shoulder. "So suck Trey's cock. Right now." Elisa looked for me in the mirror, and Trinh said, "It's okay. He doesn't mind," then turning to me she added, "Do you?" Trinh inhaled the last of her cigarette and cracked the window, the wind rushing in cold and loud, and flicked the butt outside before sealing the window again.

"I don't mind," I heard myself say. Trinh lit another cigarette and watched me as I watched Elisa in the mirror. "Drive faster," I told Trinh, and she did.

As I watched, Elisa dropped from view and I could see Trey settling into the seat, sliding down a little; draping one arm across the back of the seat, the other over my wife. Trinh smiled, as if relieved, or happy, maybe, that she didn't have to talk Elisa into it. Over the drone of the engine I could hear the faint clinking sound of Trey's belt being unbuckled. Then I could hear the wet noise of Elisa's mouth, and by the look on Trey's face I knew that Elisa had his cock out and had begun.

I stared into the mirror, straining to see in the darkness, and I could make out the dark shape of Elisa's body curling up in the seat next to Trey, her head moving in his lap. "Drive faster," I said again, glancing over at the speedometer, the needle arcing past one hundred. In the mirror I could see Trey, breathing deeply, sinking further into the seat, relaxing, both arms now slung across the back of the seat. Trey's eyes met mine, and I stared helplessly at him, unable to turn away; his eyes were white slits, half hidden in the shadows, and I suddenly had the feeling that somehow he had known this would happen, that he knew from the first time he saw my wife that this would be the outcome. I suddenly wanted to hate him for his arrogance, his utter conceit. I hated myself for wanting this, but I *did* want it.

"This is…" I whispered, and then paused. I could feel Trinh watching me, waiting for what I was going to say. "I can't believe this is happening."

"Are you complaining?" she said, just loud enough for only me to hear.

"No," I said. My cock was so hard it hurt, straining painfully against my pants, and I shifted anxiously in my seat, desperate to free it.

"Why don't you just take it out?" Trinh said, well aware. "Go ahead. That's what you're here for, right?" Hastily I unfastened my pants and wrenched my aching cock out into the open, immediately wrapping my fist around it and beating it furiously as I listened to my wife's muffled moans, her mouth full with Trey's cock. How many nights had I lain awake, planning this, imagining this? Picturing every possible scenario, every situation; loving every imaginary moment. And now the moment I never imagined would happen had arrived. Here. *Now.* Enraptured, I stared, my fantasy being made reality before my very eyes, and any jealousy I had felt, any uncertainty evaporated, leaving only a consuming urge to see her do this, to see this happen.

The lights from the city had long since faded behind us and the highway was deserted except for an occasional tractor-trailer. Trinh pushed Raquel past one-ten. The semis blew by, heading into the city, the wind from them buffeting us, crashing against us like thunder, their headlights flashing through the interior of the car for an instant like lighting. I turned around in my seat, abandoning the mirror, all pretense gone now, and watched between the bucket seats as Elisa held Trey's cock up with both hands to look at it. It was huge, every bit as large as Trinh had promised it would be, standing perfectly erect, jutting from his groin, straining up toward Elisa, and Trey brushed my wife's hair from her face to make sure I got a good look.

Elisa gazed up at him as she lapped at his shaft, the weight of Trey's cock resting across her upturned face. Then, hungrily, she hauled it into her empty mouth, sinking down on it until her wet lips were sealed around its base. I could hear her grunting, almost barking as she plunged her mouth over his cock again and again, one hand cupping his fat pouch of balls, the other clamped around the thick base. I watched Trey's cock as I stroked my own, his thick, hard shaft sliding in and out of my wife's wet lips, and I watched Elisa, showing him with her concupiscent gazes and breathless moans how much she loved it. Trey was watching as well, and he was telling Elisa how good she was, how sexy she was, but at that point I don't think Elisa cared whether he thought she was sexy or not.

Trey moved his hands to the back of her head, easing her up or down, whatever felt best to him. Over and over again Elisa worked her mouth around Trey's cock, up and down, back and forth, until she realized that Trey was driving at his own rhythm, and all she need do was hold her head still as his cock pumped through her wet lips. Trey held Elisa's head firmly in his hands and pushed his cock in and out of her mouth like a piston, Elisa's lips stretching around the raised ridges of his shaft.

"Suck it," Trey demanded. "Suck that cock, you little whore." His taunts only seemed to encourage Elisa, his words barely audible over her moans. Trey moved faster, and Elisa slipped a hand under her dress and began to touch herself as

Trey told her again and again how good she was at sucking cock. Her awareness of his pleasure only seemed to intensify her own excitement, and she groaned loudly as he slid his cock into her mouth again and again, almost gagging her every time. I could see her throat contracting, her eyes watering each time he pushed the entire length of his cock into her mouth, and I was certain, given the length of shaft that disappeared between her lips, that his cock was in her throat.

I could feel Trinh staring at me from the driver's seat, gauging my reaction to what was happening. Trey was groaning, his voice desperate as he began to beg Elisa to slow down. I could easily hear Elisa's breathing, heavy and labored as Trey's urgings became more insistent, his moans louder and in rhythm with Elisa's. Suddenly Trey gasped, his fingers tangling into Elisa's hair, his face clenched in anticipation. I saw his chest heave several times as he humped up against Elisa's mouth until finally his body started to convulse. A burst of grunts escaped him and I knew he was coming in my wife's mouth. He growled out a string of expletives, calling my wife his "little cocksucker," his "filthy whore," and below him Elisa had sealed her lips tightly around his cock, sucking and swallowing until she almost burst from lack of breath.

Their noises promptly lapsed into silence, with the exception of Trey's ragged panting, and Trinh looked at me, smiling. My eyes locked suddenly with Trey's, and for a moment I looked into them. For what, I didn't know. Gratitude, maybe, as absurd as that sounded. But instead, I saw only pride. He seemed to feel conquering, victorious even, and I knew that in his mind he had just taken my wife in a way I never could; that it was Elisa, not him, who had just been pleasured, that he had been gracious enough to allow her to suck his cock; that she had been rewarded with his orgasm.

Elisa looked up at Trey like a child wanting praise, and I watched as she opened her mouth and showed him the shimmering pool of semen on her cupped tongue before she swallowed it.

"You're a lucky man," Trey told me for the second time that night, but this time Elisa seemed to flush with pride at Trey's words. She sat up, tucking her hair behind her ears, and in the headlights of an oncoming vehicle I could see a smile pursing her raw and swollen lips.

I watched the needle sweep past one-forty.

After Hours

DANTE DAVIDSON

The crisp white nurse's skirt fell to the floor with a tiny whisper, followed by a slightly louder murmur from the nurse herself. I couldn't wait to finger her pussy, to see just how ready she was for me, but that wasn't part of the plan. Not yet. This scenario had to follow a strict schedule, and I would ruin everything by rushing. I watched as she let her white blouse follow her skirt, and then I stared, fascinated, as she picked up both parts of the uniform, folded them neatly, and set them on the blue plastic chair.

She didn't know that I was watching her, which made the voyeuristic experience all the more powerful. She thought that I was waiting, appropriately, outside in the hall for her to prepare herself. But with the door cracked slightly, I had the perfect view as she took off her bra and placed the underwire contraption with the rest of her clothes. With a gentle motion, she removed her pantyhose, then slid her silky white panties down her lean thighs and dropped both of these items on top of the skirt and blouse. She stared at the pile of clothing for a moment, then rearranged the stack by tucking the panties and bra between the skirt and blouse.

How quaint, I thought to myself. *She doesn't want me to see her panties.*

Or maybe she didn't want me to see what most likely was a very wet spot at the center of them. That thought sent a shot of adrenaline through my body, and I had to pace up and down the hall to get myself under control.

Back at the door, I rapped my knuckles on the wood, knowing full well she wasn't ready, and she squeaked out a "One moment, please." I heard rustling in the room, and then watched through the sliver of space as she slid into the ugly waiting hospital gown and hopped onto the paper-covered leather table. The gown tied in the back, and she did her best to tie the bows herself, but the end results were loose tangles of the ties and gaping areas where the smooth skin of her back could easily be seen. I took in the lines from her tan, and the way her reddish hair fell just to the ridge of her shoulders before I knocked on the door again.

"Yes, I'm ready," she said. "You can come in."

I entered the room and she turned her head to look at me. She wore the expression I always see on women's faces when I enter an examination room. Women who are nearly nude and waiting for me to touch their naked bodies tend to have an expectant look, almost excited, yet tempered with trepidation. I adore this look. I did my best to put her at ease. First, I washed my hands, soaping them generously as I stared out the window to the car park below. Evening had just about fallen, and the light was a dusky blue. Few cars remained in the lot. I dried my hands and then turned to face my patient.

I thought about what I wanted: start with a little fingering of her pussy with my thumb accidentally brushing her clit. Wait to see what sort of reaction that would bring. The thought of parting her pussy lips was enough to make me instantly hard, and I did my best to quiet my thoughts. This wasn't the time—

Slowly, I walked to the side of the table and undid her wretched attempts to tie the gown closed. With care, I slid her thin gown from her shoulders, letting the fabric fall down from her breasts to her waist. I had her lay back on the table, and I took my time with her breast exam, rotating my palm over her lovely pert breasts, cradling each one in the most clinical way. She stared at me with trusting eyes, and I did my utmost to echo her look with my own gaze. I felt a confusing mix of dirty desires pulse through me. I was only giving her a simple breast exam, after all—nothing out of the ordinary—but the feelings ricocheting within me were of the filthiest variety I could imagine.

I had her sit back up and used the stethoscope to listen to her lungs. She was in top shape, but her deep, husky sounding breaths made me close my eyes and imagine the sort of sounds she'd make if I fucked her. Would those breaths come quicker? Was she the type to hold her breath at the moment of climax? I was glad to be standing behind her, where she couldn't see the undoubtedly strained expression on my face.

After several deep breaths of my own, I had her lie back down on the table. I walked to the foot of the table and sat down on the round, leather-covered stool waiting for me. Her legs were bent at the knee, and from this vantage point, I could see right up the gown to her naked pussy. It took every once of my determination to keep the lustful longing sound out of my voice when I asked her to put her feet in the stirrups and then slide her sweet ass all the way down toward me.

No, I didn't say, "sweet ass."

But I wanted to.

The speculum lay on a paper towel next to the sink, but I didn't have any use for that tool right now. I could feel her watching intently as I slid my large hands into the requisite nitrile gloves, and I could see from the look on her face that the look of a gloved hand was foreplay to her.

Eat her.

That thought pounded in my head.

Brush her clit with your face. Make her come with your tongue and sharp chin against her.

Christ, where were these thoughts coming from?

"This might feel a bit cold," I told her.

"Yes, Doctor," she said, and the words opened up a whole wealth of possibilities to me. *Yes, Doctor, anything you want, Doctor*—that's what those words meant. When I touched her pussy, she quivered all over and let out the deepest, sexiest sigh. My thumb brushed her clit, as if accidentally, and the sigh turned into a moan. Had she gotten aroused during the breast exam? Did she want me to do the things to her that I most definitely wanted to?

I pressed against her cervix and then I found her G-spot and tapped it twice. When I glanced at her face, I saw that she was embarrassed at the way her breathing had speeded up.

"Everything looks perfect," I told her, using my most reassuring tone.

"Thank you, Doctor."

I withdrew my hand and saw her cheeks go crimson at the wetness that clung dew-like to my gloved fingers. She was deeply aroused. That was clear to both of us.

"I'd like to do a rectal," I said after glancing at her chart, and I thought she'd come on the spot. "Relax as much as you can, and I'll go slow."

"Yes, Doctor," she said again, her voice a husky purr. I gazed at her for a moment, taking in her gorgeous blue eyes, creamy skin, and long gingery hair loose to her shoulders. I thought of the way she looked all dressed up in her nurse's uniform—an outfit I saw her in five days a week. But I liked her better like this, naked under a blanket made of paper, her legs spread wide, body opened to me.

While she watched with an unwavering stare, I lubed my finger generously with the KY jelly and then parted her asscheeks. She moaned as I slid my middle finger deep into her asshole. Oh, was she ever tight here. She contracted on me instantly, but I didn't reveal any reaction at the spectacular reflex. I probed her rear entry for several seconds before adding a second finger into her hole. God, I loved the way her body seemed to pulse on my two fingers, and I had an instant preview of what it would feel like when I replaced my fingers with my cock.

But not yet.

With my two gloved fingers still tight inside her, I brushed my thumb over her clit again. She was swollen now, obviously ready to climax, and I thought about letting her orgasm one time, letting her reach the finish line here at the start, before we'd even really gotten going.

"Oh, god—"

"Relax," I said again, using my most stern voice.

"Yes, Doctor," she whimpered. "Yes, Doctor—"

I rocked my fingers gently within her asshole, and I had the distinct sensation that she might be able to come from this action alone. But that was not acceptable to me. Without a word, I gently removed my hand and peeled off the gloves. She whimpered and turned her head to the side, her face showing how sad she was at the departure of my probing digits.

"I'll need to take your temperature now," I told her, reaching for the thermometer waiting nearby. "So roll over onto your stomach for me."

"You're going to do it *that* way?" she stammered.

"Of course," I told her.

Her cheeks were on fire as she rolled over onto her belly. The paper blanket fluttered to the floor as she offered me the perfect globes of her rounded ass. Again, I smeared lube along her crack, and now I slipped the cold glass thermometer into her asshole, swallowing hard as I held the instrument in place. Oh, was I ready to fuck her, but not yet.

Not yet.

This vision exceeded all my dirty daydreams. The thought that I was examining her, here, in my office, that I had actually slipped a rectal thermometer into her perfect ass—oh, these facts made me want to come in my khakis. I loved this. The way I had to hold the thermometer still. The way her hips had started to rock on the paper-covered table. I wished I had something larger to insert into her rear entry. I wished—

Then I thought about an enema, and I removed the thermometer and told her my plan. If I'd thought she'd turned red before, now she showed me what *red* really was. Her cheeks went scarlet, vermillion, cardinal red. But she didn't say no. My nurse never says no to me. I went quickly to the closet supplies for a disposable enema and brought it back to her just as rapidly. She sucked in her breath as I introduced the tip to her perfect pucker, and then she relaxed as I let the fluid flood inside of her.

"Hold it," I told her, replacing the syringe with my thumb. "I don't have a butt plug here. You'll have to hold it yourself." I kept my thumb in place for a moment, feeling like a dirty Dutch boy, and then I decided she had better void now, so that I could finally fuck her.

She was shuddering all over as I removed my thumb and helped her off the table. The gown was completely off now, and her beautiful nude body seemed to shine winningly beneath the fluorescent lights. I watched her hurry to the adjacent bathroom, saw the way she cantered on the balls of her feet. She took care of herself in privacy, before returning and climbing back onto the table, stark naked and on her belly. She knew.

I maneuvered her the way I most desired, so that her ass was exposed and ready, and I reached for the lube again and made her asshole glisten with a healthy dollop. She was out of her head, moaning and tossing her hair as I slid first one and then two fingers back inside her. I couldn't wait to get my cock in there, but I wanted to get her as ready as I was.

"Please, Doctor," she murmured. "Oh, please—"

I split open my khakis and got out my cock, and I

watched her arch her back for me, offering herself up.

"Hold your cheeks open," I instructed. "And relax for me."

"Yes, Doctor."

She reached behind herself, and parted her lovely asscheeks, and I placed the head of my cock right at her back door. All I wanted to do was slide in hard, but I took pity on her. Like a gentleman, I brought one hand under her waist to tickle her pussy. She was so wet, I could feel her juices covering the whole of her outer lips and the tops her thighs. I stroked her clit as I slid my cock inside of her, working slowly but steadily as she backed against me.

Yes, she wanted this. In fact, she fucked me, working her body up and down on my cock. I let her take her pleasure from me, and I kept my hand in place the whole time, tickling her clit as she filled herself with my cock. I closed my eyes as she rocked back and forth, and when she came, she began to squeeze my cock repeatedly, her muscles tightening and releasing until I came right along with her.

In the sterile environment of a doctor's office, we had exchanged the most base form of sexual encounter, and the heat shone between us. As we parted, she rolled onto her back and gazed at me, and the light in her eyes made me smile. My naughty nurse.

You're not supposed to have playing-doctor fantasies when you're a doctor. You're not supposed to want to peel your nurse's uniform off her nubile body and subject her to the same intensely detailed examinations you give your high-paying clients. But sometimes the very things you're not supposed to want are the things you want most. Luckily, I'd found a match for my fantasies in Nurse Jocelyn, who craved a thorough examination with the same ferocity that I yearned to part her splendid thighs and give her one.

"When will I be due for my next appointment?" she asked softly as she stood and slid back into her rumpled uniform.

"We'll have to check the books," I told my ever-ready naughty nurse.

Performance Art
OSCAR WILLIAMS

You're so proud of them, and I don't blame you. They're lovely, large on your frame but perfectly proportioned. Double-Ds, and all natural, you brag in the online profile you use to scout for potential partners. You're only five-three, perhaps 110 pounds, so I suspect no one believes you—but I know you're telling the truth, and calling them double-Ds is, in a way, being conservative. They strain against your bras, stretching the cups, showing curvaceous and enticing through the tight sweaters you wear. You love that men look at them. It's like you can feel their energy, radiating from their eyes, caressing your tits, unbuttoning your top, unhitching your bra, untying your bikini top, lifting your sweater over your head, revealing them. It's as if you can feel a man's gaze undressing you, devouring your tits. When you know a man is checking them out it's like he's stroking your nipples with his eyes, whether we're sitting in a restaurant, lounging on the beach, dancing at a club, or just walking down the street. And you invite it. You encourage it, because you love the attention. You wear revealing tops and go without a bra when you really shouldn't, relishing the caress of the male gaze over the curves of your full breasts. Women, too; nothing makes you hotter than thinking that another woman, straight, bi, or gay, has just checked out your tits.

You're all about showing off. You're a total exhibitionist, and you've got the body to indulge yourself. But it's your tits that really drive people crazy, and that's why you love them so much. When you see people whispering, wondering if your tits are fake, I know it turns you on even more. People can't seem to stop obsessing over your incredible tits. No one can believe you were born with the genes to produce such flawless orbs, but you were, and every pair of eyes that caresses them is a chance for you to brag.

And it's not just that they're so big and perfect to look at, that they're so firm that you don't need a bra, that they defy gravity as surely as if they were bought and paid for in a plastic surgeon's office but much, much more attractive of shape. Your whole sexuality seems to revolve around your tits. Your nipples get incredibly hard when you're turned on. Those pink circles are so sensitive that I sometimes make you come just by pinching them, growling at you to spread your legs wider so you can't rub your thighs together. Sometimes it takes hours. Sometimes you don't come at all, but just having your nipples played with drives you crazy. If you aren't able to come just from having them rubbed and pinched, not being allowed to touch your clit, then invariably by the time I tire of our little game you're tottering right on the edge. The first stroke of my cock into your sopping-wet pussy brings you off, making you moan and buck and thrust with orgasm.

Other times, you drop to your knees and take my cock in your mouth, sucking hungrily as you play with your own tits—and then eagerly sliding them around my shaft. You push them together and let me tit-fuck you, relinquishing your grip on them and letting me do the holding only when you're soaring close to orgasm—so you can reach down and rub your clit the few strokes it takes to get you off. When I come on your tits, you go mad, coming harder, rubbing my thick jizz into your luscious globes. Licking your fingers.

I've always loved that you're such a tit whore. I've always adored the fact that you want to show them off, that you want your tits to be looked at. I bought you a novelty shirt once that said *Look at my chest when you're talking to me,* as a joke. You didn't hesitate; you wore it everywhere for a few weeks, usually without a bra. You meant it, too, and guys who talked to you didn't know what to think. Most of them would nervously fix their eyes to yours, but I would see them glancing down, the same way they always did but this time wracked with guilt, knowing you could tell. It would make you flirt harder than ever. It would make your nipples get hard, braless in the tight T-shirt, showing through sweat-dampened cotton. It would make your pussy wet, and whenever you wore that shirt you would tear off my clothes the second we got home, would come like a waterfall the second my cockhead entered your pussy.

When we went to a topless beach with some friends, you were the first of the women to doff your top, and I could see your nipples stiffening as they moistened, sweaty in the sun. The men on the ridge with their video cameras all trained their long-distance lenses on you, and I could see the effect it was having on you. As I rubbed suntan lotion into your tits, I could feel you squirming against me, and I knew if I'd managed to slip my finger into your pussy without being seen, you would have been incredibly wet. You were indulging in your favorite brand of performance art: the big tease, to anyone who would watch. By the time I got you back to the car to drive to the burger place for a beachside lunch, you couldn't wait any longer. You sucked me off in the car, bent over with your face in my lap and your blonde hair bobbing rhythmically up and down—not caring who was watching. I pinched your nipples as you sucked me, and I let you rub your thighs together this time. You came before I did, your face pressed to my spit-slick cock, your breasts clutched tight in my hands, your nipples pulsing with each hard pinch I gave them. You finished me off with your mouth, hungry for my come.

We go to play parties occasionally—parties where S/M aficionados go to show off. You always wear something revealing over your tits—a patent-leather bra, a see-through lace top, a mesh T-shirt. You get wetter, your nipples harder, with every man that looks guiltily at them, lusting, every woman who enviously compliments your "outfit," knowing what they're really thinking: "My God, look at those tits."

When we go down into the dungeon and start to play, I always know what you want. To have your top half stripped and your tits played with until you're driven crazy. Letting everyone see just how magnificent they are in their full, naked glory. Another kind of performance art, once again focused on your favorite two things in the world: your tits.

In fact, performance art is what gave me the idea for our

little scene. I once read an article about a performance artist whose form of art was to put a box around her upper body and walk around the street, encouraging passersby to put their hands through the holes cut in the front of the box and feel her tits. I know you would love to do that, letting anyone who wanted to stroke their fingers around your perfect mounds, pinching the nipples, making you come. Except that you'd never do it, because it wouldn't be the same for you if people couldn't see them.

But it's still a compelling idea. And that's where I got the brainstorm. How to finally satisfy that need you have to let every man in the world—or at least every man in the room—fuck your tits.

I take you to the play party late, so it's already going strong and crowded by the time we get there. In the dressing room, I strip you down to your new outfit—peekaboo corset that comes up just under your breasts, leaving them bare, covering only your belly, back and crotch. It's nothing more than a string between your asscheeks. Wrist restraints aren't enough for tonight; I put on a posture collar to keep your head up straight, and slide your arms into a bondage sleeve, cinching it tight so your arms are thrust behind you, forcing you to keep your back up straight too—and present your bare breasts to anyone who cares to look.

Or touch.

With a leash attached to your posture collar, I lead you into the main lounge area. I see a trio of men dressed in leather eyeing your tits admiringly. I lead you over and nudge you in the back.

"Would you like to touch them, Sir?" you ask, as I've instructed you to do.

"What?"

"M...my tits," you stammer. "You can touch them if you like."

The three men look at me for permission, and I nod. One of them reaches out and begins to caress your tits. You moan softly. I nudge you again in the back.

"Your mouth, too," you say, your voice hoarse. "You can use your mouth on them."

The man bends low, his bearded mouth closing around your firm, erect nipple. He begins to suckle you as his friend takes the other breast, licking and sucking it as you whimper gently and squirm against me. I hold you up and force you into their grasp. One of them is finished with you; his friend takes his place, suckling your nipple and biting it roughly. I don't move to stop him, even though I can tell it's too intense for you. After all, you've got your safeword.

I slide my hand around your body, draw my fingers up your thighs and wedge them between your legs, under the crotch of your corset. You're very, very wet.

You've attracted a small crowd. I sit you on a stool nearby and hold you there while you invite other men to come suckle your nipples. Women, too; you've never been with a woman, but tonight your breasts belong to all takers.

"Say it," I whisper into your ear.

You look at me desperately, hungrily, knowing you must obey.

"I'll be in the dungeon in a few minutes," you say, your voice raspy from the pleasure flowing through your tits as strangers suckle your nipples. "Any of you men who want to can visit me and come on my tits."

An approving murmur goes around the room. I check you again and find you're even wetter than before. After a few dozen more strangers suckle your breasts for a few minutes at a time, I decide you've had enough. I lead you out of the lounge area and down to the dungeon.

I choose a central location, laying you out on a low platform at just the right height. I undo your bondage sleeve and stretch your arms over your head, buckling on the restraints and padlocking them to the top of the table. I do the same to your ankles, keeping your legs together.

A group of men has followed us down into the dungeon, waiting for their opportunity to come on your tits. Several of them already have their hard cocks out and are stroking them.

"Just the tits," I tell them, stepping back. "You can only come on her tits."

"With pleasure," one says, and leans over you, looking into your frightened eyes as he strokes his cock, aiming it at your full, firm mounds. When he shoots his load over your breasts, you whimper softly, the humiliation mingled with excitement. He rubs his cockhead over your breasts, smearing the cream into your nipples and cleavage.

Another one takes his place, climbing onto the table and straddling you as he pumps his cock over your tits.

I watch as three, then four, then ten, then twenty men crouch over you and come on your tits. You're covered soon, your breasts slick with jism. You're moaning, and when I come around to the end of the table and slip my hand up into your crotch, you almost come at that moment.

As men continue to use you, jerking off all over your tits, I unclasp your ankles, spread them apart, and clip them to the corners of the table, spreading your legs. I can see your fear: Am I now going to let the men fuck you?

But you've exhausted all the men in the party. Female submissives shoot you angry glares, their masters' orgasms having been co-opted for your degradation. Your tits are covered with cream, glistening with it, your corset soaked. A pool of it has formed under your shoulders. I unsnap your crotch and pull the leather-lined spandex up, revealing your pussy. I take out my own cock and, climbing onto the table, slip it between your swollen pussy lips. I enter you with a hard thrust, and your eyes go wide as you lift your hips to meet me. I start to fuck you, giving you your much-deserved reward, and a cheer goes up from the men who just shot on your tits. I come down on top of you and my chest rubs against their semen, reminding you of how you've been used. I pound into you and it's not long before you come, thrusting under me, begging me to fuck you harder. Your moans of orgasm bring another cheer from the men, approving of the way you've been rewarded for giving them your all.

When you're finished coming, I pull out, crouch over you, and unload my cock on your breasts. Streams hit your face and I rub them in too, feeling you lick my fingers clean as I push them into your mouth.

There's a faint round of applause as I zip up and unclasp your restraints. I quickly wipe down the table and smear the excess semen onto your breasts again. I put your bondage sleeve back on and lead you up the stairs, your breasts dripping come, your face red from shame and post-orgasmic pleasure. When we reach the showers, I soap you up and hose you down, then lead you into the dressing room.

You put your street clothes back on and I lead you into the world, knowing your ordeal will weigh heavily on your mind from now on, dominating your thoughts whenever a man looks at your tits. In the car, you look at me and smile, humiliation giving way to release, giving way to fondness.

I kiss you on the lips, and your tongue grazes mine. I put the car in gear and we drive away.

Alice

M. CHRISTIAN

It started with the laundry—now how ironic is that?

It obviously was a kind of blind spot for Al. Ask him to take out the garbage, drive five hundred miles to help out a friend, weed the backyard, vacuum, even cook (he made a mean-ass clam chowder he was particularly proud of) and it would get done—so quick and so neat, in fact, that half the time jaws would drop and eyes would pop at how well done it was. No muss, no fuss: just a well-executed chore or perfectly performed task.

Just don't ask him to do the laundry. Domesticity might not be pretty, but the way Al faced stripping the bed, picking up crumpled clothing, hauling baskets downstairs, stuffing the washer, adding soap—the whole laundry procedure in fact—you'd think he'd been asked to give a sponge bath to Karl Malden.

Jeannine hadn't been bothered by it at first. "Your usual

breaking-in stuff," she thought to herself, said to some of her friends when they asked how their experiment in living together was progressing. "Nothing to worry a war crimes tribunal about."

Four months later it was, "Okay, it's starting to really bug me," she thought and said as she clenched her smooth hands into tight, white fists.

At six months she was wondering how to dispose of his body.

To be honest, he tried—and in many ways that simply made it worse. Huffing and puffing like a kid asked to eat his broccoli he'd make such a big production out of it that Jeannine didn't know whether to make him stand in a corner or give him a Golden Globe for overacting. Even when Al seemed to want to do it, earnestly "helping out around the house" on her birthday or when he'd done something spectacularly dumb and needed to do some housework Hail Marys, it didn't work out. Her favorite red dress, white shift, socks, the linen, dry clean onlys, even a suede jacket went in—and what came out went straight to Goodwill.

Despite Al's laundry issues, he and Jeannine had it pretty good: Al's underground comic, "The Snitch," was doing remarkably well—well enough that he didn't need a real job yet; Jeannine's store, Deco Mojo, was paying their rent and a little more; and unlike a lot of their friends, they'd been together for a little over a year with no sign of breakup or even nasty drama.

In all their time together, the months before and then after making the big leap of cohabitation, Jeannine and Al had a pretty cooperative relationship: some gives, some takes, fair play all the way around. Al did the shopping this week, Jeannine the next. This month Al paid the phone bill, next month Jeannine did. Except for the issue of the laundry, they kept everything fair and even between them.

That's not quite true, though. Everything was fair and even except for the laundry and one other place: the bedroom.

That's also not quite true—mainly because for Al and Jeannine the bedroom was only one of the places where they fucked around. The outdoors, you see, did it for Jeannine. The more out the better, especially when there was a real risk they'd get spotted by someone—extra especially when they could be spotted by more than just one someone. Parking garages, baseball games, movie theaters, hiking trails—they'd tried them all.

Al called it "eye-porn": the way Jeannine reacted to people looking was just like the way most guys reacted to looking at anything and anyone sexy. He loved it almost as much as Jeannine did: crawling up the fire escape to the roof, giggling and whispering like schoolgirls; laying out a blanket on gravel still warm from sunlight; a kiss, more kisses, clothes off, hands roaming, cock very hard, pussy very wet; fucking long and slow, then hard and fast knowing that either someone could be looking at them at any second or that hundreds—maybe thousands—were doing just that.

But what did Al like? "I'm not complaining, mind you," she thought and said to some of her friends when they'd first moved in. "Not at all."

Four months after that, "I just can't figure him out," was the order of the day.

At six she was wondering what terrible secret he was hiding, what skeletons he had in his closet.

Then, one lazy Saturday afternoon—chores completed, laundry carefully ignored—they curled up together on their plush, painfully bright orange sofa (that Jeannine had never been able to sell) and started flipping through mail, stopping in the middle of the bills, the miscellaneous flyers, to glance at the Victoria's Secret catalog.

"Wow," Al said, brown eyes wide as Jeannine flipped through the glossy pages. "Pretty."

When they went to the museum—and after they snuck in a quick blow job in the French Impressionists—all Al said was "Nice." When they went to friends' gallery openings—and fucked ferociously in the grimy bathroom—all Al said was "Eh." "Good" was what Al called his world-renowned chowder, and how he described their sex life. In all their months Jeannine had never heard Al call anything else by that one word of praise. Until, that is, page seventy-nine of the Victoria's Secret catalog.

That night, after much thought, Jeannine smiled to herself. The next day, with the dreaded laundry, it was time for Al's skeleton to come out of the closet—and play.

"Perfect. Absolutely perfect. Or else," she said, obviously uncomfortable with even the idea of a threat—but even more obviously excited by it.

"Or else?" he said, as uncomfortable as she was with the threat—and just as excited.

"Or else you're going to be very intimate with some of my more intimates, Al. Do you get me?"

Al was speechless. But his face said what his voice couldn't.

"Good. Now, get it all done right, Al: fabric softener, the right temperature, no mixed colors, no running, nothing wrong. Perfect. No mistakes, Al." She cast him a cool glance. "I'm going out for a few hours—got some store stuff to take care of—and when I get back I expect the laundry to be done like it's never been done before."

Then she went out, with even a wider, more wicked, smile on her lips.

"Let me see," she said, four hours and some-odd minutes later. "Show me what you've got."

"Ah, sure—" Al said, nerves making him hesitate, stammer. "Sure thing, babe."

"Don't call me 'babe'—not yet, at any rate. Now show me. And this had better be good."

"Yes—" he started to say something that started with *b* but caught himself, substituting a quick "be right back," and a smile.

The first basket was full to overflowing with sheets, pillowcases, blankets, and towels. Jeannine tried to keep the smile off her face as he pulled out each neatly folded bundle. Creases almost made her giggle with joy, seams made her flash some pearly white teeth—but she fought to keep her face stony and firm.

"Now the next one," she said.

The next basket was packed with slacks, jeans, blouses, socks, boxers, bras, shirts, and panties. Al may have screwed up every other attempt at laundry, but this time he gleamed, shone, sparkled, was absolutely spotless. She may have barely kept the smile from her face before but now it took every ounce of her control to keep from laughing and giving him a big hug—and the laundry had nothing to do with it.

But she had to find something wrong. That was the game, after all. "What's this?" she said, holding up a pair of panties.

"Um, er—it's your...panties."

"That's right, it's my favorite pair: soft, pearlescent, pure white with the frilly waistband and the tiny blue flower right in the middle. Right there. See the flower? But there's something about this flower, Al—something very, very bad."

Al swallowed hard but didn't say anything.

"You see, Al, my favorite pair of silky panties has four little green leaves next to that sweet little flower. Four. Not two, not three, not five—four. Now, Al, I want you to take these and tell me how many little green leaves there are next to that so-sweet little flower."

Al took the panties in suddenly moist hands, turned them carefully until the little flower was turned toward him. Just as Jeannine had never heard Al use the word *pretty* before—not at the museum, not in a gallery—she'd never really seem him hold something reverently before.

"Three," Al said, glancing up from the panties to look her in the face. His eyes were wide and gently moist.

"That's right, Al. Three. Not four—three. One of my leaves is missing. That's not a good thing. Not a good thing at all. I asked you to do something and you didn't do it. I'm afraid, Al, that you'll have to be punished."

Al's face lit with a soft smile. "I understand." He seemed to want to add something else (Ma'am, Sir, Mistress, something like that) but didn't know what to say—yet.

"Good. Now strip."

Al's smile grew, took on a sweetness and a subtle *thank you,* and he did as he was told.

Next to one of the baskets went his hurriedly shed shirt, shoes, pants, socks, and underwear, until he stood in front of her, tall and lean, all long bones and tight muscles, and very, very hard.

Jeannine looked at his gently bobbing cock. It took a lot of control not to reach out and stroke it, suck it. "Very good," she said, her voice catching in her throat. She doubted she'd ever seen him as hard. "Very, very good. Now, Al—" she tossed him the sheer panties "—put these on."

At first Al didn't do anything. He just stood in front of her, very hard, with a strange expression on his face. Later, when she had time to really think about it, Jeannine would realize that among the emotions that were zapping around inside her boyfriend's mind—desire, suspicion, shame, fear, to name a few—the one that finally won out, that made him reach down and put one foot, then the other, into the satin undies and slowly, sensually draw them up his body, was relief.

"Very nice," Jeannine said, surprising herself at her own sincerity. He really did look...not pretty, but definitely very sexy: his very hard cock tented the white material like he was trying to shoplift a javelin, and the sheer material was already growing damp at the end with pearly pre-come. Again, it took all of Jeannine's control not to just lick the end, taste the salty bitterness. "Very sexy, Al—no, that's not right. You're not really Al, are you? Not right now."

Al hung his head slightly, pulled his elbows and knees in, shrinking, getting younger, the rough and tumble Al fading away as Jeannine watched.

"Alice?" Jeannine said, the inspiration like a small shock. "Your name is Alice. Isn't that right…Alice?"

Al—no, because her boyfriend was gone; Alice, her girlfriend with the white satin panties, very big clit, and very small boobs, nodded slowly, happily.

"You're very pretty, Alice, in nothing but your white panties. Very sexy. Do you feel sexy, Alice?"

Alice smiled, radiantly, saying, but not with words: *Yes, very much so.*

"Turn around, Alice. Show me your sexy little body. Show me what you've got, slut."

Alice chewed a thumbnail, eyes wide and moist.

"Do it, Alice—or do you want me to be upset?" Jeannine wanted to laugh, to cry at how excited they both seemed to feel. It wasn't a game she'd played before—or would ever have thought about playing with Al—but with Alice it seemed right, natural, and most of all, way too much fun.

Alice's eyes grew even wider. Then, slowly, shyly, she turned around, giving Jeannine a hesitant view of her boyish body.

"Very sexy," Jeannine said, suddenly aware of her own wetness. "I really like you in my panties. In fact, I think you look even better in my panties than I do. They're yours now."

"T—thank you," Alice said; even her voice was soft and almost innocent.

Jeannine leaned forward and grabbed hold of Alice's huge clit in a powerful grip. Alice was startled, but Jeannine hung on and wouldn't let her pull away. "You forget your place…Alice. Do you want me to be displeased?"

"N—no," stammered Alice, hands falling to Jeannine's. Touching, but not trying to pull them away.

" 'No,' what? Who am I, Alice? What do you call me?"

Alice's face burned bright red. Her lips quavered but no words came out.

"Say it, Alice—or I put you to bed without any supper."

"Mistress...," whispered Alice. Then, with a bit more force: "Yes, Mistress," like a weight had been lifted.

"That's right. I'm your Mistress. Don't you forget it, either." She let go of Alice's clit. The thin girl took a half step back in response.

"No—no, Mistress, I won't forget," Alice said, composing herself.

"You'd better not." Jeannine reached out and ran her fingers up the length of Alice's very hard, rhythmically flexing clit. "So beautiful—" she said, almost whispering. Shaking her head slowly, as if to clear it, she said in a louder voice, "Now then, slut. Where were we? Oh, yes, that's right. You were giving me a show. I like a good show."

Jeannine leaned back as if to inspect her new plaything. "Why don't you show me how hard that clit of yours really is. Rub it for me, stroke it through your new panties. Do it. Do it now."

"Yes, Mistress," Alice said, her voice honey and all manner of sweetness. Palm down, she dropped one hand to the front of her panties and slowly started to rub herself.

"That's it," Jeannine said, gently parting her own legs in response, as if Alice's clit was somehow connected directly to her own. "That's it."

"Thank you, Mistress, " Alice said, her eyes glazing over

in pleasure. As she rubbed, stroked herself, the front of her panties got wetter and wetter. Soon, the pale material was almost transparent, giving Jeannine a perfect view of the thin girl's monstrous clit. "Thank you...," said Alice.

"Oh, yes, you slut. You love this, don't you, slut? You love it, being the nasty little girl, putting on a show just for me. Yeah, that's it; rub it, rub that sweet clit for me. Make those panties nice and hot and wet and sticky. Stroke it for me, stroke it...."

Alice bit down on her lip, her breath coming in shorter and shorter hisses until, finally, she didn't make any sound at all but her body tensed as if a kind of wonderful voltage slammed through her. Rigid, locked tight in a shuddering orgasm, the front of her panties were suddenly soaked with her sticky juices.

In a barely controlled fall, Alice dropped down first to her knees and then face-first onto the carpet. She lay there for a long time, her body quivering and quaking with release, breaths now heavy and slow.

"Very, very good, slut," Jeannine said reaching up under her simple skirt to hook a thumb into the waistband of her own everyday panties. "That was quite a show. Quite a *nice* show. I'm very impressed." The panties came off, soaked through. She tossed them aside. "In fact, come here, Alice," she said, her voice a husky whisper, "and taste how impressed I am."

Slowly, weak only in body, Alice got to her knees and moved over to Jeannine until her face was parallel with Jeannine's downy pubic hairs.

Now it was Jeannine's turn to really smile, as the game got even better for her. Leaning down, she parted her plush lips, giving Alice a view of her very wet folds and pulsing clit. "Taste," she managed to get out before her voice got completely caught in her throat.

Alice did. Alice did, indeed. Nuzzling up between Jeannine's strong thighs she flicked her tongue over her clit. Hard and fast, slow and soft, Alice licked. Jeannine, standing above her but at that instant miles way, moaned and bucked, dipped and swayed in response.

Finally, the pressure that Alice had been applying to her peaked and she cried—her version short and sharp and loud compared to Alice's almost silent and long one—and slid down to sit, hard, on the floor at Alice's feet.

While her body was still working, she threw her hands around Alice, her girlfriend, and Al, her boyfriend, and cried hot tears of pleasure and wonderful discovery.

Some stories really do have happy endings. Al's comic work continued to do well, receiving both critical and financial success. Jeannine's store became a hallmark of the neighborhood. Al and Jeannine, and Alice and Jeannine were very happy together—and their whites were whiter, their colors brighter than ever before.

Old Friends

DEXTER CUNNINGHAM

"Are you excited to finally meet Gina?" asked Brooke.

"Yeah," I said, not sounding very convincing.

"I'm sure you two will hit it off," said my wife, beaming broadly. There was the faintest hint of mischief in her look, and I wondered what was going on in her head. Then Gina walked off the plane, and my eyes went wide.

Of course, I'd seen pictures of my wife's best friend from college. Early in our relationship, Brooke had subjected me to every last snapshot, leading me through her big books of photos in that way new girlfriends sometimes do. I'd seen pictures of Brooke and Gina frolicking on the beach, bikini-clad; grinning together at Disneyland, wearing mouse ears; and drinking fruit drinks together at frat parties. Through it all, I'd acknowledged in my own mind that Gina was attractive. But of course I'd been much too polite to say that to my new girlfriend, who had later become my wife.

Now, however, I couldn't disguise the shock and admiration that flooded me. It was all I could do to keep my tongue in my mouth.

Gina was gorgeous. Some girls blossom after college, I guess. Her fine, Italian features were framed by a magnificent mane of jet-black hair and punctuated with small horn-rimmed glasses that gave her the bookish look I find so sexy. With her, though, the look was more female executive than librarian. That fit with what I knew about Gina: she was an advertising analyst with an MBA, successful at her job and dedicated enough that even at twenty-eight she remained single.

But what floored me wasn't just her beautiful face, full kissable lips or the rich glow of her olive-tan skin. It was the way her body looked under that tight, flattering business suit, all executive chic. Gina was *built*, the curves of her large breasts and full hips providing such a contrast to Brooke's wispy, slender form and angular bone structure. Both were incredibly sexy, but I guess I was so surprised to see Gina looking like such a sexpot that I couldn't hide my sudden, unexpected attraction.

Of course, Brooke and Gina had already planned my descent into depravity—without giving me the details, Brooke had assured me that plenty of attention had been paid to my deepest fantasies. That probably added something to the sexual tension between us.

"See?" said Brooke with a wicked smile. "I knew you'd think she was hot."

"Bubby!" shrieked Gina like a schoolgirl, using Brooke's college nickname. The two girls squealed as they rushed together, hugging excitedly. I couldn't help but notice the familiar way my wife let her hands rest on Gina's hips, nor the fact that they kissed on the lips—more than once.

"You must be Bob," said Gina, extending her hand.

"Gina," I said. "I've heard so much about you."

"Just the good stuff, I hope," said Gina.

Brooke hugged her close and kissed Gina on the side of the face. "With Gina," she cooed, "there's only good stuff to tell."

"Stop!" giggled Gina, and I reached for her bags.

For the next three days, I was all but forgotten as Gina and Brooke shared recollections of their wild and crazy college days. They stayed up late drinking wine and giggling, and I found myself sleeping alone. Brooke had taken the week off work, and while I was gone during the day the two of them cruised the city, which Gina had never visited before. Brooke showed Gina all of our favorite haunts, and by midweek I was feeling vaguely neglected.

Worse, though, Gina had proven to be pretty casual about making the house her own. She was sleeping on the couch, which created a few embarrassing moments. As I left for work early one morning, I saw that the blanket on the couch had slipped down below Gina's magnificent D-cup breasts, so different than Brooke's firm B-cups. I could see the outline of them clearly under the damp cotton sheet, her nipples firm and evident underneath. Her breasts moved up and down as she breathed softly in her sleep. I stopped dead in my tracks and stood there, staring, my cock stirring in my pants.

After a minute of that, Gina opened her eyes. "Hi," she

said, her voice sexy and flirtatious. She didn't move to cover her breasts.

I looked away nervously and said, "Good morning," rather crisply. Then I hurried out the apartment door. As I stole a glance back at Gina, I saw that she was watching me, a smile on those full, lush Italian lips.

But nothing prepared me for what happened when I came home from work that Friday. As I walked in the front door of our apartment, leafing through a stack of bills from the mailbox, I stopped and listened.

There was moaning coming from the bedroom. I recognized Brooke's moans right away—after all, I'd made her utter them often enough. And it didn't take long for me to figure out that the second set of whimpers, moans and grunts belonged to Gina.

I dropped the bills on the floor and walked softly to the door of the bedroom, which they'd left open.

There, sprawled on the bed, were my wife and her old friend, stark naked and locked passionately in a sixty-nine.

Gina was on top, her gorgeous ass deliciously facing me. Her legs were spread wide around my wife's face, and Brooke was eagerly eating her old friend's pussy while Gina humped just as eagerly up and down. Brooke's legs, too, were spread wide around Gina's face, and the old friend seemed to be giving as good as she got. Their hands roved all over each others' naked bodies, caressing as they ate each other out.

The room reeked of sex, telling me that they'd probably been at this all day. Their clothes lay scattered across the floor, as if they'd doffed them urgently, unable to wait to get each other into bed. *Our* bed. My wife was making love with a woman in our bed, right in front of my eyes.

I felt my cock quickly grow hard until it throbbed painfully. My cock swelled as quickly as my anger.

I don't know if I shifted or moved my feet, or if Brooke just sensed I was there. But she turned her head and looked back at me, her eyes wide in shock.

"Oh, God," she moaned. "Bob..."

I pulled the bedroom door shut and turned to leave the apartment.

Brooke caught up with me on the landing outside, still stark naked. She grabbed me and said, "I'm so sorry," trying to embrace me.

"You're standing here naked like a whore," I growled, my anger rising as I saw my wife's body glistening with the sweat Gina had coaxed out of her. "Like a fucking whore."

"I...I'm sorry," said Brooke, reddening more deeply. "She...she came on to me. I didn't mean for it to happen."

I felt my anger flaring, exploding into flames. "You bring a fucking slut into our house and then act surprised when she tumbles you into bed. Don't be a fucking idiot, Brooke."

"There's no need to be a bastard about it," snapped Brooke. She looked around, realizing that the neighbors could probably see her, standing there, naked. "When you're ready to talk about this, come back in the house."

She went back into the apartment. I chased after her and grabbed her shoulders from behind, pushing her onto the couch. She stumbled and fell, shrieking.

"Bob, you're being such a prick about this. It's really not that big a deal."

"Not that big a deal, is it?"

I could see Brooke's anger rising to match mine. "Gina and I used to fool around in college," she said defensively. "When she came on to me, I figured it wouldn't be a problem if I did it for old times' sake."

I turned toward the bedroom, seeing Gina standing there in the doorway, her hands up on the jamb, her face twisted in a cruel smile. I let my eyes rove over her gorgeous body, admiring her full breasts with their firm nipples, now so erect from the passion of lovemaking. Her pussy was shaved smooth, her lips showing full and sex-swollen between her legs. There was a tattoo of a rose where her pubic hair had been shaved. Her face glistened with the juices of my wife's cunt.

I could smell sex, rich and ripe, the scent suffusing the apartment.

"It's true, Bob. I came on to her.."

"You shut up," I said, pointing my finger at her. "If it's not a big deal, Brooke, then I'm going to fuck Gina, too."

Brooke's eyes went wide. "Wait—wait, don't be hasty, Bob, I—"

"I'm not being hasty," I said, turning to Gina. "What do you say, Gina? You want to save your best friend's marriage and spread those legs of yours?"

Gina smiled. "In an instant," she said. "Brooke tells me you've got a nice big cock."

"Come find out," I said, unbuckling my belt.

"Wait, wait," said Brooke. "Gina, don't do this."

Gina started toward me. When she put her arms around me, her naked body smelled moist and ripe with sweat. Brooke sat on the couch, stunned, staring at us as Gina pressed her lips to mine and wrapped her fingers around the bulge in my pants.

She turned to the seemingly horrified Brooke. It was only later I realized that if I'd been watching more closely, I might have caught the look that passed between them—and Gina's wink.

But at that moment, all I saw was Gina's naked body, her tits pressed to me, her hand curving around my cock.

"Don't worry, Brooke," said Gina. "I have to do it. To save your marriage."

Brooke's expression changed, going from horror and anger to pleasure. She smiled.

"All right, Bob," she said. "Go ahead and fuck Gina. I'll watch." Brook sat down on the couch, tucking her feet under her.

Gina unbuttoned my pants and worked the zipper down over my hard cock. She dropped to her knees, pulling my cock out.

The scent of the two women's naked bodies filled my nostrils. I was going to fuck Gina good, so good she'd scream. I was going to punish Brooke by making her watch me do Gina. It was a hateful thing to do, I knew, but my jealousy was driving me.

Brooke got off the couch, put her arms around me and kissed me fully on the lips. When her tongue slipped into my mouth, I could taste Gina's pussy, rich and tangy on my wife's mouth.

"I'm sorry, Bob," said Brooke when our lips separated. "I tried to be good. I was kind of hoping you'd make a move on her so I wouldn't have to feel guilty about it. Please tell me you're not mad."

"I am," I said.

At that moment Gina's lips closed around the head of my cock and began to slide up and down the erect shaft. I gasped and moaned softly as Brooke took my hand in hers and placed it on top of Gina's bobbing head. The two women guided me to the couch and sat me down; as Gina repositioned herself between my legs, I reached down and took hold of those magnificent tits I'd been spending the whole week fantasizing about touching. Brooke put her hand on mine and guided one of my thumbs to Gina's nipple. As I pinched gently her breathtaking face twisted in an expression of ecstasy, her nipples already sensitized from her long lovemaking session with my wife.

Brooke began to kiss me hungrily, our tongues mingling as she reached down to wrap her fingers around the base of my cock while Gina sucked the head. Brooke unbuttoned my shirt and began to suckle my nipples; I lay back on the couch.

"I'm still mad," I said. "Make it up to me."

"Oh, we will," said my wife mischievously, sliding down my body and joining Gina between my legs.

The two of them hungrily sucked on my cock. Gina licked her way to the top of my cockhead, swirling her tongue around the glans while Brooke took my balls into her mouth and lavished affection on them with her tongue. Gina's skilled fingers moved their way up to my nipples and played with them as she sucked me. Ever since I'd seen Gina at the airport, I'd longed to see her magnificent, full lips wrapped around my hard shaft. Her big, beautiful eyes looked up at me as she sucked my cock, telling me with their sparkle that she was enjoying this even more than I was.

Brooke came up for air from between my legs, leaving

my balls sticky with her spittle as she massaged them with her hand. "Come to bed with us, Bob," she cooed. "We'll make it up to you, I promise."

Gina took one hand and Brooke took the other, and the two of them led me into our bedroom.

There's nothing like old friends, I decided, for keeping a marriage interesting.

Gina and Brooke kissed and fondled me as they slipped off my clothes. They pushed me naked onto the bed, which was still damp with their lovemaking. Gina got between my legs and ran her full lips up and down my cock again while Brooke settled down onto my face, leaning forward so she could enjoy my cock alongside her best friend. I greedily ate my wife's cunt. Brooke's moans mounted in volume with each stroke of my tongue on her pussy. She was gushing with arousal; I lapped up her juices as the two of them worked my cock. Soon Brooke's hips were grinding in time with my thrusts, and I knew she was close to coming.

"Roll over," sighed Brooke, lifting herself off my face.

"Why?" I asked.

Brooke looked down at me and giggled. "Just do it," she said. Gina's mouth came off my cock. I let them roll me onto my stomach. Brooke straddled my back. I felt her seize my wrists and push them into the black fabric straps I'd installed for the occasions when Brooke was in the mood for something kinky. I'd used them on her many times, strapping her spread-eagled to the bed before fucking her silly—but she'd never used them on me.

Gina was giving my ankles the same treatment, and

before I knew it I was face down, my limbs spread, securely fastened.

"Hey," I said weakly. "You can't get at the good stuff if you tie me this way!"

Gina disappeared as Brooke slid down my body and began to kiss and nuzzle my neck, her legs spread around my ass.

"Oh yes we can," she said, seizing my hair.

I could feel my cock throbbing against the sex-damp sheets, and it had just begun to dawn on me that I shouldn't have let these two women tie me up. "Hey," I growled. "I liked what we were doing before. Let me up."

Gina was beside the bed, handing my wife a ball gag. I opened my mouth to protest, and Brooke used that moment to stuff the ball gag into my mouth. I tried to spit it out, but she got the strap around the back of my head and pulled the buckle tight.

As I struggled against the bonds, it occurred to me that Gina had more than just the ball gag. I looked at her in horror. Gina was wearing a harness, into which was fitted a huge black dildo.

I tried to scream a protest, but the ball gag prevented it. I'd done a good job of installing the straps; I was bound and helpless. I heard the big, heavy bed frame creaking as I pulled against it in protest. I watched as Brooke leaned forward and wrapped her lips around the head of Gina's strapped-on cock. Her mouth glided eagerly up and down the shaft, the way she'd sucked my cock just a moment ago—the way she'd sucked my cock so many nights in the past.

Her lips came away from Gina's cock and strings of spit stretched from her mouth to the head.

"I bought this especially so Gina could fuck me with it," said Brooke. "But now I see she's got another task ahead of her. I'm never going to have the marriage I want unless we teach you a lesson, Bob. Don't you agree?"

I screamed a desperate protest behind the gag, but it only came out as a pathetic, muffled groan. Gina looked down at me and smiled, pretty as a peach, her beautiful lips still glistening from my cock and my wife's pussy. Then Brooke seized my hair and roughly pulled back my head. Gina slapped my face, hard, shocking me.

"Oooh," she said. "I like that." Her hand went to her cock and stroked it firmly. "It makes my dick hard."

Gina slapped me again, and I felt shame and humiliation wash over me. If they'd just take the gag out, I'd apologize for getting so angry—I'd beg Brooke to forgive me. Of course she could fool around with her old friend—I knew it didn't mean anything. I knew it was just for fun.

But they didn't take the gag out, and Brooke made it quite clear she had no intention of forgiving me.

Her hand tangled in my hair, she kept my head forced up, my face turned to Gina. Gina slapped me again, harder this time. And again. And again, harder, with the back of her hand, hitting me so hard my head spun. I felt sobs surging up in the back of my throat; Gina hit me again and again and again until I couldn't hold them down. My eyes filled with tears and sobs wracked my body.

"The little bitch starts to cry," Gina said mockingly. "He wasn't crying a minute ago when he told me I had to fuck him. Still want me to fuck you, Bob? Still want to make your wife's girlfriend put out for you?"

I couldn't answer; my eyes were blinded with tears and my whole body shook from the sobs that assaulted me. Brooke held my hair while Gina slapped me again, again, again, a dozen more times, harder each time as she wrenched my sobs out of me. I cried even harder when she pinched my cheeks between her thumb and forefinger and Brooke yanked my head back again. Gina hovered over me, pursed her lips, and let a great string of spit slip out from between them. The spit hit me, warm and wet, right on my cheek. Then she hawked, pursed her lips again, and spat, harder this time, a thick glob striking the bridge of my nose and oozing down.

"Oh, maybe he thinks if he cries enough, I'll go back to sucking his dick. Do you think I should go back to sucking his dick, Brooke?"

Brooke laughed, pulling my head back even more roughly. She hawked and spat, a big glob covering my face. I sobbed hysterically, my crying reduced to pathetic whimpers by the big gag in my mouth.

"I think he's the one who needs to suck dick," she said. "You shouldn't ever suck him again. I say we turn *him* into a cocksucker."

"Agreed," said Gina. "He obviously needs it."

With that, Brooke pulled the buckle of my ball gag and yanked it out of my mouth. I opened my mouth to scream, but before I could, the gag was replaced by Gina's cock. She shoved it into me so hard I couldn't help but swallow it; when the head spread open the tight entrance to my throat, I gagged, my stomach seizing up. Brooke held my head tight so I couldn't move. Gina forced her cock into my throat, not even caring that I was gagging and choking around it, my throat spasming around her shaft as she fucked my face.

"Not much of a deep-throater, is he?"

"He'll learn," said Brooke.

Gina mounted the bed, leaning against the headboard and spreading her legs so she could hunker down and pump her hips, properly fucking my throat open wide. Brooke let go of my hair and Gina seized it, keeping my head in the right position, throat stretched out and straightened, for her to fuck it. Brooke climbed off of me and I heard a drawer opening; somehow, I knew what was coming. I heard the snap of a latex glove, the gurgling sound of lube being poured on it—the lube I used when I managed to talk Brooke into letting me fuck her in the ass.

"He's always been real big on anal sex," growled Brooke as she roughly pried open my cheeks, exposing my sensitive asshole. "I let him put it in me there, now and then, just to shut him up."

"Let's show him what it's like," said Gina, fucking my face more roughly than ever. She pinched my nose so I couldn't breathe, and I felt my lungs burning and my head pounding as she controlled my breath, only letting me gasp for air in the moments when her cock slid out of my throat.

Brooke slicked up her hand and I felt her fingers forcing their way into my ass. I squealed deep in my throat behind Gina's cock, but my wife wasn't interested in my protests.

"Look, the little piggy's still hard," she said, her free hand caressing my balls and stroking my shaft. "He's always wanted me to make him my bitch. Isn't that right, Bob?"

"Of course he has," Gina answered for me. "Why do you think he's such an asshole all the time? He knew if he was enough of a dick you'd finally snap—if he pushed hard enough you'd eventually flip him. He's been waiting for it all these years, baby."

"Oh, yeah, darling," sighed Brooke, stroking my cock. "This is what you've always needed, isn't it? To be ass-fucked and raped in your throat?"

There was no answer possible—and Brooke didn't care.

She was pumping her fingers deep into my ass, moving them in circles so my ass stretched wider with each stroke. "That's two fingers," she said. "Now let's try three. Think you can take it, Bob?"

Gina was still pinching my nose and fucking my throat; there was no chance of my giving an answer. All I could do was lie there as my wife forced three fingers into my tight ass, stretching me open. She added more lube and chuckled.

"I think this little pig is going to take more. He's lucky I've got small hands. Here's four, darling. Open wide!"

With that, Brooke roughly shoved four fingers into my ass. I felt my sphincter stretching, my ass opened wide by her hand. I struggled against the bonds, but with all four limbs tied and Gina deep in my throat, there was little I could do. I felt more lube being poured between my cheeks, and my ass stretched further as my wife began to fuck it roughly with her hand.

"Think I can get my fist in here?" asked Brooke playfully. "I don't know, he's pretty tight-assed...."

"Oh, you can get it in there," laughed Gina. "If you shove hard enough."

I uttered a helpless groan of protest as I felt my ass stretching still more. Brooke forced her thumb into me, pointing her fingers just so, pumping in and out as she added still more lube, twisting her hand in rapidly widening circular motions as she forced my ass open.

"Get ready, darling," she cooed. "You're about to become my fucking bitch. They say a man's never the same after he's been fucked in the ass. I bet it's even truer once he takes a fist in there."

I squealed, and Gina pinched my nose harder, ramming her cock deep into my throat to shut me up. Brooke shoved, and I felt my asshole stretching, protesting—and then giving way. Her hand sank into me and my whole body shuddered as I took her fist. I heard Brooke giggling, and Gina leaned over me so she could high-five Brooke's free hand. I felt lube splattering over my ass. Brooke pushed deeper into me, her fist filling me, sliding in, I thought, almost to the elbow.

"Sweet Jesus," said Brooke, stroking my cock. "He's still hard."

"Think he deserves a hand job?" asked Gina.

"Absolutely not. Untie his hands."

Gina's cock was still deep in my throat as she leaned over and pulled the buckles open. My hands hung limp, my arms stretched out to the side. I didn't move, afraid Brooke's hand in my ass would hurt me if I tried.

And afraid the pleasure flowing through me would stop.

I'd never been fucked in the ass before. I'd certainly never been fisted. And I'd never dreamed it could make my cock so fucking hard.

I felt Brooke's hand against the head of my cock. She used her fingers to guide the tight stretch of a condom down my shaft.

"Beat off, darling," she said. "Beat off with my fist in your ass."

I didn't move, just lay there, not believing what was happening as Gina slowly eased her cock out until the head rested between my lips. I couldn't move. I was frozen. It was one thing to be violated by my wife, forced to take her fist in my ass. It was the worst thing I could ever have dreamed of. But for her to know how much I was loving it, to know that I could stroke myself to orgasm while I was being so brutally taken—that was even worse.

"Come on, Bob," Gina cooed. "I know how much you love to stroke off. You think I don't know that you've been jerking off all week thinking about my tits? Come on. Stroke it."

"Don't play hard to get," said Brooke. "I know how much you love to jerk off. You think I don't know when you're doing it in the bathroom? When you sneak off to the garage and look at your *Hustlers?* Come on, Bob. Give up. I know you want to come. Do it."

My hand traveled slowly down my body and wrapped around my latex-sheathed cock. I moaned as I began to stroke it and Brooke and Gina both laughed. Then they started fucking me, harder than before, more brutally than ever. Gina's hips forced her cock down my throat again, making me gag and choke just as Brooke began to pound my ass, fucking her hand in and out of my asshole.

It only lasted a few seconds. Then I heard myself grunting rhythmically, my groans rendered staccato by the movement of the thick dildo in my throat. My cock pulsed and my entire body exploded with pleasure as I succumbed to the most intense orgasm of my life. My asshole clenched tight around my wife's fist as I came and came and came, filling the condom with what felt like gallons of come.

"That's a good boy," said Brooke, easing her hand back. She gently worked her hand around until she could slide it out of my ass. I heard the snap of her glove, and Brooke tossed the discarded latex across the room.

Gina pulled her cock out of my throat, and I gasped desperately for air, sobs attacking me again. Gina seized my hair and slapped my face again, harder—three times, four, half a dozen.

"It's no good crying, bitch," said Gina. "We know you loved it."

Gina came around the side of the bed as Brooke reached under me and gingerly unrolled the condom. I had thought my ordeal was over, but when Brooke climbed onto the bed in front of me, leaning against the headboard, I realized that it had just begun. Gina knelt behind me and guided the thick head of her cock to my fucked-open asshole. She drove into me so quickly that even my spread hole seized and clamped around it. But there was no resisting—Gina began to violently fuck my ass just as my wife clamped her legs around my face.

My arms still hung limp, untied, at my sides. My legs, however, were bound to the bed, forcing me open wide. There was nothing I could do to respond to Gina's violent, hateful invasion of my asshole.

Nothing, that is, except lift my hips and raise myself up to my knees, pushing myself onto her cock.

"Look, he's learned his lesson well," said Gina. "He's a little ass-bitch now. You can give it to him every night, and he'll fucking beg for it."

"It always happens," sighed Brooke as she grabbed my hair and forced my head back. "Once you ream them out, they're good little sluts for the rest of their lives. Now eat, darling."

I hadn't realized that she still had the condom—I'd thought she just didn't want me to make a mess when I came. But she had other things in mind, I realized as she forced the rubber ring of the condom's end between my lips and behind my teeth. She let go of my hair, roughly forced my mouth closed and, deftly using one hand, rolled the condom like a tube of toothpaste. I tasted my own come, felt it oozing into me, lukewarm goo from a rubber tube. I choked at first, not expecting the strong taste. But Brooke wouldn't take the condom away until she'd squeezed the last drop into my mouth.

"Swallow, dear," she said.

I swallowed, the taste overwhelming me and making even my cock-opened throat close tight. I managed to gulp it down with some difficulty, but as I finished, Gina slapped my ass hard, making me surge against her as she grabbed my hips and shoved me back onto her cock.

"*He's* fucking *me*," she laughed. "Come on, bitch, fuck yourself onto my cock."

She had my hips firmly between her hands, pulling me back to meet each thrust. I could have struggled now; I could have resisted. But I didn't; I let Gina's firm hands guide me up and down on her shaft.

As I felt my cock stirring, getting hard again.

"Ready for another go?" said Gina. "I think he's more virile than you let on." With that, she slapped my balls, and I gasped as my wife grabbed my hair. "I thought you said he didn't fuck you so good," said Gina.

"His cock's all right," she said. "But men are so obsessed

with their pricks. It's their tongues that they should learn to use better."

Brooke shoved my face into her pussy and growled: "Show me how much you love me, bitch."

I began to tongue her cunt as Gina fucked my ass harder. She spanked my balls with every few thrusts, but even the seizing pain that rocketed through me with every rough blow on my nuts didn't stop my cock from pulsing to full erection. My tongue worked up and down as I suckled on my wife's clit, and she twisted her hand up tighter in my hair as she forced my face more roughly against her cunt. Her hips worked in time with my rhythm, and she began to moan as she neared her orgasm.

"I'm sorry," gasped Gina suddenly. "I've *got* to fucking come."

She got my ankles unstrapped in a moment, pushing me onto my side and twisting my lower body so she could get at my cock as I continue to eat Brooke's pussy. Gina wedged her thigh under my hip and straddled me, guiding my cock to her entrance. She slid onto my cock, her pussy wet and open as she leaned back, hanging partway off the bed. Her hand pressed tight against her clit and she rubbed fervently as my hips began to grind.

Brooke came loudly, moaning as she gripped my hair. I kept licking faster, just barely managing to coordinate my thrusts into Gina's pussy with my tongue against my wife's clit. When Brooke shuddered all over and finished coming, she slipped out from under me and pushed me hard onto Gina. Gina squirmed underneath me until she was spread, missionary-style, under my thrusting body, her hand still pushed between us working her clit.

Still quivering from her orgasm, Brooke curled up beside me and nuzzled the back of my neck as I pumped into Gina. "Fuck her good, baby."

I was close to coming but Gina was even closer, and her hand came away from her clit just as she came, wrapping me in her arms and grabbing my ass to pull me roughly into her. I pounded faster and faster, feeling Gina's cunt tightening around my shaft as I thrust into it—and then she moaned loudly, the moan turning into a scream as her intense arousal drove her over the top.

I went rigid as my second orgasm ripped through me. I came in Gina's pussy, clutching her tight as Brooke stroked her hand down my sweat-sticky back. When I'd finished coming, Brooke put her arms around both of us and kissed Gina hard on the lips. Gina was so ruined from her orgasm that she could barely respond. As my soft cock slipped out of her she gasped.

"How's that for an anniversary celebration?" asked Gina. "As rough as you hoped?"

"Rougher than I'd imagined it could be," I said. "And everything I've ever wanted."

Brooke's hand found my ass and gingerly stroked the tender, moist hole, still oozing lube.

"It's true," she said. "There's nothing like old friends to keep a marriage interesting."

"You're lucky it's only five years," said Gina. "Just wait till your silver."

"I'm quivering in anticipation already."

Brooke playfully slapped my lube-slick ass.

"Just 'cause the scene's over, don't start getting smart,"

she said. "You're still my bitch."

I rolled off of Gina and took my wife in my arms.

"Of course I am, darling," I said.

"Don't get cute."

"Never," I said, snuggling close to her. "Never, ever."

House Rules

SARA DEMUCI

"Come on," Michael said, loud into my ear so I could hear him over the music. "You *can't* pass this up!"

And I didn't want to. Michael and I had come to the fetish ball knowing there would be a cordoned-off play area; we'd even joked about the possibility that we might play in it. But I hadn't expected it to be so crowded—every piece of equipment packed tight with players, and the bar behind the cordons crammed even tighter with spectators.

But Michael and I had found a place to sequester ourselves so we could watch this one beautiful mistress play with a gorgeous, muscled young stud as we swayed to the pounding trance beat. She'd had him bent over the spanking bench, and was flogging his ass. I'd gotten quite wet watching them, and Michael had been behind me, cradling me in his arms, so I had been able to feel quite clearly that Michael was as turned on as I was.

Now, the mistress had finished with the young stud and sent him away.

And she was looking right at me and crooking her finger.

She was breathtaking—with a gorgeous, aquiline face; long dark hair and a slim body packed into a tight corset; G-string and high-heeled boots. She had a flogger in one hand and a paddle in the other, and she was unquestionably summoning me, though I couldn't have heard her say a word.

Michael knows how much I love to be spanked, but I'd never been flogged before. My knees went weak as I looked at the mistress and made a "Me!?" sort of gesture. She gave me the most intense bedroom eyes I've ever seen, and I melted.

Michael pushed me gently toward her. I walked forward as if in a dream.

Then the mistress snapped her fingers and pointed right at Michael.

"Him, too," she mouthed, her words shrouded by the music.

We passed the safety monitor and went into the cordoned-off play area. It was crowded, but the mistress had cleared a tidy space no one dared violate. I hadn't even thought about the fact that we couldn't negotiate if we couldn't hear each other—and that turned me on even more. What was I walking into?

She had to bend forward and talk right into my ear, loud, to be heard over the music. "I'm Xenia," she shouted.

"Lisa," I told her.

Michael didn't say a word.

"I'm going to play with you, Lisa," shouted Mistress

Xenia. "Do you like to be spanked? Flogged?"

"J—just spanked," I shouted nervously.

She nodded, put her lips close to my ear. "Then that's what you'll get."

I nodded back at her, my pussy feeling hot as Mistress Xenia ran her hands down my side, playing with the way my lace-trimmed PVC G-string met my garter belt. She spread her palm and drew it over my shimmering bustier, feeling my nipples poke through it.

She put her hand on my shoulder and moved me out of the way so she could lean over and talk into Michael's ear. When she pulled away, Michael took hold of my shoulders and Mistress Xenia took my hand. They guided me toward the spanking bench, and I saw Mistress Xenia nod to someone, who brought over a chair.

Mistress Xenia pushed me down over the spanking bench while Michael took the chair.

Then he pushed my face into his lap and started to stroke my hair.

Mistress Xenia circled my wrists with buckling restraints and clipped them to the side of the spanking bench. Now I was helpless; I couldn't get free if I wanted to. I struggled against the bonds, getting more and more turned on. I shivered as I felt Mistress Xenia's hands running over my ass. She slapped the insides of my thighs and I obediently spread my legs, leaning heavily on the bench. I felt her bending down behind me, putting leather restraints around my ankles, too. She fastened my ankles spread wide, forcing me to keep my legs open for her.

The first blow came with her open hand, right on my

sweet spot. She was pressed up to my side, embracing me tightly as she started to spank me. The nearness of her body made me tingle. She spanked me again. And again, softly, softly, then harder, building up pressure as I raised my ass into the air for her. She could tell I liked it—it was making me so wet. I love nothing more than being spanked, and I could feel the blows of Mistress Xenia's hand reverberating right into my pussy.

Michael was excited, too; I could feel his hard cock against my face. I was so turned on I would have done anything. But I never expected to do what I did.

As Mistress Xenia spanked me, Michael unbuckled his belt and unzipped his pants.

Then he took out his cock and guided my mouth onto it.

I felt a stab of fear—there were strict prohibitions against sexual activity. What about the house rules? Was the monitor watching? Was the *crowd* watching? Even over the music, I could hear them clapping and cheering. They *were* watching. Everyone crowded around could see me sucking my husband's cock. Everyone could see me bent over, ass in the air, Michael's beautiful cock sliding between my lips as I bobbed up and down on it.

I wriggled my ass and Mistress Xenia spanked me harder.

I could feel my pussy throbbing as I sucked Michael's cock. I was incredibly wet, and Michael knew it. Mistress Xenia knew it, too. I moaned as I felt her hand on my pussy. That was forbidden, too. She plucked the G-string out of the way and started to rub my cunt, feeling how wet I was. Then, the crotch of the G-string tucked to the side leaving my pussy exposed, she spanked me again. Harder. Right on my sweet spot, making my bare cunt ache each time. She pushed her body up against me. This couldn't be happening. This was like every one of my fantasies, but it wasn't allowed—was it?

Michael held my hair up behind my head so the crowd could see me suck him. So they could see his long, hard cock sliding between my lips as I struggled against the four-point restraints.

But Mistress Xenia had more things in mind for me.

I felt her fingers on my cunt, probing me, and I was embarrassed at how wet I was. We hadn't negotiated this; she didn't know I would be okay with it. Why did she do it, then? Maybe because she could tell I wanted something more?

She slid her fingers into me—first two fingers, then three—and started to slowly fuck my cunt.

I squealed and tried to pull away, but Michael and the restraints held me, and I surrendered, letting Mistress Xenia fuck me as I serviced him. But then her fingers slipped out of me, and I was afraid she might have been asked to stop. *Please. No. Please don't stop.*

But Michael didn't stop. He kept guiding my head up and down on his cock, and the taste of his pre-come was like ambrosia. I suckled at it hungrily as I wondered where Mistress Xenia was.

Then I felt her body pressing up against mine. Her thighs against mine. Her hands on my hips.

Her cock at my entrance.

I could feel the roughness of the straps. She was going to fuck me. She had gone away because she was putting on her strap-on.

She teased my cunt open with the thick head of her cock. I moaned and fought violently against the restraints as she entered me—the struggle excited me more. That made the crowd cheer louder.

When she entered me, I came—right away. I felt her cock sliding into me and my whole body convulsed in orgasm. Michael could tell; he pulled my head up and listened to me moan. I let myself go, totally, moaning and screaming so loud everyone could hear me even over the music. Then as Mistress Xenia started fucking me harder, my loud moans turned into soft ones; my pussy was so sensitive now, after my orgasm, and I wanted more, wishing I could reach back and open my pussy wide for her cock. But I was bound, and as I struggled against the bonds I only felt my pleasure heightening.

Michael guided my mouth back onto his cock, and I started sucking him in earnest, wanting his come.

Mistress Xenia reached under me and rubbed my clit, hard, not warming me up—knowing I didn't *need* any warm-up. She rubbed so hard that for an instant I wanted her to stop—and then she fucked me deeper, all the way into my cunt, filling me, and I wanted her to never, ever stop. I wriggled my butt back and forth and pulled hard against the restraints, making the whole spanking bench shake. That only made her pound me harder as she rubbed my clit in little circles, faster, faster, faster as her hips forced her cock into me again and again.

I came again, even harder than before, but this time my moans weren't audible to the crowd—because my mouth and throat were filled with Michael's cock.

I felt the first spasm of his long shaft and tasted the bitterness I so loved. Just a hint, at first, which made me suck him harder, bob my head up and down faster. Then a thick pulse of come filled my mouth and I moaned and gulped, wanting it all. His hips ground against me as my lips clamped around his shaft and he filled my mouth with his juice. I drank it all, not spilling a drop, wishing it could go on forever.

My head was spinning; I was so high on endorphins I felt like I was in another world. Mistress Xenia unbuckled the restraints as I covered Michael's softening cock with tiny licks, wanting to taste it as long as I could.

Michael fastened his pants and the two of them helped me off the spanking bench. Mistress Xenia still wore her cock, and I wanted to get down on my knees and suck that one, too. She pressed her mouth to mine and kissed me deeply.

Then she kissed Michael, too, and pressed a card into his hand.

She put her lips to my ear and spoke just loud enough for me to hear her over the pulsing music.

"Next time," she said, "we play without *any* house rules."

Her hand gently squeezed my ass, making my pussy quiver.

The Fifth Day

AYRE RILEY

On the first day, three painters arrived at our house. This was a big event. Adam and I had discussed upgrading our decor for quite some time. Now that summer was here, we'd decided to go forward, having our fence repainted as well as redoing the trim, doors, and windowsills on our cottage-style bungalow. I chose a pale gray for the fence and a slate blue for the trim. Adam found the painters by way of an ad in the local paper, and I couldn't believe how excited I was when they showed up. But my thrill at finally giving our house a much-needed facelift was quickly surpassed by a different emotion altogether.

Two of the painters were a couple, as was made obvious by the way they kissed at every possible exchange—handing over paintbrushes, going up and down past each other on ladders set side by side; each interaction called for a sexy smooch. The girl was a lanky strawberry-blonde who wore her shoulder-length hair braided into Pippi Longstocking-style pigtails. The man she was with was dark-skinned, with corded arms and a flat, hard stomach he showed off just after their lunch break by pulling his damp cornflower-blue T-shirt over his head and tossing it to the ground before climbing up the ladder again. All day long, the couple spoke to each other as they worked, teasing and laughing, making plans for the weekend and discussing their previous weekend's activities, actions that apparently involved going to outdoor barbecues up in the hills and drinking way too much pineapple-infused vodka.

The third painter was younger than the other two, perhaps only about nineteen to their mid-twenties. He sported a slim physique and dirty-blond hair that was cut short everywhere except in the front, so that a forelock fell constantly in front of his eyes, causing him to toss his forehead to send the hair back into place. I found this move oddly mesmerizing as I watched him from the upstairs window in my home office. And oh, did I watch him. I watched every motion, every stroke of the brush against the tall, wooden fence. I memorized each gesture, each shrug, each time he licked his full lower lip, as if he were considering which place to work next, as if painting a house were as important as conducting surgery.

Although they were all far more attractive than was necessary for their profession, it was this third member of the party who caught my eye. He was so good-looking, almost beautiful, that I couldn't help but drink in his statue-like features. Yet he was almost eerily quiet, so that I found myself wondering what he was like away from the job site. What did he talk about when he spoke? Who did he hang out with? Where did he like to go on weekends? The other two let their personalities shine. They were young and free and given to spending off-time partying—at beaches, parks, their friends' houses. But painter number three hardly said a word. He nodded occasionally to them, but refused to join in their joking conversations. His attitude didn't strike me as angry or pompous. He simply appeared as if he were more interested in his own private thoughts than in his coworkers' steady banter.

What were those thoughts? I wondered. What could he be spending all those hours under the hot summer sun thinking about?

When my husband came home from work on that first day, he found me in the bedroom, touching myself as I visualized that fine young blond painter caressing my entire body with a soft clean brush. I imagined the handsome man whispering to me that all day long he'd thought about my naked body beneath his own, and that as he'd stroked the wood with his brush, he'd thought only of stroking my body with his fingertips, his mouth and his cock. I pictured his teeth against my skin, biting me, marking me. I imagined his hands, rough and hard, around my waist, holding me in place while his cock thrust firmly inside me.

Adam had no idea of my fantasies, but he also had no problem stripping out of his work clothes and joining me on the bed. He was hard from the moment he'd entered the door and caught me playing with myself. This has always been one of his favorite sexy scenarios.

"So goddamn hot," he said as he took his position on the bed with me. "What a nice surprise for me."

On the second day, the painters arrived before Adam went to work. He got a chance to see the pretty girl in her cargo pants and lipstick-red tank top, got to watch her climb up a ladder and start where she'd left off the evening before. Adam's dark eyes took in her sublime ass, the curves of her hips, and then he looked at the man who positioned his ladder at her side, staking his claim with a smile at my husband, as if to say, "Fine to look, man, but don't try to touch." I felt the same way. Who was I to judge Adam's approving gaze when my own interest was fully captivated by the quietest member of the team? The young painter chose an area about twenty feet away, and he slid on a Walkman, once again apparently content to entertain himself, not needing the constant banter of the other two.

Adam didn't even look at my painter. He gave me a quick kiss on the lips good-bye, and said he'd be seeing me after work—in a low, teasing voice adding that he hoped he'd be seeing as much of me today as he had the day before.

"So fucking sexy, baby," he whispered in my ear before gently biting the lobe. "Surprise me again, will you?"

I hardly heard him, but I nodded quickly, just to help him out the door. I had plans for my day—plans to watch paint drying. In fact, I spent my whole day trying to look as if I weren't watching the painters. I sat in my upstairs office and did my best to appear busy. In reality, I got not one thing done. All day long, I imagined inviting the young painter into my bedroom and asking if he thought I should change the color of the walls—or change my panties, or strip down and change the whole feeling of the day by giving him the blow job of his young life.

"You need anything, Joe?" the girl called to him at lunchtime, but Joe just shook his head.

Joe. Now, I had a name. A name made everything all the more real for me.

When Adam came home, I was in the shower, using the handheld massaging device to bring myself to my third orgasm in fifteen minutes. The hot water was about to give out, but I didn't care. Hot or cold, all I needed was the gush of water on my clit as I placed my palm on the glass wall to steady myself and imagined Joe in the shower with me, fucking me up against the wall, fucking my ass after he'd finished with my pussy. I saw the two of us, slippery with soap and come, getting as dirty as possible in a room designed to keep people clean.

Adam said, "What's all this?" as he opened the door and joined me. "What have we here, Cecilia?"

My breath was gone, my body limp. "Nothing," I said. "Nothing. Nothing."

On the third day, I came in my office while gazing out the window. Things were spiraling in my world now, and I couldn't explain my actions, but I couldn't stop them, either. I knew my desk and computer console provided me with ample coverage, and I slid my hand under my vibrant pink sundress and caressed my throbbing clit as I watched the boy work.

He had his headset on again, and he painted steadily, only occasionally breaking for a sip of water or a rest beneath the shade of our one-hundred-year-old apple tree before climbing back up the ladder, focused again on his work. I knew to time the grazing of my clit with the moments when he'd shake his hair out of his eyes so that I could gaze at his face when I ultimately came.

Something needed to be done, I told myself. I couldn't

go on like this, could I? Normal people didn't behave in such a wanton way. By the time Adam came home that night, I was so loose from climaxing that I didn't want my husband to fuck my pussy. Instead, I offered him my ass, bending over my desk as he took me, looking into our dark yard and visualizing the painter standing on a ladder right outside of the window and watching us.

Would his expression change when he watched my husband part my heart-shaped rear cheeks and fuck me from behind, sliding his greased-up cock deep into my rear hole? Would he lose that intent expression, or would he become even more focused on the intense action before him? We had to be more exciting to watch than paint drying, didn't we?

The fourth—and last—day the painters arrived to work was a Saturday, and I had a plan. I'd done my curly auburn hair in a loose bun, put a bit of extra attention into my makeup, and bought the most seductive little two-piece I could find. Not specifically skimpy, but sexy, a bikini top that tied in the back and fell scarf-like over my breasts. It was covered with a palm-tree motif that made me feel as if I'd left sunny Sonoma and found my way to Hawaii.

I gave myself a silent pep talk before exiting the bedroom, then went out to the lounger, as if I was solely after a tan, and I kicked back and watched Joe go to work.

Lord, was he sweet looking with his blond hair falling over his face so that he'd have to shake it out of his eyes every few strokes. His hard-muscled arms were so tanned, so tough. I was wet already—honestly, I had been wet since putting the bikini on in the first place. The question was this: When would he notice me?

That was Adam's question, as well.

"You look amazing," my husband said, bringing out lemonade for everyone. "But what do you think you're doing?" This last part was delivered in a dark whisper, and I shot him my most wide-eyed, Bambi-esque expression. "What do you mean?" I asked innocently.

"You're flirting," he said, insistent. "I know you. I know what you look like when you're flirting."

"Just tanning," I corrected him, trying not to peek over his shoulder at Joe, trying to keep my gaze locked on my husband's.

"It's okay," Adam said, bending next to the deck chair and reaching for my suntan oil. "If that's what you want, it's okay. If that's why I've been coming home to find you all soft and wet, then it's fine. Just let me know what you're thinking, darling. Clue me in to the plan—"

I stood and walked back into the house, knowing Adam would follow right after. In the cool shadows of our kitchen, I confessed. "Don't know. He just turns me on."

"The young one?"

I nodded.

"How far were you going to take this?"

"Fantasy-level." My blush was ferocious, but Adam seemed only after the facts.

"What about if we go further than that?"

"What do you mean?"

"He looks at you, kiddo. You have to know that. He'd have to be blind not to notice you."

That was delicious news to me, but I didn't know how to proceed with Adam. "So—" I started.

"So?" He let it hang there, between us, an unanswerable question. As long as we had been discussing a face-lift for our house, we'd also been discussing a face-lift for our relationship. Late at night, Adam and I would tease each other with images of inviting another lover to join us in the bed. Sometimes, we flirted with the thought of a slim cheerleader type, other nights we fantasized about asking some he-man stud from the gym to be our "third wheel." Now, it looked like we were on the verge of something new.

At the lunch break, the couple departed, as was their standard routine, probably off to snag a quickie, I thought, in the back of their truck. Joe stayed on, and Adam brought us all lunch. We talked, the three of us, and I thought I saw the lust I felt reflected in the young man's eyes. He still hardly said a word, but when he spoke, his voice was deep and husky, like a jazz singer's.

"Would you like dinner sometime?" I found myself asking. "Sometime like tonight?"

Joe gave me a quirky half-smile. "Yeah," he said, "sure. But the thing is, I have to tell you something—" As he said the words, he blushed.

The other two painters came back then, and he shrugged and said, "Tonight."

Adam and I were over the top with excitement. I fluttered uselessly around the house, getting ready. But nothing could have prepared me for Joe's surprise. When I opened the door, there he stood, wearing faded Levi's and a leather vest, open to reveal a scarlet tank top, low cut enough for me to see that Joe wasn't really "Joe," but a "Jo."

"I was trying to tell you earlier—"

Adam stood behind me, and rather than let us flounder there on the front step, he said, "Come on in, everyone. We don't want to hang out here all night."

Adam didn't have a problem at all with the change in events, but my mind reeled. All week, I'd thought of the young painter as a he. Now, with the revelation of this butch dyke, I didn't know what to make of my visions. But Jo did.

She put her hand on my knee and gazed at me. "You're so beautiful," she said. "I had trouble concentrating on my work, all week long—"

"Cecilia can do that to you," Adam agreed. "She has a way of making you forget what you were supposed to be doing."

"That's not it at all," Jo said, sweetly contradicting my husband. "I know what I'm supposed to be doing," Jo insisted, and she got on her knees in front of me and slowly slid my sundress up to my thighs. "Christ," she sighed. "You're just lovely."

I trembled ferociously. What was going on? My fantasy involved me and this hot young stud of a painter. Instead, I was being caressed by a "studette," by the hottest boy I'd ever seen in my life, and that boy was a girl.

"Get over it," Adam whispered to me. "Doesn't matter at all, what you're thinking about."

"But—"

"Doesn't," he insisted.

I looked into Jo's eyes and saw that Adam was right. It didn't matter whether this new lover was Joe or Jo, I was as attracted to her as I had been all week. Truthfully, maybe more so, because the surprise floored me, rocked me from the inside out. Still, I didn't know precisely how to proceed.

Jo did. She parted my legs further and gazed up the line under my dress, her eyes on my panties. "Take them off," she said.

"You do it."

"Gladly." She reached her hands up under my dress and gripped the waistband of my bikini-style panties. Slowly, she slid them down my thighs and off my legs. Then she parted my thighs even wider and brought her mouth to my exposed pussy. The pleasure of her mouth on my cunt flared through me like a wildfire. I couldn't believe how hot I felt at the electrical moment when her tongue made contact with my clit. Adam couldn't seem to believe it, either. He watched every second of the action, as mesmerized as I had been by Jo painting.

"So lovely," he said under his breath as Jo rubbed her head back and forth, tickling me all over with her soft short hair. She knew a lot about going down on a woman. She used her tongue expertly and assisted with her fingertips, parting my slippery pussy lips and holding me wide open for her voracious mouth. I thought of my fantasies during the week, watching her work, envisioning her cock—

That last thought made me sit up straighter.

"Don't worry," she said softly. "I pack—"

How had she known my fears of not being fulfilled? I don't know. I just sighed and whispered, "Perfect," as she moved her body, straightening up and letting me see the bulge beneath her jeans.

"Can I see it closer?" I asked, and I heard Adam suck in

his breath. I was getting bold, but only because I was so turned on I could hardly stand the suspense.

"Why don't I let you feel it?" she replied, popping the fly of her jeans and moving me with a graceful motion, so that I was on my stomach, facing my husband. I felt her pushing my dress up over my ass, and then I felt the head of her synthetic cock, parting my swollen pussy lips and giving me the first taste of being fucked by a woman.

The sensation was completely different from being with Adam. Jo's hands on my hips were soft and warm. She moved me gently, to an inner rhythm, and then she slid one hand under my belly, moving down until her fingertips could capture my clit. I felt her body pressed against mine, felt her small breasts against my back—even through the fabric of her shirt and my dress. I groaned at the teasing caresses of her relentless fingertips, and then I started to come.

Adam groaned when I groaned, and he moved forward on the couch. I saw that he'd taken out his cock, and I started to suck him as Jo continued to fuck me. I'd imagined the young painter shooting inside me. That fantasy changed as I realized Jo would come her own way, with her pussy pressed against the base of her toy, and that toy deep inside my pussy. Adam was going to come in my mouth, and I loved that I was the connecting rod between the two of them, that my holes were filled by my two lovers' cocks.

That's the image that brought me off a second time, coming as I swallowed Adam's juice, coming as Jo whispered something indiscernible beneath her breath and slammed her body against mine. I thought about watching her paint our house, the steady unshakable expression on her face. I thought of the way she remained focused and intent while she worked. Then I glanced over my shoulder and saw the same look on her face now, as she came.

On the fifth day, the job was finished, and the painters didn't come.

But Jo did, and that's all that mattered.

Rest Stop

FELIX D'ANGELO

I pulled up outside the rest stop, right by the men's room. I put the car in park and turned it off. Steevi looked at me nervously.

I smiled at her.

"You know what I have in mind," I said.

She shook her head. "I'm…I'm not sure, Sir."

"Make a guess."

She looked at the entrance to the men's room, at the dilapidated door hanging off its hinges. "You…you want me to go in there," she said. Her face was flushing deep red. Her nipples stood out clearly in the tight white minidress she wore. She plucked nervously at the hem of the minidress, trying in vain to pull it down more than an inch past her crotch. Her thighs were bare, her knees shrouded in the knee pads I'd had her purchase just yesterday at the sporting goods store. I could almost see her pussy, and I knew it wasn't protected by hair or panties. I kept her bare, exposed, vulnerable. I could see her nipples becoming more evident as they got harder. Her face flushed deeper red and I could see her cleavage getting pinker.

"Good guess," I told her. "And then what?"

"I…I don't know," she said.

"Make a guess," I said, reaching out to caress the thick knee pads she wore.

"You want me to get down on my knees."

"And?"

She hesitated, looking down at the ground. I leaned over, reached between her legs. She obediently opened them, making the hem of her dress ride up above her pussy so I could see it. When I drew my fingers up her slit, I found it incredibly wet. I slipped my fingers into her, making her moan. When I drew them out, I put them to her mouth and she obediently licked them clean.

"And suck cock," she said.

"That's right," I said. "About midnight, this rest stop gets hopping. It's the only rest stop on this road with a men's room that doesn't get locked at night, because every time they lock it people just break the door off the hinges. Straight guys come here every night to get their dicks sucked by other straight guys. Think it'll be a big thrill for them to get a woman's mouth on their cocks?"

My hand went back between her legs and I caressed her juice-slick clit. She moaned. Her arousal was obvious, and when I kissed her she was hungry, her mouth sucking at my tongue as I savaged her. When I pulled back, she smiled, trying hard not to display her fear.

"Yes," she said. "I think it'll be a great thrill."

"Then get in there," I said. "Your boyfriends will start showing up soon."

She hesitated, obviously toying with the idea of using her safeword. She always has that option, but in our two years together Steevi has never used it more than once in a given month. I push her as far as she'll go, always knowing that she'll stop me if she absolutely has to.

But she so rarely does.

Steevi opened the car door, got out, and walked toward the men's room, tugging down the hem of her minidress.

"Take the center stall," I told her.

She looked back at me, her nipples standing clear in the light of my headlights. She looked glorious in the tiny dress, her firm body wrapped tightly and exposed for all to see. Except there was no one to see it—yet.

Steevi turned and headed toward the darkened door.

When she disappeared into the darkness of the men's room, I killed the headlights, pulled my laptop out of the back and set it up on the seat Steevi had occupied. I booted up and fired up the software that would show me the scene captured by the wireless infrared camera and microphone I'd installed earlier that afternoon. It had cost quite a pretty penny to get one of that kind of quality, but it was worth it.

I had placed the tiny camera immediately above the two bathroom stalls, allowing me to see both of them from directly above. Steevi had to know I was watching. I'd used this trick before, though never with such edgy certainty. She'd sucked strangers, but she'd never done it in such inglorious environs.

I could feel my cock hardening in my pants.

The fact that this was the most deserted stretch of highway in the state, and that our friends would be traveling a hundred or more miles to reach it, did little to lessen my arousal. After all, you never knew when a stranger might happen by—a real stranger, not one of the men Steevi and I played with regularly. And you might see a cop uniform that wasn't bought at a leather shop on Santa Monica Boulevard.

But everything else about this was perfectly planned. Steevi would know each cock in her mouth, but she wouldn't know she knew—not until she tasted it, and maybe not even then. After all, I liked to find new partners for her, and part of her own fantasy was that she never knew when a brand-new, unfamiliar cock would find its way into her mouth.

Steevi had closed and latched the men's room stall. She must have gotten the picture as soon as she saw the glory holes smashed out of the panels on each side of her center stall. She knew she'd be taking on two dates at once. With the stall door latched, she lowered herself onto her knees and waited, her face up against one of the glory holes.

About eleven-forty-five, another car pulled into the lot—a big pickup truck with a beefy, flannel-clad guy driving. He looked me over, as if to make sure I wasn't a cop. Maybe he thought I was a guy waiting to go in and give head. Either way, he disappeared into the bathroom.

Almost immediately another car pulled up, this one a sedan. There were three young guys in it, out for a thrill, and they joked and teased each other about being faggots as they got out of the car and headed into the bathroom. Our friends, getting into the act even more than I expected.

I watched, everything illuminated in reddish-gray by the infrared camera. The beefy guy was first. It was almost pitch black inside the bathroom, so he mustn't have known he was about to get sucked off by a woman. He stepped into the stall and unzipped his pants, took out his cock and took a long, luxurious piss, a thick stream hitting the toilet as the teenage guys crowded into the bathroom. Without even shaking off very well, he turned and shoved his cock through the glory hole. It connected with Steevi's face, a face I'd fucked so many delicious times before. Steevi didn't hesitate; she wrapped her lips around the guy's cockhead and started bobbing up and down, servicing him.

The three young men crowded into the other stall, pushing and shoving each other as they argued over who was going to be first. Finally one pulled out his cock and stuck it through the hole.

Steevi reached behind her and took hold of it, getting it hard as she sucked off the beefy guy.

His hips started to pump, fucking Steevi's face as she got her next cock ready. I admired the way her mouth worked up and down on his shaft, one hand milking his balls while the other stroked the next guy hard. From what I could see the beefy flannel guy had a good-sized cock, but Steevi took it all, no doubt swallowing it down her throat. Within minutes the guy let out a long, low sigh and Steevi clamped her lips around his shaft. I knew she was swallowing.

The guy zipped up, left the stall. One of the young men heard him leaving and took his place. By the time he put his hard cock through the hole, Steevi had turned around and knelt to suck his friend's cock. She was going at it fiercely, but she heard the other guy's footsteps and reached behind her to keep him ready as she sucked off his buddy.

The first one came almost immediately—premature ejaculation, no doubt. Steevi stayed down low on his cock until he'd pumped her mouth full. Then she turned around and her hand guided the new boy's cock into her mouth. She started to suck.

Two more cars pulled up. I was too fixated on the screen at first to notice who was in them, but when I glanced up I saw that there were several guys in each car. They crowded into the bathroom. I looked back on the screen. Steevi finished up with the second teenager and moved on to the third as the new men crammed into the bathroom stalls and took out their cocks.

Someone finally noticed the third hole I'd cut in the door of Steevi's stall. One of the guys, apparently less shy than the others, pushed his cock through the hole and Steevi obediently began stroking him off with one hand while she kept another cock hard with her other hand. Her mouth continued to work on the third young stud until he groaned and shot in her mouth.

Steevi looked straight up and swallowed, her eyes wide. Did she know I was watching? Despite the poor resolution of the infrared camera, I could see the glistening on her chin from the faint lights through the window. Her face was covered in come. She was drooling it.

More men crowded into the stalls, waiting their turn to get sucked through the glory hole. Steevi obediently moved from one to the other, using her hands to keep the others hard and ready so she would waste no time when her mouth finally got to them.

I timed several of the men with the clock showing in the bottom right corner of the laptop's screen and found it was less than three minutes from the moment Steevi's mouth touched their cockheads to the moment she drew her lips off of them, dribbling semen. They flooded out of the bathroom door and jumped into their cars, the ones who came in groups slapping each other on the back at the free blow job they'd just gotten.

Then I felt my heart in my throat. I looked up to see a pair of black sedans pulling into the rest stop parking lot. At first I panicked—until I realized these weren't unmarked police cars at all. They were rentals, and the uniformed "cops" inside were supposed to be here.

There were four cops total. They adjusted their belts as they walked past me. One of them nodded. I knew him well, of course—but he still looked mighty intimidating in uniform.

Steevi had almost finished the men in the bathroom—a total of twelve so far. There were two men left waiting to have their cocks sucked. They were too distracted to notice the cops. One of the men stood with Steevi's mouth wrapped around the base of his shaft, working hungrily; the other with Steevi's delicate, long-nailed hand stroking him into readiness for her mouth.

She swallowed one man's load and moved on to the other. The one zipped up and pushed past the cops, nodding to them.

Two "cops" crowded into the vacant stall. One took his place behind the guy getting his cock sucked, waiting for the glory hole. The other unzipped and put his cock through the third glory hole. Steevi reached out and took it, stroking him hard as she finished the cock she was on, swallowing eagerly.

The guy pulled back, zipped up, and nervously pushed past the cops, running for the door.

Steevi didn't even know they were "cops." But I did, and it made my cock throb even harder than before. In the gray-pink light of the infrared I could see when she stretched her head back to massage her sore jaw that her eyes were closed.

One cop unzipped and put his hard cock through the vacant glory hole. The other two grabbed the hole and punched it, cracking it wider until it was oblong enough to fit them both at once. Steevi faced four cocks.

She took one cock in each hand and started sucking the first cop's. He groaned as her lips eagerly worked up and down on his shaft.

It was only a minute before he came. Steevi missed some of his come, dribbling it down her chin and onto her breasts, soaking the thin minidress she wore. She kept reaching behind her to stroke one cop's dick and turned her attention to the oblong glory hole that offered two.

She went from one cock to the other. One cop reached through the hole and grabbed her hair, guiding his cock into her mouth at the same time as his friend's. The two of them fucked Steevi's face at the same time as her hand twisted behind her to keep their fellow cop hard and ready for her.

Both cops shot at once, filling her mouth with their semen as she groaned and gurgled deep in her throat. Semen ran down her chin and soaked her dress. Her hair was matted with it.

She licked them clean; they pulled out, zipped up, and went to wait in their "cruiser."

Steevi turned to take care of the last cop. Her head bobbed

up and down on him, and he reached through the glory hole to hold her face so he could face-fuck her better. Steevi moaned as he pumped her. It wasn't long before he came in her mouth and she swallowed.

The cop buckled his belt, zipped his pants, and left.

The two cruisers pulled out of the parking lot; no other cars showed up. The cop cars had probably scared them away.

Steevi stayed on her knees, her face against the glory hole, dripping come. I left the laptop on the seat, locked the car, and went inside.

I had to break the latch to force the stall door, but I moved fast enough that I don't think Steevi was sure it was me. I pushed her over the toilet and she leaned hard on the pipes as I pulled up her short dress and forced her legs open. She lifted her ass in the air as I pulled my rock-hard dick out and shoved it into her.

She was gushing. Juice ran down her legs as I entered her.

I started fucking her, pushing down on her ass to keep her low so I could hit her G-spot just right. I knew how to make her come, and I knew any residual doubts about whether she wanted this would be shattered in her own mind by the explosion of an orgasm. I pushed one hand into her mouth, smearing the streams of semen all over her lips, and grabbed her hair with the other, pulling her head back so she had to lean hard against me as I pounded into her.

She let out a great gasping moan and I felt her cunt contracting around my shaft. She was coming, and she didn't even try to hide it. She let out great sobs of release as I fucked her, and I knew that now was the time to drive my dominance home.

I pulled out of her cunt and yanked her skirt up higher, moving my cockhead between her cheeks.

"No," she gasped. "N—no—no!" But she didn't call out her safeword, didn't do the one thing she knew, beyond a doubt, would put an end to the scene.

I drove into her hard in one thrust, taking her ass and making her squeal with surprise. I pushed her hard against the toilet pipes, listening to her sob and shudder as I fucked her dry hole.

"Rub your clit," I growled.

"N—no!" she gasped. "P—please!"

"Rub it!"

She reached between her legs so quickly I knew her protest had just been a resistance to the ultimate humiliation of coming a second time. She began to rub her clit eagerly as I fucked her ass, my hand in the small of her back keeping her steady as I pounded into her. I was fighting not to shoot my load; her incredibly tight ass always made me come so quickly. But I managed to hold off as I took her anally, making her rub herself to the second orgasm I knew she so badly wanted.

"Oh God," she sobbed. "Don't make me—oh!"

Then she came, and the spasms of her asshole around my cock were even stronger than those of her first orgasm. She kept rubbing violently, bringing herself off until I wasn't sure if she'd come twice more or three times more, one after the other as she did sometimes when she was really, really turned on. It was all I needed to let myself go, pounding my cock into her ass and erupting in a flood of semen deep inside her. I groaned, letting her know that I was going off inside her, and as I did she pushed her ass back against me, demanding my load, and I knew she felt the flood of hot liquid as I injected her with my come.

"Th—thank you," she whimpered. "Thank you...."

I pulled out, tucked my cock away just like the others. Zipped up and turned to leave the bathroom.

I was already in the car before Steevi followed me, tottering on unsteady legs. Her dress was torn, the neckline opened so I could see one pink nipple hanging out as her white skin shone in the headlights. She swayed on her high heels and came to the side of the car, leaning up against the window, panting.

I reached over and unlocked the door. She stumbled as she pulled it open, leaning hard on the door and tumbling into the seat. I barely got the laptop out of the way.

She curled up in the passenger seat, her face dripping semen, her eyes wide and glazed.

"Thank you," she whimpered. "Thank you."

I started the car, put it in reverse, and pulled out of the parking lot.

On the long drive home, Steevi dropped off to sleep, her tit still hanging out, her dress still pulled up and semen running down the backs of her thighs. I pulled over to the side of the road and repositioned her so I could put on her seat belt.

I looked into her sleeping face, slick with other men's come, her hair matted with it.

It had been hard for me. For every aspect of it that had turned me on, there had been jealousy, rage, confusion. But when it came right down to it, I loved her. And she had begged me, in page after page of her diary, detailing this, her fondest fantasy for more years than she could count.

The diary she had pleaded with me to read, whispering to me that I had permission to do anything—*anything*—she'd written about in it. How could I let her down?

Steevi began to snore softly, delicately, as I pulled back onto the interstate and headed for home.

Forbidden Fruit

PEARL JONES

It started with a hothouse cucumber. Shauna never bought the waxed kind; she didn't like the way they felt, preferred the kind where you can eat the skin. Her husband thought it was funny, plastic-wrapped food. He came up behind her while she was unloading the groceries, laughing as he saw what she held.

"For your protection?" he murmured into her neck.

She leaned back against him, smiling. Shrugged. "Like you, for my pleasure." Turning in his grip, she reached for the new pack of condoms. She decided to put the condom on him, but she'd never done it before, fumbled a bit. They were both laughing by the time it was on, still hot, still excited, having fun. Like children, for all their five years together.

"I am the Hulk!" Dave growled. "Large and green." He gripped her ass, picked her up, set her on the table; her legs wrapped around his waist. Teased her a moment longer, thrust in, hard and long. She bucked up against him, moaning into his mouth.

"My very own superhero," she sighed. The cucumber rested on the counter; he looked at it and grinned.

Dave had to go out of town on business. Creeping out of bed quietly, leaving her asleep, he chuckled silently all the way out the door, imagining the look on her face when she saw his "present": a plastic-wrapped cucumber with a sticky-note attached. *Think of me,* it read.

She did more than that. Opening her eyes, seeing the vegetable, reading the note, she sighed, filled with her love for him, then, grinning, stripped off the plastic. She put a condom on the vegetable, to make it feel more like him, filled herself with it. It felt almost like him, coated in latex, hard and slick; she screwed her eyes shut, tilted it high, pulled it out, pushed it back. Her other hand brushed her breast the way he did, teased the nipple, stroked the sides. She quickened her strokes, mimicking his pattern, changed the angle of thrust again, higher, deeper inside. Almost enough to hurt, but not quite. Intense. Pinched her nipple, wishing it was his teeth. Brushing her clit just a few times, she came.

"I love you," she sighed, eyes closed, and fell asleep, still surrounding the surrogate. Waking, she had to laugh. *Him, not the cucumber,* she thought.

She never told him about her early-morning adventure; perhaps he guessed from the way her fingers shook, watching her fill the fridge a few weeks later. Maybe it had always been in his mind. He made plans, his own hands unsteady as he thought of her, of what he'd do. Colors filled his mind, green and orange, yellow, white. The deep not-quite-red of her flesh. The purple of his own engorged head.

He came up behind her as she bent over, reaching into the vegetable bin. There were cucumbers there she didn't remember buying; she craned her neck to look at him. "You?"

"Mmn." He smiled down at her. His eyes lit up, drinking her in, and her body warmed, nipples coming up—she knew that look, what it portended. Her heart sped in her chest.

"If you've finally learned where the grocery store is, perhaps you might be taught to shop?" She moved to rise, but he bent over her, pressing himself hard against her ass. Her breath caught, cheeks heating in the refrigerator's chill.

He reached around her, hand brushing the side of her breast as if in passing, selected a smallish cucumber from the bin. Free hand on the small of her back to keep her in position, he drew the cucumber back, stripped the plastic away with his teeth. Somehow never losing his grin. Her skirt was only knee-length, easy enough to dip beneath the hem. He used the tip of the vegetable to tease her. When she was ready, he told her to close her eyes, used it like a dildo, then replaced it with his cock. One chill, one hot, both hard, both satisfying. When he pulled out, put the vegetable back, she thought she'd scream. When he replaced it with himself again, she did.

When she came, he slid the cucumber home, pressed it all the way into her. "It's holding my place until later," he told her, "after we shop." They went to the grocery store, but didn't buy much in the way of groceries. More cucumbers, and carrots, and bananas. Raspberries. A melon, oranges, peaches, grapes. A mushroom brush, when she brushed the soft bristles and smiled. Some Popsicles, which he tried to sneak into the cart. She saw, and raised an eyebrow, and then laughed, kissed him there in the aisle and threw the box in.

They raced home. He lifted her by the waist, put her on the counter, leaned in to give her a deep kiss. She rucked up her skirt, put his hands where she wanted them. "Oh, my. Did I do that to you?" He pulled her panties down; she could feel the moisture, blushed. "So, what do you think I should do now?" He loved to tease her, knowing she didn't much say what she wanted. She'd blush, and look away, but then she'd make some signal, put his hands where she needed them to be, rub against him. He expected her to do something of the sort now; instead, he got a quick cold shower. She grabbed the hose from the sink, aimed it at him, turned it on. "Don't you know you're supposed to wash the produce before you eat?"

That sounded like directions to him! He wrestled the hose away from her, turned it between her thighs, then decided he might as well do her whole form. He soaked her, then peeled her clothes away, rinsed her off again.

He kissed his way down from her neck to her heels, making nibbling, munching sounds. Torn between laughing and moaning, she tried to draw him up her body to where she wanted him, but he refused. "My mother taught me never to start with dessert."

"I'm not asking you to!" she cried, writhed, trying to keep her balance. The counter wasn't the widest bed she'd ever had. "I just want you to eat your vegetables!"

"In that case..." he kissed his way up the inside of one leg, and got to work. The base of the cucumber barely protruded from her lips; he used his nose to push it higher, sucked her flesh, ran the flat of his tongue over her clit. She clenched, excited, and the vegetable pushed out a quarter inch. He pushed it back again, blew his breath hot to make her shiver.

Her spasms pushed the cucumber out again; this time, he gripped it between his teeth, pulled it most of the way out, pushed it in hard. She moaned, lifting her hips to him, and he smiled around his mouthful, brought his fingers to bear.

She reached out as she came, grabbed the nearest objects. One hand found a drawer-pull, harmless enough—the other squeezed the dish detergent, forcing the soap up and out in a fountain. Much of it landed on his back; he pulled the cucumber free, spat it into his hand (his teeth almost all the way through it). "What, you think I need another shower already?"

They played in the kitchen for hours, ended up on the floor. He put a raspberry in his belly button for her to suck out. She did the same for him. They weren't large enough to cover her nipples, but he balanced two, nibbled them and the fruits they tipped. They traded fruit-flavored kisses.

"All those years I wasted, listening to society!" Shauna smiled, staring up at the ceiling. (There were cobwebs in the corners; for once, she couldn't be bothered to care.)

"And what did society say?" Dave reached for the groceries still on the table. There was a banana…

"They told me not to play with my food!" They both dissolved in laughter, ended up entwined tighter than before, kisses and caresses heating their blood again. He reached again for the banana, but she beat him to the punch (or rather, to the fruit), retrieving a melon, a devilish smile on her face. "I've always wanted to see this," she told him, rising and moving to the counter. She grabbed a utensil from a drawer, blocking his view with her body. Though curious, he wasn't about to complain; he loved the sight of her, the line, the curves. The taut flesh just begging for his touch.

She turned around, body shaking with silent laughter. "Here," she handed him the melon, now with a cock-sized hole. Some of the flesh had been removed, cored out to give him room.

"You're kidding." He looked at her. "Aren't you?"

"No. What, you've never? When I was in school, they talked like all guys did. And I've always wondered. What it would look like, I mean."

"Besides silly?" He twisted up his face, stared at the melon. The flesh inside was pink. Almost reminiscent of her, now that he thought about it. And the hole was the right size. And her eyes were so bright, hopeful and admiring and amused. His cock twitched, deciding for him. He lay back on the floor. Then got up, sat in a kitchen chair. Shifted his weight a few times, trying to guess at the proper position. She giggled at him, knelt on the floor where she could see, kissed his knee, looked up at him through her lashes, her patented sex-kitten look. He sighed, and brought the melon home.

It was cold! Colder than he'd expected. Almost cold enough to wilt his cock. But she was cooing her pleasure, watching, and it was wet, and smooth, and tight, and it warmed as he pushed in again and again. He alternated, using his hands to pull the melon back, holding it in place and thrusting with his hips, getting more excited with each push. Body heat at last, it sloshed and yielded, a cunt from the vegetable kingdom, almost as nice as hers.

He was heartbeats away from coming when she stopped him. "Wait. Let me." She took the melon, pulled it back, replaced it with her hot mouth. "Mmm." She licked and sucked the fruit juice from him, then took him deep, swallowing, breathing through her nose. He panted, struggled not to come too quickly, but the moment her lips hit the base of his shaft, he was lost. He exploded, orgasm as intense as any he could remember, throbbing at the base of his spine, salty come pouring up from his balls, roaring up his shaft, into her drinking, sucking mouth.

"I need a bath. And a nap. And some food." Shauna sighed, leaning against his leg, tired and sticky and swollen and tender and very satisfied, but still curious, if only she had the energy. What else might be done with what they'd bought?

"Wait here," he winked, levered himself up out of the chair. She followed his progress by the sounds. The bedroom. The bath. Cabinets opening. Water running. Back to her. "Come on." He helped her to her feet, then, laughing, picked her up, carried her to the bathtub, bubbles beckoning. She clung to him as he lowered her safely, kissed him, tried to pull him in. "Nope. This one's for you."

She didn't understand what he meant at first, but he made himself clear. He bathed her, tenderly, completely, his fingers gentler than any sponge, sliding over sensitized flesh, dipping within. Pressing softly on her sphincter, making her gasp. She was very sensitive there, enjoyed some anal play, but they hadn't done much in that area. He was afraid of hurting her.

Tonight, he seemed a little more confident. The tip of his finger slid in, out, back again. She sighed, eyes fluttering closed, lost in sensation. His finger crept forward, deeper, twisted the slightest bit.

"More?"

"Oh, yes."

He pulled away. Her eyes still shut, she waited, smiling like a cat. Feeling incredibly well-loved. Splashing sounds, small waves against her body. The return of welcome pressure. She relaxed.

As thin as his finger, but longer. Her eyes opened, blinked shut again. "Oh, my. That's—" her words cut off, his fingers' knowing motions stealing her voice. Not gentle any more, but insistent, he rubbed the flesh around her clit, not touching the swollen nub, but circling it. She squeaked, and he laughed, a low sound of masculine pride, flicked his fingers sideways.

Her body clenched. The feeling was odd, welcome but strange. She was stretched, gripping the object, held open around it. It felt like it extended up past her ribs. She imagined that if she swallowed, she would taste it, and while part of her wondered what it was, mostly, she didn't care. She felt reformed, reshaped around it, and each flick of her husband's hands taught her more.

He teased her for long minutes that felt to her like hours. Mini-spasms shook her body, splashing water from the tub. Her teeth chattered; she was aroused, excited, desperate to come. "Please," she sighed, and he laughed again. Leaning over the side of the tub, he kissed her, thrust two fingers inside, curled them high to hit her G-spot. One hand curled behind her head, necessary precaution. She arched her body high, might have hurt herself had he not been there.

But of course, if he'd not been there, it wouldn't have happened.

She rested in the water until it cooled, dreamy expression on her face. Maybe drifted off for a moment or two. He wandered away, came back smiling again, drained the tub, put her in the shower. Got in himself, rinsed her off, began to soap himself. "Oh, no," she shook her head, "that's my job." She took the sponge from him, began to work. Soaped, rinsed, ran her hands down his sides. Used her nails to trace his spine.

"No," he took her hands in his own. "Not now." It was almost a ritual with her. First the tracing, then the circling to his balls, a massage, then her mouth, her tongue. He was still a little sore from recent orgasms; more than that, he was hungry. And he had plans for what remained of the night. He kissed her pout away, got them dried off, led her to the bedroom.

She had to laugh. There was a bowl of fruit on the pillows. A bucket of ice, champagne chilling. A fruit knife she dimly recognized as having been a wedding gift. And two of his silk handkerchiefs. "Napkins," he explained. "Shall we dine?"

"There are no plates..." Her intonation made it almost a question.

"If you will," he bowed, playfully formal, took the bowl of fruit away, pulled back the covers to expose new satin sheets. Her jaw gaped, but she let him help her into bed, watched as he opened the champagne. No glasses, either.

He drank from the bottle, moved to her, leaned in to kiss her and gave her the sparkling wine from his lips. She swallowed, remembering their wedding night. He'd done that then, too, a few times since. Back to the bottle, another mouthful, to her again.

"Ready for something to eat?" Her eyes traveled down his body. "No, I was thinking of something less salty." Smiling, he grabbed a bunch of grapes from the bowl, held it above her lips. She took one with her lips, then reached for the fruit. "Let me." He put her hands on the headboard, held the grapes to her mouth. Her eyebrows raised, but she said nothing, just ate the grapes.

And the melon cubes he fed to her, though she found it hard to swallow through the laughter, trying to find some taste of him in the fruit.

The peach he sliced, fed to her from his mouth. That taste was easier to find; her breath sped, her pulse raced. "My turn," she grabbed the back of his neck, pulled him down, kissed him hard and tugged him down onto her. She could feel his cock beginning to rise. Laughing, she wriggled out from beneath him. "No, stay there."

When she was sure he would, she climbed out of bed. Champagne, as he had served it to her. Grapes. There were some melon cubes left; she looked at them, nodded. Set one between her teeth to feed to him. Then a second and third and forth inside her cunt. "You'll have to work for your dinner. I'm sure you won't mind." She straddled his head, lowered herself gently. His hands came up to her waist, and he dove into his task.

She felt each cube as his tongue drew it forth, shuddered and shook and moaned, near coming again. But as soon as the last cube was gone, he stopped. She lifted her hips. "Still hungry?"

"Always. There's a banana in the bowl."

Her body spasmed just at the thought of it. She peeled it, inserted it very gently, trying not to squish it, resumed her seat, resting her hands on the headboard. He ate very slowly, making each bite last. By the time he was certain there was nothing left, she was a quivering wreck, as desperate to come as if she hadn't come several times in the past hours, as though it had been months, years, since her last orgasm. Drenched head to foot in sweat, clinging to the headboard for balance, animal sounds escaping, shocking even her, she begged and pleaded with him to help her. To make her come.

"Hands and knees." His breath was as ragged as hers, his cock stiff and proud again. He drank in the sight of her, the sounds. His wife, his love, shaking with need. And him the cause. The taste of her, the scent, in his mouth, on his skin. The heat of her, mere seconds away. She half-fell off him, waggling her hips like a dog. *Come get me.*

He reached into the bowl, retrieved a parsnip. Like a thick, albino carrot, deeply ridged. He'd scrubbed it while she was resting in the bathtub, coated it with salad oil. He placed a kiss on the base of her spine, pressed it against her anal rim. She leaned back, welcoming, and he pressed it almost all of the way in. He'd chosen this one on purpose; its base had a natural flare. Her sphincter contracted around the relative thinness, holding it secure.

He nuzzled his cockhead between her lips, finding the optimum angle with the ease of long practice. Very gingerly inserted himself, a half inch at a time. Her keening began before his head was fully in, got higher and louder with each centimeter until he nudged her cervix, then broke.

She'd never felt hotter, wetter, tighter, more welcoming. He gritted his teeth, holding back his orgasm. He wanted her to come first, sawed himself in and out. Three times, four, five. She started to yip, pocket-pet sounds. He pulled all the way out, pushed back in hard. Pulled out halfway, tugged at the parsnip, pushed it back. "Yes. Yes. Yes!" High-pitched yelps. Rictus grin tearing at his face, knowing he could hold back no longer, he pushed himself back in as hard, as deep as he could, angled to hit her G-spot with his cock. The base of the parsnip poked him; he ignored it, pushed harder still. Her flesh shivered around him as she came. He exploded with the first contraction, and she milked him dry.

They fell, exhausted, still together, parting slowly, naturally. He moved to clean up the evidence of their passion, stripping the condom away, beginning to pull out the parsnip, but she made a sleepy noise of discontent. Smiling softly, he left the vegetable where it was, rose to collect a pitcher of ice water, some crackers and nuts, more fruit. She'd be hungry when she woke. Grinning, he grabbed another cucumber, and a few carrots. Just in case.

On the table, a box of melted Popsicles sagged, forgotten.

Sometimes It's Better to Give

BRYN HANIVER

"I'm sick of being fucked."

Julie's husband, sitting across their living room in his recliner, lowered his paper and raised an eyebrow at her—she never used rough language.

"You heard me," she added.

He nodded. "I did indeed—but last night causes me some doubt."

He had a point. Last night she had been insatiable, demanding him in her mouth, her pussy and her ass, only reluctantly letting him come. He'd fallen asleep with one of those exhausted smiles she loved.

But she'd lain awake for hours, restless and twitchy, trying to figure out what else she wanted. The twins were at summer camp, getting into trouble as only fourteen year olds could, but that was somebody else's trouble for two weeks. She and Gerry had a rare and cherished stretch of privacy and time for each other, and sex for the first three days had been energetic and deliciously loud.

Something was missing though, and she sensed Gerry felt it too. There was a restlessness. It wasn't that either of them was losing their looks—the streaks of gray in his beard and temples had made him even more handsome, and she kept herself in excellent form with swimming and yoga. She felt damn good, and Gerry had never stopped telling her how sexy she was.

So what was missing? Last night she had thought long and hard, finally succumbing to a fitful sleep. This morning, perhaps as a result of dreams bubbling through her subconscious, she knew.

"Okay, you're right. I'm not exactly sick of being fucked. I'm sick of—only being fucked."

"Right," Gerry said, slowly, waiting for more info. He taught history and English, didn't speak much, and had the patience of the ages.

"Sick of always being the fuckee, and never the fucker," she continued. "Of receiving, but never giving—so to speak."

"And you propose to ameliorate this issue by...?"

A small shiver went through her—he knew damn well exotic words turned her on. A decade ago she'd nearly creamed her jeans while taking the GRE.

"Get dressed," she told him. "We're going shopping for strap-ons."

They made a day of it, having a nice lunch in the next town over and then visiting a sex shop that was out of range of Gerry's high school students or her associates at the lab. It was a big shop, and the variety was a bit overwhelming.

As she took a harness and one of the exchangeable dildos from the rack, Gerry looked a little pale.

"I'm reluctantly deferring to your desires on this," he said, voice low so the other half dozen people browsing the wares couldn't hear. "But I have two conditions."

"I'm listening."

He looked at the wide display of colors and shapes on the wall, then turned to her. "The business end can't be too big—or even remotely realistic looking."

"Something like this?" she asked, grabbing a long, smooth and purple dildo called Silk.

"Actually that's still too big."

"A compromise has been reached. Excellent." She made a couple of thrusting movements with her hips and smiled as he turned pink and looked around to see if anyone else had seen.

Julie reached up for a very large, very realistic-looking phallus called the Champ, holding it between her breasts and giving him a wistful look.

"Still, it would be nice to try something like this on for size."

Gerry shook his head. "Actually, you can't fully appreciate the joy of having an erection unless..." He gazed off into space.

"Yes? Unless what?"

"Unless you've got a beautiful young woman kneeling in front of you, back arched, sweet ass high in the air, her head turned back to look at you, her face transformed by lust and anticipation."

Julie thought about it—she had been that woman many

times, but how would it feel to see it from his point of view? It sounded so sexy her pussy twitched.

"Fine," she said, holding up the Champ. "I'll use this to fuck the babysitter." Scooping up the harness and both dildos, she headed for the checkout.

Gerry showed remarkable restraint on the drive home. Amber, their old babysitter, was in her second or third year of college now but she was back in town for the summer, living with a couple of friends two streets over. They'd chatted just the other day in the young woman's yard—she'd been mowing the grass in short shorts and a bikini top.

Unlike Julie's tall, firm and fit body, Amber's was petite and well-rounded, with large breasts and lush curves. She had a friendly, beautiful smile and had casually flirted with Gerry.

As soon as they were back from the walk her husband had bent her over the couch and fucked her silly. It was great when the kids were away.

They were twenty miles away from the sex shop before Gerry finally spoke.

"You want to fuck the babysitter."

"Don't you think she's cute?" Julie replied, teasing. "Besides, you're the one who said I couldn't appreciate it without..."

"I remember what I said. I just don't think you'll—"

"Go through with it," Julie finished for him. Would she? Gerry didn't know it but she'd spent some quality time talking with Amber in the coffee shop yesterday and the young woman had been frank about the fun she was having at college—and about her sexual adventurousness. She'd also mentioned several times how good her former employers both looked, and that she'd love to "catch them up on everything."

Julie got the big dildo out of the bag and began stroking it gently, smiling as Gerry's eyes remained riveted to the road ahead. "I'll invite her over for dinner tonight," she said. Gerry remained quiet.

Dinner went remarkably well. They had dressed carefully—Gerry wore teacher semiformal, looking quite dapper, while she had chosen a smart blazer top and loose-fitting trousers. Amber showed up in a snug, summery dress she saucily called a "baby tee." It was short-sleeved, cut high, and clung tightly to her full breasts. Julie thought it made her look scandalously young and sexy, though the purplish color was probably something only a college student could pull off, and reminded Julie of a ripe plum.

Conversation flowed, and Amber was more than warm toward her former employers—she was deliberately flirtatious. After dinner and some excellent wine, Julie figured it was time to take charge. Beneath her loose pants, the mid-sized Silk dildo was strapped on, pressing up against her abdomen and lending her some courage.

Amber was leaning up against the bar in the living room, looking at the latest pictures of the twins. Julie walked up behind her and put an arm on either side, trapping her.

"As you might have guessed," she said softly near the young woman's ear, "I had a reason for inviting you over tonight."

Amber didn't turn or tense up, she just said "Oh?"

Julie leaned into her a bit, feeling the dildo as it pressed against her taut stomach and the top of Amber's ass.

"Oh!" the smaller woman said. "My, my." Now she turned, her hand reaching down to rub the dildo through Julie's trousers, pressing it against sensitive skin. Without getting a chance to think too much about it, Julie melted into her first serious kiss with another woman, soft lips and gentle tongue tasting of wine, larger breasts pressing against her own.

Gerry, who she knew had remained skeptical throughout dinner, let out a sigh at the sight. Julie wasn't sure how long her tongue danced with Amber's, but eventually she got hold of herself enough to break the kiss and step backward.

Amber was smiling up at her. "Well then, Mrs. Johanson. What are *your* plans for the evening?"

Julie stood up straight and said, "Fucking."

Amber raised an eyebrow at her. Julie allowed her lip to curl into a small smile. "There are two beautiful bodies with five inviting holes in this room, and I'd like to fuck them all."

Amber's jaw dropped slightly, and she looked over at Gerry. He shrugged. "It's her party tonight," he said.

A smile spread across Amber's face as she stepped forward and slowly dropped to her knees in front of Julie. Opening the front of the trousers, she took the smooth purple dildo out and slowly licked the tip. Looking down, Julie was mesmerized.

"It's very feminine," Amber said. Tilting her head slightly, she took the entire length of it to the back of her throat, then slowly pulled back, resting her head on Julie's hip and looking up her. The sight had been remarkably erotic—Julie could feel herself getting squishy.

"Have you ever done this before?" Amber asked her.

"No." Julie whispered. She could feel the young woman's

warm breath on her thighs.

In response, Amber deep-throated the purple dildo again, this time maintaining eye contact. Julie watched as the phallus, her phallus, disappeared and then slowly reappeared. She'd wondered what it looked like to her husband when she gave him head and now she knew: it looked sexy.

"Gerry, get your mouth over here," she said.

He knelt beside Amber who graciously held the dildo for him, licking the side of it with her tongue. His tongue joined in and Julie was amused to see he seemed more interested in Amber's tongue than the dildo.

She grabbed either side of his head. "Ready for this, sweetie?"

Amber was grinning, but Gerry wasn't, though he opened his mouth for her as she pushed gently forward. Amber whispered for him to relax as more of the dildo disappeared.

When he looked up at her with resignation and trust in his eyes, Julie felt wetter than ever. She thrust slowly until the dildo disappeared completely into his mouth. What could be sexier than having your husband deep-throat you?

A few more slow in and outs and he began to get into it, his hands squeezing her buttocks as they tightened and relaxed with the thrusting. The feel of the straps and the dildo bumping against her were driving her crazy—it was time for some serious fucking.

She withdrew from Gerry's mouth and told him to pull down her pants. Stepping out of them, she walked over to the dresser, removing the Silk dildo and replacing it with the thick, realistic looking Champ. When she turned around, Amber said "Oh my." Julie squirted some lube onto it and began stroking it, still wearing the blazer. Amber stared at her.

Julie pointed to their thick area rug. "On your knees," she told the babysitter. Keeping wide eyes on the oversized phallus, the still-smiling Amber knelt down on the rug, placing her elbows and forearms on the ground. In the compromising position, her short skirt didn't quite cover her ass. Julie strutted over, went down to one knee and flipped up the girl's skirt.

Amber hadn't worn any underwear. Catching a whiff of a clean, musky scent, Julie was caught off guard by a rush of lust. When Amber arched her back and rolled her hips slightly, Julie stared. It was so submissive, so inviting—having been in that pose many times herself, she knew just what the young woman felt.

"Please fuck me," Amber whispered. Overwhelmed with desire, Julie knelt behind her, put her hands on that smooth white ass and pulled Amber's pussy wide open with her thumbs. Amber moaned, and then gasped as Julie used one hand to guide the head of the big dildo in. The young woman was sopping wet, and whimpered as her lips stretched slickly around the thick shaft. Grabbing Amber's hips, Julie pushed it all the way to the hilt, her own hips colliding with the girl's ass.

She pulled slowly back, fascinated by the intimate view of puckered asshole, sliding labia and emerging penis. When she got near the end, she could feel Amber push back against her.

The young woman's hunger made Julie's clit burn and lent power to her hips. She thrust forward firmly, reveling in the cry of passion it elicited from both of them. Getting a better grip on Amber's hips, she began to ram in and out of her, fucking her faster and deeper with each thrust, the slap of skin and the grunts of lust egging her on. In what seemed like a very short time Amber's whole body convulsed and she shot forward, facedown onto the rug, twitching with orgasm.

"Wow," Julie said. Glancing over at Gerry, she smiled at his dazed look. "How'd that look?" she asked him.

He just shook his head. Amber was moving now and Julie turned to watch her sit up and pull her dress over her head. Completely naked, she lay back and spread her legs. Their eyes locked and the younger woman said "More?"

She looked achingly beautiful and sweet and slippery. Julie edged forward on the thick rug, moving between legs which opened wider to accommodate her. Amber guided the big dildo in herself, groaning as it filled her, then reached up to unbutton Julie's blazer. Julie knelt, mesmerized by the sight of her big penis buried in Amber's labia. The view from this angle was entirely different from what she was used to. Julie gasped as Amber freed her breasts and then began pulling her down by the nipples.

Julie was overwhelmed by the intimacy of it, the feel of their naked breasts mashing together, Amber's soft lips on hers, the young woman's body squirming underneath her as the angle of the dildo changed. It was too intimate, but she couldn't escape the passionate kiss—when Amber's fingers reached around and found Julie's engorged labia she twitched, driving the dildo deeper.

Breaking the kiss with a gasp, her babysitter stared up into her eyes and whispered, "Fuck me hard, Mrs. Johanson." Clutching the young woman's shoulders, Julie did just that, timing her thrusts to the stroking she was receiving. Amber's legs clamped down on her and she could feel an orgasm brewing. As the pace increased Amber came, shuddering beneath her and trying to squirm away, but Julie was stronger and on top, holding her tight, ramming deeper into her at an angle that ground the big dildo against her own clit. In a frenzy of thrusting Julie threw her head back and yelled as her own orgasm shook through her.

"Wow," Amber whispered into her ear. Julie had collapsed onto her, both of them still panting. "Could you pull out now Mrs. Johanson? It's still awfully big."

Julie rolled off with a groan, the Champ coming out with an audible pop as she sprawled onto her back. She looked guiltily at Gerry, but he had a huge grin on his face.

"Bet you want to fuck the babysitter too," she said.

Amber giggled and Gerry rolled his eyes. "It's your show tonight," he replied.

Julie sat up. "All right then. Time to fuck some ass. Go get the lube, and get naked." She shrugged out of her open blazer as Gerry brought her the bottle of lubricant and began to strip.

Amber sat up abruptly. "You are NOT putting that," she pointed at Julie's immense dildo, "in my ass."

Julie grinned. "Don't worry, either of you. The remaining two holes will be fucked with the Silk and plenty of lube." Hands still shaking a bit, she removed the Champ from her harness as Gerry finished removing all his clothing. His erection looked as large as she'd ever seen it.

"Fetch the Silk," she told him imperiously. As he went to the dresser she held up the Champ—it glistened in the soft light, still slick with Amber's orgasm. She caught the young woman staring at her.

"Taste me," Amber said softly. Maintaining eye contact,

Julie impulsively ran her tongue up and then down the big dildo, following its realistic shape, savoring the tangy flavor, similar to her own and yet different.

Amber stared longingly. "Can I fuck you?"

Julie shook her head. "Nobody fucks me tonight." She took the Silk from Gerry. "Now both of you, on your knees in front of me."

As they complied, she attached the smooth purple dildo. By the time it was mounted between her legs there were two inviting asses in front of her, one slim and firm, the other round and tanned. As she slathered lube onto her dildo both her husband and the babysitter were looking back over their shoulders, eyes apprehensive.

"Ladies first," Gerry murmured.

Julie chuckled. "Okay smart-ass—here it comes."

Serious now, he said, "Be gentle."

She was at first. With lube-covered fingers she rubbed him, pressing the sensitive area between his balls and his ass, slipping a finger into the tight hole. This was familiar territory. The dildo swaying between her legs wasn't though, and she eased it in very slowly, reading the tension, acceptance—and finally, lust—in her husband's body language.

After two long, slow thrusts and retractions, she grabbed his hips. "Are you ready?" she asked, her voice low and gravelly. Instead of speaking, he pushed back against her.

Julie fucked Gerry. Shallow at first, she pushed deeper with each thrust, accepting his need to keep it slow. When she began to bite the back of his neck he shuddered—and picking up the pace, she took him through one of the powerful internal prostate orgasms he occasionally had when she fingered him.

From the sound and feel of it, this one was considerably more intense than usual.

He collapsed onto his side, exposing an erection that got bigger when she pulled out. "Christ," he whispered, his body shaking, "that was—different."

Amber was staring at them, one hand unconsciously fingering her swollen clit. "Give me a second to wash up," Julie told them, "and then we'll both fuck the babysitter."

Gerry groaned and Amber kept staring as Julie walked to the bathroom and quickly soaped and rinsed the dildo. Swaggering back into the room, naked and erect, she started giving instructions.

"Gerry—on your back. Amber—slip this condom on him and then hand me the Champ." When she had the big dildo in hand she rubbed its length along her sopping labia, bathing it in fresh juices, shuddering at the sensation. Amber just stared.

"Amber, I want you to straddle my poor, swollen husband and take him into your pussy. That's it—face to face." She watched as the young woman lowered herself onto Gerry, both of them moaning as she enveloped his raging erection. She stepped up beside them. "Lube me," she said, and Amber, now impaled on her husband, turned sideways to rub the Silk with more lubricant.

"Now lie down and lift your ass a bit." Gerry sighed as those big breasts pillowed against his bare chest. Julie knelt beside them. "Since this is about fucking and not kissing, would you mind wrapping your lips around this?" she said sweetly, holding the slick Champ up near Amber's lips.

Amber grinned before opening her mouth and taking

the large head of it in, her tongue hungrily lapping at Julie's flavor.

Leaving it with her, Julie moved around to the back. It was an amazing view—she could see her husband's shaft disappearing into Amber's folds, and just above was her puckered brown hole. It quivered—and Amber gasped—as Julie fingered in some lube.

Kneeling carefully between their legs, Julie began to push the strap-on in. Amber tensed up and Gerry groaned—Julie retreated a bit, felt the young woman relax, and then began to push again. She was burning with desire and quickly developed respect for her husband's gentle restraint when he had anal sex with her. This time Amber stayed relaxed and the dildo slipped in past the tight ring of muscle—Julie used her hips to push it in slowly, moaning when they finally pressed against the other woman's ass. Beneath her, Amber was breathing in shallow gasps and Gerry seemed to be holding his breath.

Leaning forward, melding with them both, she whispered in her husband's ear. "Are you ready to give the babysitter the fucking of her life?"

His hips responded for him—she felt them drive up and in. Amber's cry was muffled by the big dildo in her mouth, but she squirmed provocatively between them and Julie began to thrust. She saw Gerry's eyes go wide—she knew he could feel her. Between them, their sweet young babysitter went wild, her hips thrashing and her mouth taking the Champ right to the back of her throat. Julie thrust and thrust, watching with awe as first Gerry, then Amber began to come. She rode them as they did, holding them together, grinding herself against the butt of the dildo and the ass of her babysitter until an immense orgasm washed up from the two squirming bodies and swept her into darkness.

Julie's vision came back to a tangle of limbs on the rug. She was on her back, her husband's head nestled between her breasts, his eyes closed. She could feel Amber's breath in her ear and her warm skin alongside. Tucking chin to chest, she saw the dildo jutting up between her legs—one of Amber's hands cupped the base of it, the other was draped across Gerry's shoulders.

"You know," Amber whispered, lips brushing Julie's ear, "I'm around for another three weeks. Maybe I could try fucking?"

Gerry's eyes opened, and Julie smiled.

Daddy's Boy

ELIZABETH COLVIN

"Come on, boy. Come over here and tell Daddy how much you appreciate his hospitality."

I take the cigar out of my mouth and smile at him.

Lounging in the armchair, I reach down and unzip my leather pants. I pull out my cock and start stroking it. My boy looks at the big, thick shaft of my cock and licks his lips.

Then he goes down on his knees and plants his mouth on the head of my cock. He takes my shaft into his mouth until the head nudges the top of his throat. Then, without hesitating, he swallows, forcing the shaft down his throat without even a hint of a gag reflex. That sends a shudder through my body; I can feel my pussy aching. He starts working on my cock, sucking it like an expert.

I don't look much like any daddy I've ever known. The tight leather pants, big black boots and Harley Davidson T-shirt could belong to a daddy, sure. But there's no disguising my broad hips or the way the pants hang so low on them, revealing my flowery tattoos and my navel ring. And I haven't strapped down my tits, which are big enough to stretch the T-shirt and, even with a sports bra underneath, show my nipples as they get hard in response to the sight and feel of my boy's mouth on my cock.

But it doesn't matter, because I'm a daddy; I've got the big, thick cock to prove it. Silicone, yes; maybe not as sensitive as a real daddy's cock. With this daddy's cock, it's not just a matter of licking and sucking around the head or teasing the underside of the shaft. Sucking this cock is a lot more work. My boy has to push and work his head around and suck my cock harder, pushing the base of the dildo against my clit to make my pussy throb in response. But I don't care and my boy doesn't care, either, because my boy knows I'm his daddy. I've got the cock to prove it—and the armchair.

And a boy is exactly what he is, tonight. Torn jeans, so faded they're almost white, hug his lithe body, showing off the big bulge in his pants, swept to the right and getting bigger as he sucks me. His tight white T-shirt, so tight it's almost see-through, shows off his perfect chest. He looks like some boy hustler I picked up on the street, offered a place to stay in return for a blow job. The big white athletic shoes are a decidedly adolescent touch.

The whole package makes my pussy so wet I can hardly stand it.

And when he looks up at me with his mouth around my cock, there's no question that this is my boy, servicing me.

"Come on, boy, suck it better than that. Earn your keep."

He launches more eagerly into it, his mouth pumping

up and down on my cock and forcing it deeper into his throat. He's obviously a skilled cocksucker; he doesn't even hesitate when the head of my cock presses against his throat. He just swallows, knowing that's what I want. I want to feel him take it all the way, feeling it in his belly, just like he will when I put it up his ass.

His eyes turn back up to me and I grin down at him, flicking ash off the end of the cigar. "I think it's time you sucked a little ass, boy."

I pull him off of my cock and turn around on the armchair, pulling my leather pants down over my hips. When I've got them down around my knees, I bend over, pushing my ass out for him. He leans in and obediently presses his face between my cheeks, his tongue sliding into my ass. I have to stifle a gasp that I know will sound way too feminine, and I barely manage to replace it with a manly grunt as I reach back behind me to grab his hair and push his face more firmly into my ass. His tongue works its way deeper into my asshole. He alternates between teasing the entrance with big long swirls of his tongue and pushing hard into it like he's fucking me with that limber little organ. I want to reach down and rub my clit; I want to come so bad it's driving me crazy. But instead of rubbing my clit I reach down and begin to jerk off, stroking my cock, pumping it hard up and down, and that only makes me want to come even more. When I push the dildo down I can feel the base against my clit, almost direct enough to make me come, but not quite. God, I want to fuck him so bad.

I'm so turned on I can hardly speak. But I manage it, barely, working hard to maintain a gruff rumble in my voice instead of a girly squeak. I turn my head and look down at him over my shoulder. He's beautiful, his mouth planted between my cheeks, licking me. His eyes are turned up toward me, and I look into them as I growl at him.

"You take it up the ass, boy?"

His mouth comes away from my ass and he says, "If I have to, Daddy."

"You have to, boy," I tell him.

He moves back and I get off the armchair, still stroking my cock. I watch as he shucks his white T-shirt, showing off his beautiful chest. I run my hand down it, working my cock faster. He unzips his jeans and peels them off, kicking his way out of his white athletic shoes. He's not wearing socks. I look at his gorgeous cock, standing there hard, the tip glistening.

"You can suck it if you want," he says weakly, not meeting my eyes.

I grab his hair and pull his face close to mine.

"No kissing," he says, sounding petulant and whiny. "I don't do that. I'm not a faggot."

The sound of that helpless plea sends a new surge of arousal through my pussy and into my cock. I've got him right where I want him.

Ignoring his protest, I press my lips to his and thrust my tongue into his mouth. He lets me for a moment, then begins to respond with his own tongue against mine. I kiss him deeper, then spin him around and shove him against the armchair. He climbs onto it, knees pressed to the thick, padded arms, legs spread, ass in the air. He reaches back and parts his cheeks as I grab the bottle of lube on the end table.

I pour lube between his cheeks and work two fingers into his ass—not even bothering to start with one. He gasps as

I penetrate him, and I reach between his legs to feel his cock pulsing with excitement.

"You like that, boy? You like taking it up the ass?"

"If I have to, Daddy," he says nervously.

"You have to, boy," I tell him. "You have to like it. And I know you're going to."

I add some lube to the head of my cock and push his back down till he's crouched down low and his ass is in the right position. I nuzzle the head of my cock against his tight entrance. His ass opens right up as I thrust into it; he lets out a shuddering gasp as I drive it in to the hilt.

I start to fuck him; for some reason, this position pushes the base of the dildo against my clit at just the right angle. Or maybe fucking my boy in the ass just turns me on more than anything. I reach up and grab his hair, listening to him moan as I shove my cock roughly into his ass, each thrust harder, building up speed.

His hand is underneath him, pumping his cock. His hips start to work, pushing him onto my cock. It's like he's trying to get it over with at first—then, as his hand quickens on his cock, like he wants it. He shoves hard onto me, his ass opening wider as it engulfs my cock. I pull his hair, making him squeal. At one point I reach down and spank his ass, which makes him fuck back onto me with even more urgency.

I don't even feel it coming, really. I've been working the dildo into him, pressing the base against my clit for so long that when I finally reach the breaking point I barely know it. It happens when he lets out a little whimper and I feel his body shaking—he's coming, shooting his load all over Daddy's armchair. I start to fuck him harder, faster, as his lips go slack and he leans hard against the back of the chair. I pound into him and that drives me over the top, my own orgasm sending my pussy and clit into tight spasms, my ass tightening as I feel the cooling moisture of my boy's spittle where he tongued me. I collapse on top of him and the chair groans under our combined weight as my body surges with pleasure, my high-pitched moans as feminine as it gets—but my boy doesn't seem to care.

He reaches back and strokes my hand where it still grips his hair. "Did my tight ass get you off real good, Daddy?"

"You have no idea," I said, still panting hard.

"Oh, I think I have some idea," he smiled, and squirmed around under me to hold me in his arms. He began to stroke my long hair gently and whispered, "Thank you, Daddy. Thanks for fucking me so good."

I curled up in my boy's embrace, sighing contentedly.

Watch and Learn

ISABELLE NATHE

"What a dump—"

"Let's see," I said, wrinkling my brow. "That's Bette Davis, right?"

"No, honey, that's me."

"But you sounded just like her," I insisted as I gazed at my best friend Maxine from the muddled collection of semi-warm laundry on the sofa. I was using the deep pile of colorful clothing as a nest. In the heat of the summer afternoon, I simply couldn't be bothered to fold the clothes. Besides, they made such a nice little pillowy lounge. Feeling Maxine's eyes on me, I snuggled back against the vibrant fleecy sweatshirts and sweatpants, then tucked one of my husband's stray black dress socks behind the crook of my arm.

"Even so, Elsa—" Maxine continued, her voice rich with disapproval.

"Bette Davis said it in that movie," I insisted.

"And I'm saying it about your house."

I giggled as I took a sip of my spiked lemonade. Heat makes me feel sleepy and relaxed. In the state I was in—a combination of languorous laziness and mild inebriation—it was simply too difficult for me to clean. That was my surface excuse, anyway. But really, whenever Maxine came over, I found plenty of reasons for being slovenly: too hot or too cold. Too tired or too wired. There was always some reason I could dig up for being under-prepared for her caustic judgment.

"Get to work right now," my buddy insisted.

"I don't wanna—" I said, and I tried to keep the bad-girl sneer out of my voice, but failed. I knew that I sounded just like a teenager who'd been told in no uncertain terms to get her bedroom into shape. In fact, I'd *been* that sort of teenager only several years before. I guess I'd never grown up.

"Baby, you really don't want to get me started," she said, starting already.

"But I'm too hot," I whined, giving up on any pretense of behaving.

"You're *going* to be too hot. Your ass is going to be so fucking hot, you won't be able to sit down."

"People always say that," I murmured sadly, "but it's never true."

"It'll be true this time. Trust me."

I just shrugged, knowing that was precisely the way to get what I wanted. Max was at my side in a heartbeat. "You always test me," she said. "You think you're being cute and coy and all-around adorable. And you are. But you shouldn't test me."

She sat down on the one clear cushion on the couch, hauled

me out of my lovely laundry nest, and positioned me over her stern lap. My pussy quivered with excitement. I couldn't believe I'd already angled myself a spanking, and she'd only been in the house for three minutes. But after she lowered my Wednesday panties down my toned, tanned thighs, she stopped.

"What day is it?"

"Friday," I muttered, my face against the sofa cushion, ass lifted upward, very ready for the first stinging spank to find its mark.

"And you're still wearing your 'Wednesday' panties?"

"Yes," I admitted. Although I'd been sprawled amongst the clean laundry, I hadn't actually done much bathing myself in the past few days.

"Dirty girl," she hissed. "I'm not going to spank you until we get you a wee bit cleaner." With that, she repositioned my panties, then pushed me off her lap. I lay on the floor, looking up at her like a sad puppy. "Behave, Elsa," she hissed, and then yanked me by the ear after her down the hallway to our bathroom. She started the faucets on the tub and efficiently stripped me of my floral sundress and panties.

"Bend over the tub," she demanded, eyes flaming. "I want to see for myself what state you've gotten yourself in. Christ, kiddo. *Wednesday* panties on a Friday—"

I did exactly as she said, and Max parted my rear cheeks and got her face right in there. I could hear her breathing in deeply.

"Oh, you dirty girl," she whispered, and then her tongue licked my hole, and I convulsed fiercely against the cool porcelain of the tub. "You're just filthy," she said, and I could hear the rich sound of pleasure in her voice as she began to clean me with her tongue. I couldn't believe how wet my pussy was as her lips pressed firmly against me. She licked and lapped and I ground my hips forward and back.

For an instant, I wondered whether she would let me come, but I should have known better. Max would never reward me so soon. Not with the way I'd behaved for her—misbehaved, really. But that didn't mean she made me suffer. She let me enjoy the sensuous swirl of her tongue in my rear hole until I was crooning her name over and over. "Max, oh, Max, oh, Max—"

But after several more delicious spirals of her tongue against my asshole, she had me stand and hurried me into the water.

"It's hot!" I yelped.

"It should be hot. You need a serious scrubbing."

She used a loofah and a pale yellow washcloth to suds me all over, and then she had me face the turquoise tiled wall as she soaped my ass. She worked the soft bath mitt deep between my cheeks, and I groaned at the probing I was undergoing.

"God, do you like being touched back there."

I groaned again, harder. She was speaking the truth from many past pleasurable experiences.

"Arch your back, baby," Max instructed. "I want all access."

I did as she said, and Max let the mitt slide off her hand so that she could thrust two fingers back into my asshole.

"Oh, yes," I whispered, loving the way she touched me.

"I'm just bathing you, baby," Maxine laughed.

When she was satisfied with my level of cleanliness, she took me back out of the tub and roughly dried me off. With me still naked, and her still fully clothed, she led me down the hall to the bedroom, where chaos reigned king. The sheets were bunched at the bottom of the bed and clothes were strewn everywhere.

"It looks as if your dryer exploded," she said.

"I've been busy—"

"No excuse, honey," Max said, "you knew I was coming here today," and she left me alone while she retrieved her huge black leather satchel from the hall. When she came back, she started pulling out the largest dildos I'd ever seen.

"No—" I started.

"What's our deal?" Maxine asked fiercely.

"I don't say 'no' to you," I repeatedly dumbly.

"And what do you get in return?"

"To be your little house slave."

"What sort of a house slave?"

"A dirty little house slave," I said automatically. She'd trained me that well, at least.

"Bend over, my dirty little house slave, and show me your anus."

As always, the word sent a quiver through me, but I immediately obeyed her request. Of course I did. This is the exact action I fantasize about late at night. I envision myself bent over at the waist, showing Max her favorite part of my anatomy and my favorite part as well. She likes to touch me and inspect me back there as much as, if not more than I like my ass to be probed and licked and disciplined.

In seconds, I had my supple cheeks stretched wide apart, and I felt a pang of total surrender when Max once again brought her soft warm tongue to my exposed rear hole, now squeaky clean from her own careful ministrations in the tub. She licked me there for several seconds, while I mewled like a kitten, pleasure bubbling up inside me. Then she thrust her tongue into my asshole and I whimpered, "Please, Max, don't stop—"

She paused long enough to whisper, "Why?"

"What do you mean?"

"Tell me why you like it."

I was at a loss. I like everything Max does to my ass. I like how hard she spanks me, how soft she licks me, and how rough she fucks me. But I couldn't explain why.

"Tell me," she insisted, "and I'll break out my good toys and fuck you."

"God, Maxine," I sighed, "I don't know. I just like it. I like when you put things in me back there. I like when you fuck my ass. I don't know why. I just do."

"What does it feel like?" she asked, still probing with her questions and her tongue and fingers.

"Like being found out," I told her. "Exposed. Opened. Seen."

"Good girl," Max said, heading toward her bag of tricks. Before she got to the dildos, though, something caught her eye.

"Look at the layer of dust on your dresser," she gasped. "It's as if you've never heard of a Swiffer."

"We've been—"

"—busy, I know," she said, reaching into her bag again and bringing out a feather duster with a thick metal handle. "Clean—" she demanded, and I took the duster and quickly flicked the feathers over the top of the dresser. Dusting in the nude made me feel weak all over. I had an idea of what awaited me in my very near future, and with Max's hawk-like gray eyes watching my every motion, I felt on the verge of swooning.

"Now, bring it back to me." I hurried to obey, then watched, horrified, as she slid a condom over the base of the duster.

"Bend over again, my slovenly girl, and spread those cheeks as wide as you can."

I wasn't entirely prepared for being fucked with the duster, but I had no say. I bent over the unmade bed. Max readied my asshole with a handful of greasy lubrication, her fingers oil-slick against my pucker. I clenched down on the intrusion of her fingers, but she didn't stop. She continued to slowly and seriously lube me up. Her fingers made continual rotations around and around, every so often pushing further inside of me. I sighed into the mattress, loving every moment of her prep work. I knew what was going to happen, but I forced myself to stop worrying and let myself enjoy the glorious sensations fluttering inside of me. Maxine spent a long, languorous time readying my rear hole for its first fucking of the day.

When she was satisfied with my level of lubrication, she expertly lubed up the handle of the duster, getting the base all greasy with the glossy liquid. Then the duster disappeared from my view as she slid the handle of the device deep into my rear hole. I yelled out at the feeling of being filled, and at the tickling of the feathers against my skin. Max didn't stop or slow down. She worked that handle back and forth until I was crying out. My pussy was spasming at the vibrant thrusts and my asshole felt stretched to the limit.

It wasn't, of course. Max would never take me to the

limit so soon. She let the duster fall to the floor and had me watch as she lubed the next toy. But before she introduced this mammoth dildo to my ass, she said she'd have to punish my asshole.

"You know you deserve it," Max said. "Don't you?"

"Yes, Maxine."

"Now, repeat after me," Max said, " 'I won't be such a dirty girl in the future.' "

"I won't be such a dirty girl in the future," I lied.

" 'Because I'm a dirty girl, Max has to punish my asshole.' "

"Because I'm a dirty girl, Max has to punish my asshole."

" 'Thank you, Max, for loving me enough to punish my asshole for me.' "

There were tears in my eyes as I said these words. "Thank you, Max, for loving me enough to punish my asshole for me."

"Spread those cheeks, dear," Max said, and I did as she brought out a thin whippet of a switch. I whimpered in anticipation even before the switch began to line the tender skin of my exposed butthole. When she struck, I thought I might come on the spot.

"Oh, ow!" I cried.

"You deserve this, so tell me that you deserve it."

"I deserve this, Max," I bleated.

"What do you deserve?"

"I deserve to have you whip my asshole."

"Why?"

"Because I've been such a dirty housekeeper," I said.

"And because you like it."

"And because I like it," I admitted tearfully.

She let the stinging switch cut into my tender skin, first on the left, then on the right, then directly in the center. I howled at the impact, adoring every moment of the torturous pleasure. Max gave me a serious thrashing with the dangerous implement, and I bucked and cried out at every stroke.

"Now, stretch that asshole of yours wide open and get ready for my next present for you."

I did as she said, trembling all over as she stripped out of her jeans and T-shirt, then slid on her harness and buckled the large dildo in place. She had the head of it right against my ferociously smarting anus when the door to the bedroom opened. My husband, Jules, was home.

"What the fuck—" Jules said. Max didn't even hesitate; she drove that dildo home into my ass, and I screamed and then collapsed on the bed as she rocked back and forth inside me.

"Your wife," Max said calmly without ever stopping her motion, "is a slovenly girl. She can't make the bed, can't do the laundry properly. She's been wearing the same filthy panties for two days. That's why she's being punished."

"Jesus—" Jules said, leaning against the wall. I glanced over my shoulder at him and saw him wiping his forehead with the back of his hand. It was as if he couldn't believe the scene that was right before his eyes. Of course, this wasn't entirely true. Jules and I have a sexy understanding in regard to bedroom play: as long as we keep each other aware of our naughty escapades, anything goes. I'd held up my half of the bargain—well, sort of. Jules knew Max and I did the girl-girl thing—he's even watched a couple of times. But he had no idea

Max and I played like THIS. He certainly never would have envisioned me pinned to the sheets by a huge black dildo banging my (as far as he knew) innocent asshole.

"If you want to stay," Maxine continued, "you'll have to abide by our rules."

"*Your* rules—"

"That's right."

After only a moment of hesitation, Jules nodded. Obviously, he wanted to stay. In truth, he always wanted to stick around when I was having sex with another woman— what man didn't?

Maxine withdrew the cock from my asshole and walked to my husband. She had absolutely no problem striding around our room with her synthetic cock standing straight out in front of her slim-hipped body. After only a moment's consideration, she had Jules sit on the chair near our dresser, and she bound his hands and feet with his own fancy dress ties. Then she left the room for a moment. When she returned, I saw that she had my discarded jade-green panties in her hand. I watched in awe as she gagged him with my Wednesday panties.

"Breathe in deep, Jules," Max said, "she had these panties on her dirty body for two days straight."

I saw the look in Jules' eyes as he tasted me on my underpants.

"You thought you knew everything there was to know about your wife, didn't you?" Max asked.

Jules nodded.

"Did you know how much your wife likes anal sex?"

Jules raised an eyebrow. He was trying to act cool, but I could tell he was curious. VERY curious. Curious enough to let Max boss him around—anything to find out what she knew that he didn't.

"What your wife really requires is a lot of rough anal play," Maxine explained. "Not only does she like it, she needs it. In order for her to feel truly cared for, she requires a steady diet of punishment, discipline, and tender loving—and all of this revolves around her ass. She likes her asshole to be spanked and licked and fucked. She likes me to put things inside her and stretch her open. She's a horny little beast, who needs a little of everything. But mostly she needs her ass taken care of. That's what I'm doing. Do you understand?"

Jules nodded.

"Then watch and learn."

With that, Maxine came back over to me and now she lubed up a monster butt plug and forced it inside of me. I groaned intensely at the intrusion. Being filled with this toy was like having Max continually hold my butthole wide open. The stretching sensation never left me.

"I haven't forgotten your spanking, hon," she said, removing her harness and sitting on the edge of the bed. She hauled me over her lap and began to paddle my ass with a Ping-Pong paddle pulled from her bottomless satchel. Between every stroke, she rocked the butt plug in my asshole, and I cried out, so close to creaming I could hardly stand it. From the noises that Jules made against the panty gag, he could hardly stand it either.

"See how much she likes it?" Maxine teased. "She likes me to work the plug in as far as it will go, then slide it a little bit out, so that her anus is fully stretched around it. Of course, this hurts a little bit, but your wife craves a little pain with her pleasure, don't you, baby?"

I yelped in answer.

"Yes, she likes it. My lover here needs that pretty asshole of hers played with, doesn't she?"

Again, I made some nonverbal response.

"So you take it, darling," Maxine crooned to me. "You take it."

She kept on spanking me with the paddle, and I knew my ass was a deep red, but all I wanted was more. I was thrilled by the fact that Jules was watching every second of this punishment session, that he was seeing firsthand how I need to be treated. Because Maxine was right—this was the sort of scene I live for.

Max suddenly yanked the butt plug out of me, leaving my asshole gaping and my whole body feeling sad. She pushed me back on the bed, buckled the harness back into place, and relubed her cock. "You want to come on me, don't you, kiddo?" she asked.

"Oh, yes."

"Good girl."

Back Maxine slid, deep into my hole, and she gripped my hips and rocked in and out quickly. In and out. I was gasping at the speed of the sensation, but when Max slid her hand under my body and started to pluck my clit, I knew I was only seconds away from a monster orgasm. I'm sure that Max knew that, too.

"When I'm done with your wifey," Maxine continued sweetly, "Elsa and I will give you a few pointers, Jules. On your own tender asshole."

I saw the tent in his pants as she spoke, and I realized that

Max's lessons would have a permanent result in our house. No, I might never be known as a woman with the cleanest house, but I'd definitely teach my husband a thing or two about how to use a duster.

Evening Class

J. HADLEIGH ALEX

The end of the office day draws near. He phones home. It rings three times.

She answers. "Is there anything you want to ask me?" Her voice is quiet, almost a whisper.

"Yes," he says. Her mouth is close to the phone. He listens to her breath—measured, deep, with a hint of a tremble. After a pause, he asks, "Have you done your homework?"

A sigh. "Most of it," she says.

"Make sure it's done by the time I'm home," he says, and hangs up. He's made the decision, now it's just a matter of time. Come five he takes his coat from the stand and puts it on, lifts his briefcase—already packed and shut—and, like a ghost, slips unnoticed from the office.

The house door clicks shut behind him. He drops his keys into the pocket of his coat as he hangs it up—one of many ritual reversals that punctuate the day.

The house is dark, though the welcoming aroma of a spicy supper wafts toward him, and soft, yellow light spills around the study door. He takes five steps toward it, pushing the door wide in front of him as he enters.

She's sitting at the desk, head bowed over an open book, but she looks up as he fills the doorway. She makes to rise, but he waves his hand in a circle to tell her to stay seated. He walks to her desk, stands to one side, peers at what she's reading.

Her long hair, straight and black, tumbles onto the pages, and he can't read the words. He places one hand on her shoulder and eases her back from the studious hunch she's adopted. As he does so, his gaze takes in the view down the front of her blouse—her generous bosom revealed in the deep V-shape of her unbuttoned collar. No tie this evening; is that mere fashionable variation, or rebellion? No matter, this he will decide later.

He takes her chin in his hand, lifting her face up so that he can see her eyes. Her soft skin is warm against his fingertips. He repeats his earlier question.

"Have you done your homework?"

She blinks, and he feels the rippling tension in her neck as she swallows. "Most of it," she says, in an echo of her previous response.

"That's what you said when last I asked you," he says. "Have you done no more?"

She blinks again, and makes to shake her head, but still he grips her chin, and he feels rather than sees the movement.

"My dear," he says, letting her face fall. "You know that isn't good enough."

She nods, and her black tresses brush the book once

more, like curtains at an open window. She doesn't look at him, but stares at the floor.

"You know, as well...," he continues, walking over to the clear expanse of his rosewood bureau, "...what this means, don't you?" He opens a drawer.

Her hands grip each side of her desk as she stands up. "Yes, sir. I do."

He hears the catch in her throat.

He looks at her. The writing surface hides her legs, but not the gray, pleated skirt curving around the contours of her hips. It's short enough to reveal a flash of thigh above the desk's varnished, ink-stained wood.

"Come here, girl." He points to his bureau, immaculate and clear, an embossed leather inlay its only decoration.

She sighs, shuffles sideways from her desk and walks slowly toward him. Her legs are bare. No stockings, not even white ankle-socks, hide the lissome sweep of her calves, or the subtle promise of her thighs soaring up behind the hem of her skirt. On her feet, patent-leather high heels accentuate the wily provocation of her walk.

He shakes his head. Will she never learn? How much discipline do such lessons take? He *tut-tuts* to himself and moves his hand above the bureau. "You know the procedure," he says.

She looks at him across the vast leather and rosewood expanse, then her gaze drops to its surface. She nods. She places her hands on the dark, polished wood, then leans forward, letting her palms slide toward him as she lowers her body to the bureau. When her hands have almost reached his side of it, he grasps her wrists and pulls them toward him;

she lets out a gasp as he yanks them so that she can grip the edge of the desk. The tails of her blouse pull free of her skirt's waistband, revealing the pale skin of her lower back.

Now that she's stretched out across the leather, he reaches into the bureau drawer and removes a transparent plastic ruler. He brings it down with a crack, just millimeters from her face, and she flinches at its resounding proximity.

"Homework not done. Not wearing a tie. Nonregulation shoes." With each recitation of her misdemeanors he slaps the ruler down. "You know that means extra punishment." Her head twitches with the slightest nod.

He walks round to her side of the bureau and stands behind her. She's bent across the surface but her legs are straight, the gray fabric of her skirt barely covering her rear.

With finger and thumb he takes the hem of her skirt and pulls it up, high above her waist, revealing her backside. An involuntary whistle escapes his lips at the sight: this timid girl is wearing a sheer, lace thong. The pastel pink fabric, tailored to a tiny triangle below the small of her back, disappears between her cheeks, the twin globes of her bare buttocks presenting a perfect target for her imminent chastisement.

"Not a word, now," he says, letting the wide plastic blade oscillate in the air as he takes aim. And then he strikes; the ruler swishes down, catching her exposed cheeks full and flat with a satisfying smack, sending ripples radiating down her thighs.

"Ow!" Her cry is gasped out, then stifled almost before it's audible.

"Silence!" He bends close to her head and speaks into her ear. "You know the rules." Only strokes received without a murmur will count toward her punishment. Her transgressions this evening have already mounted up; she can ill afford to add to her tally.

The second stroke is harder than the first, but precisely registered, and though she takes it without crying out he can tell it's an effort. Her body shudders in response to the blow and she screws her eyes shut. The third and fourth strokes follow in quick succession, and each time she convulses her reaction, but in silence. Her cheeks are now beginning to respond, lighting the ruler's path in ruby neon.

The fifth blow he delivers from a greater height; she hears the hiss of air as it descends, and tenses up, clenching her cheeks in anticipation. But this serves only to harden the ruler's target, the plastic making firmer contact, sharpening the pain.

She's breathing heavily now, and despite the movements of her bottom as she squirms her body in acute discomfort, he lands the sixth stroke with confirmed accuracy, bringing her protesting cheeks to a rosy glow. Her scorched backside radiates a satisfying heat into his palm as he holds it close, testing his handiwork.

"Good girl," he says, and she relaxes into the surface of the bureau. "But now we must take account of certain facts." He sees her body jerk with renewed tension as she realizes her punishment isn't over. "This underwear," he says, tracing his finger along the edge of the lacy fabric where it plunges between her cheeks, "is entirely out of order, and must be removed."

He stands behind her bent body and tucks the fingers of both hands behind the waistband of the thong; he crouches, pulling the thong downward, letting the narrow string slip over her reddened flesh. The string pulls out from its snug captivity deep between her buttocks, the waistband rolling itself into a thin cord as it travels down to her ankles.

He stands, and takes the waist of her pleated skirt in one hand, and with the other unzips it at the side and pulls it away. He pauses for a moment over the sight of her naked rear, then walks once more to his side of the bureau, where her hands still grip the edge, stretching her body across the leather.

"It's time we saw precisely what we're at," he says, leaning forward to reach over her head and grasp the tails of her blouse. With a fluid motion he pulls the white cotton up her back toward her shoulders, and the front of it rides up between her chest and the bureau's leather inlay. His insistent pull causes the garment to catch on her breasts as they press into the leather, but he continues the rough divestment until the fabric has gone over her head and traveled to her wrists. On his guidance she releases her grip, hand by hand, and he peels the blouse away.

She now stretches naked across the leather, her hair pulled up by the removal of the blouse, revealing a pale-skinned back narrowing to a slim waist, and hips that broaden to a pair of luscious, rounded buttocks streaked in angry red.

For the second time he reaches into the drawer, and removes a long, narrow cane. In his hand it feels light, but sharp, as he whips it around above the girl's prone form. She moans at its hissing passage through the air. This won't be the first time her skin has felt the sharp crack of the cane, and her body tenses at the memory, anticipating its relentless scourge.

He takes aim, eyeing up his target—her reddening cheeks drawing his gaze to the epicenter of her shapely form. He raises his hand high, pauses for accuracy, and with one quick swish brings the cane down in a precise slash, to land squarely on one buttock. The resounding smack echoes through the room as the painful jolt radiates from the point of contact, rippling across her skin—the natural vibration combining with an involuntary muscle spasm.

He can see the pain. She strains to keep it within her, screwing her eyes shut, as if opening them would let the sensation stream out of her in agony. But while she holds it in, he wastes no time and brings the cane down on the other cheek, making a harsh red line to mirror the first. Once more she shudders her resistance in agonized silence, letting a rush of breath escape her open mouth.

He looks her over, sees the sheen of sweat on her skin and the droplets forming on her spine, running together, gathering in a tiny pool in the small of her back. On the bureau, the leather is moist where her perspiring skin moves against it.

He returns his attention to her crisscrossed backside, and readies himself for his next strokes. The cane is a precise instrument, its surface texture just right for its purpose. He must judge the force to use on her—a swinging blow, as powerful as possible, without actually breaking the skin. This is what he gives her, landing a precise inch away from the cane's first strike. She jolts in agony once more, and he knows she can hardly bear it. But the regularity of her punishment cannot be interrupted. She must lie there, willing to receive the just rewards for her transgressions.

The air above her snaps in two as he brings the cane down again, completing the second pair of stripes. Once more he surveys the damage. Her red cheeks stand out in contrast to the sober study decor, and the pale flesh of her back and legs quiver in time with her snatched, shallow breathing. It's clear that she's reacting to the severity of her chastisement, and that she's only a couple of strokes away from completing penance for her sins.

And so he administers the first of the final strokes, swishing the cane down from high above his head, to land perpendicular across the first two strokes on one buttock.

She convulses as it hits. The bite of the cane is precise, raising a further welt across her cheek, with a bright spot at each of the stroke's intersections with its two predecessors.

The final stroke sends an equal spasm through her as it bites into the other cheek, finalizing the scarlet symmetry.

She's done. She's paid her price. Her backside's patterned lines bear witness to her ordeal. He lays the cane down on the bureau, and gently places his palms on those neon-striped globes. The heat from them is unbelievable. He squeezes the soft flesh, allowing his thumbs to slide into the welcoming crevice between her cheeks.

He spreads her. She moans as he exposes the hidden recesses within, pressing one hand deep into her. His fingers find her moist, and swollen. He removes his hand, lifts it to his face, smelling her heavy scent. It's time. She's ready.

He steps back from the welted redness of her tortured butt and quickly undresses, and in a moment he has his heavy, expectant organ pressing between her buttocks' soft flesh. He can feel her heat on him. He leans into her, grasping her waist in his hands, gripping her yielding body. His hands slide up between the bureau's sweat-smeared leather and her hot skin, and her breasts succumb to his caresses, her nipples hard between his fingers and thumbs.

His erection continues to jut into her, straining to find its way. With care he leans back, sliding his hands down over her back, to rest for a moment on her radiant buttocks, then to slip between them, spreading those fulsome globes.

Her flesh is parted. She's exposed, revealing her slick pink slit, and he maneuvers his hardened shaft toward its target. He pauses at her entrance, relishing the expectation of her secret grip on his purpled engorgement. And then he pushes home, sliding the bold rod of flesh into her, feeling her heat, her pressure, her muscular containment as she takes him within her.

She's hot, and wet. His progress, though unimpeded, is resisted just enough to bring him to a delicious height of sensual pleasure as he plunges and withdraws in measured strokes.

He keeps his rhythm, but he can feel her tension as she comes before he does, her muscles alternately gripping and releasing him, her slick wetness growing to a flood around his member. But still he pumps her, maintaining his unhurried oscillations, drinking in the pleasure of her responsive flesh engulfing his.

She's gasping now, and letting out unintelligible squeaks as he continues his measured thrusts. Her gasps grow deeper, her squeaking grows to pronounced cries, and all the while he's getting closer to his own fulfillment. Her orchestrated arousal tells him she's near, and so he concentrates, slowing his thrusts, feeling her body tense and relax, aware of his own impending climax as the fire of his orgasm travels up the shaft of his organ to the pressured head, its stretched skin so sensitive to every nuance of her engulfing flesh, until, as the well of his climax rises, his member throbbing inside her, he grips her body and comes in a flood of pulsating pleasure. As his tidal wave breaks within her, it is enough, the final sensation, to send her over the edge into ecstasy, and she convulses, letting out a lasting, helpless sigh.

The end of the office day draws near. He phones home. It rings three times.

She answers. "Is there anything you want to ask me?" Her voice is quiet, almost a whisper.

"Yes," he says.

Picture Perfect

DONNA GEORGE STOREY

I didn't mean to shave it all off. At first I was trying for a whimsical heart shape, but I couldn't seem to get the curves even. Then I sculpted a fur patch like those models in men's magazines, but it looked too much like Hitler's mustache. In the end I went all the way—the Greek statue look. It's harder than you think to get yourself all smooth down there. I stood with one leg propped up on the side of the tub, studying my cunt like exam notes. I'd never looked at myself so carefully down there before. What surprised me was the color—the deep, almost shocking pink of the inner lips. The skin looked so sensitive and dewy, I was scared to get close with that nasty razor, so I left a little fringe. There was no room for mistakes.

I called Brian at work to tell him about my art project.

"Hey, Kira." I knew someone was in his office by his offhand tone, but I went ahead and told him anyway.

"I just shaved my pussy."

There was a pause.

"Oh, is that so? Listen, honey, I'm in the middle of a meeting right now. I'll call you back when I can. Okay?" Only a wife would have picked up the faint tremor in his voice.

Unfortunately, Brian was a model employee—not the type who would stand up in front of the boss and announce, "Sorry, I have to go. My wife just shaved her pussy." It would probably be hours before he could get home. That left a whole afternoon alone, just me and my bald snatch.

I went over to the full-length mirror. My heart was pounding. I hadn't felt this naughty since I was a teenager doing "homework" up in my bedroom with my panties around one ankle and a pillow pushed between my legs, ear cocked for the sound of my mother's footsteps in the hall. Which was silly because I was alone in my own house and all I was doing was looking at myself, my new self: the white triangle of smooth skin, the fold of tender pink flesh now visible between the lips. There was an indentation at the top of the slit, as if someone had pressed a finger into it. I had an overwhelming urge to play with myself. Just an appetizer before I jumped Brian's bones tonight. I touched a tentative finger to my clit. I was already wet.

The phone rang.

"I'm taking the afternoon off," Brian told me. His voice was husky. "I'll be home in twenty minutes. Don't you dare touch that shaved pussy of yours until I get there."

When I hung up, I had to laugh. My husband knew me well. Very well.

There were no *hi-honey* kisses or *how-was-your-day*; the moment Brian got through the door, he pushed me back on the sofa and yanked open my robe. He made a little sound in his throat, half gasp, half moan.

"Wow, you really did a job on it."

I smiled. "Didn't you believe me?"

He gaped, eyes glowing. *Pussy power*—suddenly the words took on fresh meaning. Gently he nudged my thighs apart. I shivered. He bent down. I thought—and hoped—he was going to kiss me there.

"You didn't get all the hair off."

"Hey, it's a tricky job."

He frowned. "Don't move."

He left me lying on the sofa with my legs spread like a virgin sacrifice. My pussy was getting chilly, but my breath was coming fast and I had that naughty teenage feeling again, arousal so sharp it was almost pain.

Brian returned with a towel, a canister of shaving cream and a razor. He'd changed into his bathrobe, which did nothing to hide his bobbing erection. He came back again with a basin of water, which he set carefully on the coffee table. The last trip brought the video camera and tripod.

I felt a contraction low in my belly.

"Spread your legs wider."

I caught my breath, but obeyed.

He patted a dab of shaving cream between my legs. The coolness made me squirm.

"Lie still."

He was acting awfully bossy, but I didn't want any slipups. I held my thighs to keep them from shaking.

"Relax, Kira," Brian said, more kindly. Guys are always saying that when they're about to mess around with your private parts. Still Brian did have plenty of experience with shaving, so I closed my eyes and took a deep breath. The room was quiet, except for the scraping sound of the razor and the occasional swish of water. At last he rinsed me with a washcloth, smiling as I wriggled under his vigorous assault.

He leaned close to examine his work.

"Picture perfect," he declared.

Five minutes later, I was sitting naked in our armchair, watching my own twat, larger than life on our new plasma TV screen. My legs were modestly pressed together, but Brian had me lounge back so you could see the slit, shorn of its covering. He knelt, pointing the camera straight at me.

"Did you get turned on when you were shaving?" His tone was soothing now, like a friendly interviewer on a weekly news magazine.

"Yes," I admitted in a small voice.

"Did you masturbate?"

"No." A few flicks didn't count, right?

"You wanted to, though."

I swallowed.

Brian clicked his tongue. "Why don't you do it now? Don't you want to know if it feels different when it's shaved?"

My cheeks burned, but I ignored the question and turned to the screen. "It sure looks different."

"Yeah. It really does look like lips. The skin gets pinker here and pouts." He reached over and pinched the edges.

I bit back a moan.

"We could put lipstick on it. Deep red like a forties movie star."

"No, that's too weird," I said and immediately regretted it. Why was I being such a prude? After all, I'd started this with my little experiment in the tub. Suddenly bold, I glided my middle finger up and down along the groove. "This is an easier way to make it redder."

Brian grinned. "Yes, indeed. Let's get the full view." The camera zoomed in expectantly.

I hesitated. I'd played with myself in front of Brian before, but now a stranger was in the room with us, a stranger with a round, staring eye. "Go ahead, honey. I know you're turned on. Your chest is all flushed." I inched my thighs open, glancing at the TV. To my embarrassment I was already quite ruddy down there and shiny-slick with pussy juice. The fleshy folds and hole filled up the screen. My finger, laboring at my clit, looked strangely small.

"Does it feel different?" Brian was back to being the cordial journalist.

"A little."

"Tell me."

"The mound is really smooth, like satin."

"Is it more sensitive?"

"Yes, I think so. The outer lips are tingling. Or maybe I'm just noticing it more." I looked up at him. "What's with all the questions? You sound like you're interviewing my pussy for a dirty documentary."

Brian laughed. "What if I was?"

"Now wait a minute." I sat up and snapped my legs together.

He turned the camera to my face. A frowning twin gazed back at me from the TV.

Brian, on the other hand, was still smiling. "What if there was a guy in the city, a dot-com billionaire, who collects videos of married ladies pleasuring themselves?"

My pulse jumped. "You're joking right?"

"For his eyes only, discretion guaranteed. He pays well for it."

"Oh, yeah? How much?"

"Three grand for a genuine orgasm. That won't be a problem for you. We might get even more because you're all shaved down there. Just think, Kira, we could go on a nice vacation for a few very pleasant minutes of work." I moaned and covered my face with my hands.

"Don't worry. I'll edit this part out. He specifically requested no faces. Just sweet pussy."

Would my own husband really sell some rich voyeur a movie of me masturbating? I never thought he had it in him. And I never thought I'd find the idea so fiercely arousing. Funny all the things you discover when you shave your pussy.

Brian put the camera on standby. His eyes twinkled. "Jake and Ashley did it."

"No way."

"Lie back. I'll tell you about it."

There I was with my pussy on the screen again, a sprawled-leg Aphrodite, her naughty parts tinted dark rose.

"Ashley let Jake talk her into this?"

"Better than that. She went with him to drop it off. The guy tacks on a bonus if the lady and her husband join him for a drink."

I pictured Brian's best friend's wife, with her spiky blonde hair and lip ring, swishing up the stairs of a mansion in a black party dress and heels. That wasn't so hard to believe. "What was the rich guy like? I bet he was a creep."

"Jake said he was the perfect gentleman. Fortyish. Friendly. He served them a glass of champagne and hors d'oeuvres made by his personal chef. They chatted a bit, then left with an envelope of cash. Easiest money they ever made."

"I don't think I could meet him." So why did I see myself walking up those same mansion steps, Brian at my side, video in hand? I wasn't as wild as Ashley. I'd have on something prim: a lace blouse, a velvet choker with a cameo, a long skirt. I'd wear my hair up and keep my eyes down, blushing under his billion-dollar gaze. The perfect lady. That rich guy would get a boner the size of Florida just looking at me.

"Jake said the guy only did one thing that crossed the line. When they were leaving he took Ashley's right hand and kissed it like he was a baron or something."

"What's wrong with kissing her hand?" I had a weakness for old-fashioned manners.

"Well, it's the hand she uses to masturbate, of course. Like you're doing right now."

Without my realizing it, my hand had wandered back down between my legs. I jerked it away.

Brian laughed. Holding the camera steady, he reached up and guided my fingers back to my pussy. "Don't be bashful, honey. He wants to watch you do it. So do I."

And the truth was, I wanted them to see, the two pairs of eyes floating before me, Brian's the greenish-gray of a northern sea, the rich guy's golden and glittering.

"Where does he watch it? In his home theater?" Under the veil of my lashes I studied the screen. My labia jiggled lewdly as my finger strummed on. That's what the rich guy would see as he sat on his leather couch in his silk dressing gown. A wine-colored gown, the same color as his swollen dick. He'd pull it out and stroke it as he watched.

"A home theater, yes," Brian said softly. "State of the art."

"Why are you doing this? Don't you care if your wife shows her cunt to some horny billionaire?" The words came in gasps.

"The joke's on him. We'll take his money and get a suite in the fanciest hotel in town and fuck all night." Brian sounded winded, too, as if he'd just finished a run. Then I realized he was jerking off.

"I'm not a whore." I was half-sobbing, from shame and pleasure.

"Of course you're not, honey. You're a nice, pretty married lady. That's what he wants. Someone he'd glimpse at the gourmet grocery store or the espresso bar, buying a nonfat decaf cappuccino. I see guys staring at you. If only they knew the truth about my sweet-faced angel. If only they knew you want it so bad you shave your pussy and let men take pictures of it."

Sounds were coming out of my throat, sounds I'd never made before, high-pitched whines and animal moans.

"You're the hottest thing he's ever seen, but no matter how much he pays he can never have the real you."

"Oh, god, I'm gonna come," I whimpered.

A hand closed around my wrist and wrenched it away.

"He'll pay an extra thousand if you come while we fuck."

"Did Ashley do it?" I panted. I knew what the answer would be.

"Jake said she had the best orgasm of her life."

Brian hurriedly fixed the camera to the tripod, adjusted the height, then lifted me to my feet and took my place on the chair.

"Face the camera," he said.

My knees were as soft as melted caramel, but by gripping the arms of the chair I managed to position myself properly. On the screen Brian's penis reared up, my smooth snatch hovering above.

"Sit on it."

I lowered myself onto him with a sigh. Then I was up again, a woman who couldn't make up her mind. Up or down? It was there in full color: Brian's rod plunging in and out, his balls dangling beneath like a small pink pillow. "Now turn around and ride me."

In a daze I straddled him, my knees digging into the cushion. Just last week, we'd done it this way on the sofa. We pretended it was prom night and we were sneaking a midnight quickie while my parents snored in the bedroom upstairs.

"Do you like to fuck with a shaved twat?"

"Yes," I confessed. "I like to rub my bare lips on you." Which was exactly what I was doing, lingering on the downstroke to grind my exposed clit against the rough hairs at the base of his cock.

"You're so wet. That rich guy can hear it. Your hungry lips gobbling up my cock."

Brian began to twist my nipples between his fingers.

"It's an extra five hundred if you show him your asshole."

I grunted assent and bucked harder. In that position, the rich guy could see it anyway.

Then he whispered in my ear, "And another five hundred if you let me touch it."

I froze mid-thrust. "Please, Brian, don't," I whispered back. I didn't want the rich guy to hear. We'd recently discovered that when Brian diddles my butt crack when we fuck, it feels like a second clit. I loved it, but I was embarrassed and wanted it to be our secret. Brian knew he could make me blush just talking about it.

"Why not, baby? Because he'll know you're a bad girl who comes when I play with your pretty ass?"

"Please," I begged. My asshole, however, seemed to have other ideas, the brazen little show-off, pushing itself out, all plumped and ticklish.

"Please what, Kira? I know you want it, but I won't touch it until you say yes."

"Please," I gasped. "Yes."

"That's a good girl. Nice and polite."

Good girl, bad girl, I wasn't sure what I was, but it didn't matter. My torso rippled like a column of heat between his hands, one tweaking my nipple, the other going to town on my quivering bottom. Our bodies made rude noises, swampy, squishy sounds—or was it the rich guy whacking off? He probably used a special custom-made lotion to make his dick all slippery. He'd be close to the end now, pumping his fist faster and faster, his single nether eye weeping a tear of delight. He'd gotten everything he wanted. The cool lady in the gourmet grocery store was unzipped and undone, a bitch in heat, writhing shamelessly on her husband's cock for his viewing pleasure.

But I had one little surprise left for him.

"What if you spank it? Is that another thousand?"

"Two thousand." I could tell Brian was close, too.

"I want him to see it. Spank my naughty asshole," I yelled, so the rich guy could hear.

The first slap sent a jolt straight through me that quickly dissolved into pleasure, foamy fingers of a wave creeping into the hollows of my body.

"Again."

Smack.

Each blow hammered me deeper onto Brian's cock. I pushed my ass out to take the next one, to show that rich guy I could do it. He was so turned on, I could feel his eyes burning into my back through the screen. But it wasn't just him. There were others watching—my parents, my tenth-grade science teacher, the postal clerk who sneaks glances at my tits, a Supreme Court Justice or two—dozens of them, their faces twisted into masks of shock and fascination. And beneath, in the shadows, hands were stroking hard-ons or shoved into panties, damp and fragrant with arousal. They liked it, all of them, and I was watching them as they watched me in an endless circle of revelation and desire.

"I'm...gonna...come."

"Come for him. Now!" Brian bellowed. The last slaps fell like firecrackers snapping, and I jerked my hips to their rhythm as my climax tore through my belly. With the chair springs squeaking like crazy and Brian grunting, *fuck your shaved pussy, fuck it,* that rich guy got himself quite a show.

I'd say it was worth every penny.

Afterward, I pulled Brian down to the carpet with me. Our profiles filled the screen. He'd seen me and I'd seen him and we fit so well together and I loved him more than anything. I told him that. Or maybe I just kissed him, a deep soul kiss that lasted a long, long time.

The rich guy got that part for free.

Dinner Out

SKYE BLACK

I've been hurting for it so long that the smell of you hits me as soon as I enter the house, and I feel my body respond with the kind of hunger I've been nursing with melancholy sadness for a whole week. I unbutton my blazer in the kitchen, kick off my pumps in the living room, strip off my blouse and my skirt in the hall. By the time I nudge open the door of the bedroom and see you in bed, sprawled out sweaty and naked in the tangled sheets, my pussy is already aching. The moist sheets splay across your belly and your skin glistens in the slanted light from the window. You're asleep, snoring lightly. I don't even take off my garter belt and stockings before I climb into bed with you. And I don't even kiss you hello before I press my body against yours and cradle your cock, half-hard as you sleep.

Your eyes pop open and I shiver as you look at me with naked lust. Your cock hardens quickly in my hand and my pussy responds with such a hot flood of juice that before I know I'm doing it, I've burrowed under the covers and taken your cock in my mouth. The taste of it fills me with a rush of sensation and my nipples harden painfully in my too-tight bra. I want to take it off, but I find I can't do anything except wrap my fingers around the base of your cock and push you deeper into my mouth until I feel your swelling head against the entrance to my throat. When I reach down to my panties, it's to slide my fingers into them and feel my wetness, coating my fingers so I can reach back up and push them into your mouth. You bite my fingertips, hard, then lick my fingers clean and seize my hand to bite the heel of it while I suck you. I whimper softly, my noises muffled by the fullness of your cock in my throat as I bob up and down on you. I wore a thong today, thinking of you. It hurts me to take your cock out of my mouth, and my slick lips draw a glistening string of drool and pre-come from your cockhead as I sit up and straddle you, plucking the tiny crotch of my thong out of the way so I can sit down on your cock.

Your hands cradle my hips as I push onto you, my pussy so wet that it engulfs your cock in one hot, easy motion. In an instant I feel the familiar push of your cockhead against my G-spot, and I moan as I start to stroke my clit. I look down into your eyes and love you more than ever, wanting you to come inside me, wanting to come hard on your cock. And I'm close—very, very close.

Your hips rise up to meet me and I pump mine rhythmically; I feel my orgasm approaching. I'm on the very edge of it when you roll me off of you and tumble me onto the bed, face up, under you, legs spread. The feel of your weight almost makes me come right then, but you slide out of me and hold your cock erect, an inch from my cunt.

Moaning, whimpering, desperate, I inch my hips up and try to push myself back onto you. You tease me, pulling back. When I thrust myself hard at you, hungrily seeking your cock, you look down into my eyes and laugh.

You shake your head.

"Not yet," you say. "Get dressed. I'm taking you out to dinner."

"Baby, I'm so close," I whimper.

You smile broadly, climbing out of bed. "I want you aching for it. Get dressed."

I stretch out, sliding my hands into my wet thong and rubbing my clit. "Please?" I whisper.

"No," you say, getting back on the bed and grasping my wrists. You kiss me tenderly on the lips, your tongue stroking mine. That only makes me want it more, and I struggle against you, trying to get my hands back between my legs. I rub against you, feeling your wet cock on my belly.

"Come for me, then? Come on me?" I beg you. "Come in my mouth," I whisper.

You shake your head. "Get dressed in something nice—something very nice. This is an excellent restaurant. Be sure to wear gloves, though. Satin ones. And don't change your underwear—I love what you're wearing."

I should know better than to argue with you when you want to play these games. I love them as much as you do; for every whine and whimper I give you, begging you to come, to let me come, I know I'll come ten times harder when you finally let me have it.

But now, after a week without you, I want it so bad I can't control myself. I put my arms around you as you button your dress shirt; I drop to my knees and take your cock in my mouth again, tasting my pussy's juices so sharp on your hard flesh. You let me suck you, kneeling in my bra and panties. You let me take you into my throat, rub you all over my face. You let me bring you almost to the point where you'll come in my mouth; I taste the first tiny squirt of pre-come, and the flavor overwhelms me, making me want you more than I've ever wanted you in my life. I swallow eagerly and suck you harder, waiting for your come.

But you pull back, holding my hair, forcing my head back so that my lips and tongue work, empty and aching, an inch from your cock. I look up at you and whimper, then hear myself moaning, "Please? Please? Please?"

But you shake your head, pull me to my feet, and point me at the closet. It hurts to walk, my clit is so swollen. My hands quiver as I select my sexiest minidress, a tight little black number. I need your help zipping it, and the feel of your fingers on my skin makes me bite my lip. I put on a string of pearls, a dose of mascara, a thick coat of bright red lipstick. You knot a red tie around your neck and put on your dark wool suit coat.

I wear high-heeled shoes, praying you'll fuck me in them, like you did the last time we played this game. Only this time, something in your eyes tells me that the ante has been upped more than even I can imagine.

I don't bother with my seat belt in the car; it's much more important to me to tuck my ankles under my ass and cuddle up against your warm body as you drive.

I ask you how your trip was; I wonder out loud, again, why you chose to drive from Vancouver rather than flying, especially since your work would have paid for it. "I wanted to pick something up in Oregon," you tell me mysteriously. When I ask you what it is, you tell me I'll find out soon enough. That makes my pussy feel swollen and wet. I'm so turned on I'm still leaking, thick pulses of juice oozing out of my cunt and soaking my thong until it's so wet it feels cold and clammy. But when I push my thighs together tightly, it soon warms up.

We drive into the city and into the financial district. As the sun goes down, you go slowly along the less savory streets, like you're looking for a hooker. I think for a moment that maybe you are—maybe that's what you've got in store for me, why you wanted me so aching and wet that I couldn't say no. Are you going to push me to my knees in front of a twenty-five-dollar whore in a cheap red minidress, knowing I can't deny you anything, knowing I'll slip my tongue into her cunt just to get you to fuck me till I come? Knowing I'm yours, no matter what you do to me?

I think I have my answer when you pull into an alley, a dark one leading behind the newspaper loading dock and the back end of an office building. By now it's completely dark, and the alley stretches into blackness with not a streetlight anywhere to be seen. You hit the button that unlocks my door.

"Walk to the far end," you tell me.

"Honey, what...?"

You lean over and kiss me. "No questions," you say. "Just do it."

Nervously, I get out, taking my purse. You reach over and snatch it away from me, smiling.

"You won't need this," you say. "Walk quickly and with determination."

As I start walking, I hear you putting the car in reverse. I listen to the scratch of your tires as you pull back into traffic and disappear. Now I'm lost in the blackness of the alley, shaking with my fear. I try to walk quickly, but it's hard in these high heels. Each time I pass one of the empty cul-de-sacs that sports sleeping street people, I catch their harsh scent and try to hold my breath. But there's no clean air to be drawn. Each time I pass a tiny side alley, I feel the thumping heartbeat of terror that someone is waiting there for me, waiting to hurt me. I feel the familiar bite of tears in my chest, the quiver of my throat as it closes from mounting terror.

I walk as quickly as I can, listening to the echoing click of my high heels. The fear is making the ache in my pussy feel dangerous. It's making my knees feel weak. It's making my nipples hard, harder than they ever could have gotten from arousal alone. None of this feels good, however; it's all sheer terror; sheer pain; sheer hateful, forced surrender. I feel my eyes moisten and I choke back a single sob, then a second, then a third. I walk faster. Past another open, blackened alley.

I'm trying to watch for it. I'm trying to be aware, awake, alert, observant, but my tears have blinded my eyes, rendering me helpless—paralyzing me. The arm comes out from blackness and seizes my hair, jerking me back against a hard, unfamiliar body. For an instant I pray it's you, and then I smell the filth and the ancient, soured sweat. I open my mouth to scream. The arm closes around my throat, and I see the hand in front of me in the shadows, black-gloved. I hear the click and a glistening stream of silver erupts in the darkness, reflecting a single band of light from high, high above. Then the arm pulls me back into darkness, and all I can do is feel the blade against my throat.

"Don't scream," I hear the raspy voice. "Or you're finished."

Now I know why you drove through Oregon; switchblades are legal there. You push me forward across a cold metal garbage can, bending me over as you seize my hair. The tears grab me and I hear myself sobbing even as my pussy floods to feel you pushing hard against me from behind. I can feel your cock in your pants and it terrifies me even as it makes my clit throb. You grasp my hair tightly and I feel the cold steel of your blade sliding between my dress and my skin.

It's not even a ripping sound. The blade is so sharp it barely makes any noise at all. The only way I know you've cut my dress from back to hem is when it falls off of me. You slice each strap neatly, holding my hair so tight I can't do anything but squirm and sob. My dress is in shreds, and I feel the cold night air against my flesh. You cut each strap of my bra and it, too, falls in ruined pieces. Then my garter belt, garters first, low, close to the clasps, then waistband. My stockings fall. You pull me up, hard, by my hair, so that I'm standing there, almost naked. All I have on now are satin gloves, a string of pearls, and my thong and stockings. The stockings have already slid down to my knees, weighted by the garter clasps. You reach out and stab the remains of my dress with your knife, flick the ruined garment into a puddle of urine. With it goes my bra, or what's left of it, and my garter belt is already tattered at my feet. My arms hang helpless at my sides, shaking, as you caress my throat with the tip of a switchblade I now know is sharp enough to cut silk and satin without ripping.

Your breath is hot against my ear as you twist your hand in my hair. I can smell your filth, the rough wool overcoat you wear soaked in old sweat and god knows what else. But it's open in front, so I can feel your cock pressing hard through your suit pants, long and threatening between my cheeks. Hard and ready to fuck me. Ready to rape me.

You jerk my head, pulling my hair so firmly I have to choke back another sob, fight the urge to scream. Some part of me thinks you really might slit my throat. Some part of me thinks you're really going to rape me.

You draw the knife tip down between my breasts, taking a moment to tease my nipples. The fear has hardened them until they hurt enough to make me cry on their own. But the tip of your knife makes them ache in a different way, flushing shame and humiliation through my body, making my chest hot as my full breasts quiver with my sobs.

You finish with my breasts, draw the knife down over my soft belly, pressing just hard enough to let me know that, pressing any harder, you would gut me. My arms hang limp, my entire body helpless in your grasp.

You slip the edge of the blade under the front of my panties. I think you're going to cut them off. Instead, you twist my hair harder, so hard I gasp.

Then you bring the knife slowly back up my belly, circling each of my nipples and letting it come to rest at my throat, where it scares me the most.

"Take them off," you tell me.

I shake. I don't move. I stand there frozen under your terrible assault, knowing the word I should say to stop this, the word that will let you know you've gone too far. I look into the shadows and think I see distant shapes—men watching. Waiting their turn.

You press very gently against my throat, making me feel the prick of it.

The word is on my lips, in my tongue, but my lips are too tight and my tongue is too swollen with excitement and fear. I can feel my cunt throbbing with each beat of my pulse against the tip of your knife.

You shake my head with your hand tight in my hair, and I would swear I could feel the trickle of blood down the front of my throat. You growl in a voice I've never heard from you:

"Take them down," you say. "Pull your fucking panties down, bitch."

Whimpering, terrified, I force my useless hands to move, reaching to the thin string of my thong panties and pulling them down over my hips, over my ass. Peeling the crotch off of my pussy, feeling how it's so wet it sticks. Feeling how the bare flesh tingles with the freezing night air.

"All the way," you order me, and I tug my panties down to my thighs, having to stretch since you won't let go of my hair. Since you won't let me move at all, won't let me bend over.

I let go, and my panties slide down my thighs to my knees and then stop. They're so tight they lodge between my knees. You shake your fist again, jiggling my whole body against your knife. My panties drop down over my shins and bunch around my ankles.

"Step out of them," you tell me.

I do, my legs quaking. It's so much more humiliating, being forced to take my own panties off, being forced to reveal myself to you. But you've got more humiliating things in store for me, as you pull me hard against you and tell me:

"Spread your legs."

Nervously, I open them, moving very slowly so you don't cut me. I have to bend forward to spread them, but as I do you shove me hard, and in that instant you must have slipped the blade away, because I don't find myself impaled on it. Instead, I'm sprawled over the garbage can lid, legs spread, arms thrust out desperately, body shaking.

"Wider, bitch," you say.

I obey this time, shocked and terrified by the sudden burst of force. I spread my legs as wide as I can, so wide I feel my feet pushing into the mounds of garbage off to the side. So wide I feel myself helpless, off balance, opened up to you.

I realize with horror, with excitement, that it's time. You're going to rape me.

You don't go slow; you don't tease me. Your cock drives into me so fast that if I wasn't already gushing wet, it would make me scream in pain. I scream anyway, in shock and fear, even as the thickness of your cock explodes through me and makes every muscle in my body strain with sudden pleasure. You grab my hair and lean forward hard, bearing me into the garbage can as you drive your cock violently into me. I feel the prick of the knife against my throat and you growl, "Scream again and you're dead, bitch!" But my mouth is already open wide, and it's all I can do to turn that scream into a long, low moan as I feel your cock pounding into me. You've shoved me forward so roughly that my pubic bone is pressed against the rim of the garbage can, forcing pressure hard against my clit. I'm close to coming already, and the sobs have turned to gasps and moans of pleasure. But before I can come, you pull out of me and snarl, "You're so wet your pussy's loose, bitch. Let's see how you like it back here," and before I know what's happening my cheeks are spread around the thickness of your thumb, forcing me wide open. My eyes go wide and I start to gasp "No, no—!" The safeword springs to my lips but never makes it out. Your thumb slides out, replaced by your cock as you shove into me so hard that it feels like you should rip me in two—but you don't; my wet pussy is still dripping from your cock, and it forces its way into me with violence matched only by the pleasure it drives through my naked body. I open my mouth wider than ever, so wide I feel my jaw popping, the corners of my mouth stretched painfully, and as your cock sinks into my ass I push back onto you, fucking myself onto it. Your hand comes around and you seize my hair to keep me from moving, and I feel the coldness of the knife sliding up my thigh. I would scream, then, as I feel the sharp tip of it pushing between my lips, but there isn't even time for me to scream—because I'm right on the edge of coming. As you shove the knife into me, your cock filling my ass, your violent pounding ripping me every bit as much as a knife blade ever could, I let out an uncontrolled, desperate scream of orgasm, terror mingling with pleasure and heightening every sensation coursing through my naked body. Sobs wrack me as you drive it handle-deep into me and I feel its cold, hard hilt pushed up against my tender opening even as it spasms with orgasm. You pound into me, another thrust, another, and then you let out a scream of your own as you shoot deep into my ass. I lie there bent over the garbage can, naked, helpless, terrified, not sure whether I'm alive or dead. You pull your spent cock out of my ass and a stream of your come oozes down my inner thigh. You're gone in an instant, and I hear your footsteps echoing as you vanish down the dark alley.

I don't know how long I lie there over the garbage can, naked, spread, ass and cunt fucked wide. Just long enough for me to come to my senses, pull myself off the garbage can, and cross my satin-shrouded arms over my naked breasts, shivering.

As I stand there in the garbage-strewn darkness, I reach down and touch my pussy. It's wide, dripping, and it aches with every touch. My clit throbs, still hard, wanting more though hurting from the rough press of the metal garbage can. But my cunt is intact, neither cut nor bleeding.

My clothes, however, are nothing more than shredded rags all around me.

I stand there exposed, frightened, feeling off balance in my high-heeled shoes and the stockings bunched around my ankles, feeling the warm brush of my satin gloves against my breasts as I struggle to hide them—from whom, I don't know. Pearls dangle between my breasts, looking odd and ridiculous.

The alley explodes in a blaze of light, and I turn, stunned, looking into the headlights. The police? A stranger?

You get out of the car, throw your suit jacket over me, and lead me otherwise naked into the car. You close the passenger side door, get in.

I curl up against you, clutching you for support. I can feel the bulge of your pocket—two bulges, actually, and I know that it wasn't your knife I was so sure was cutting me deep when you slid it into my pussy. I press my palm against the dual handles of your weapons—one metal, to scare me, one rubber, to fuck me with. How could I have been so convinced you would really put a knife inside me? It doesn't matter. In the moment you slid it into me, I was yours, totally owned by your brutal persona, and that's why I came so hard. The part of you that took me so violently really *would* fuck me with a knife, and that's why I came so hard. But the more important part of you that loves me and cherishes me made sure that evil bastard was holding a knife that wouldn't do anything except what you wanted it do—to make me come, harder than I've ever come before.

I know you'd never hurt me—now, I know that. A moment ago I was sure you would, and that's why I love *you* more than anything. You went there with me, into a place that terrified us both. But now we're back in our real life, where you take care of me. You gently push me off of you, force my limp body into the seat, pull my seat belt over me and buckle it.

"Seat belts save lives," you tell me, and put the car in gear.

By the time we get home I'm half asleep, floating on a delicious cloud of fear and sex and hunger. You pull into the garage so the neighbors won't see me get out of the car nude except for your jacket. You lead me into the house, put me to bed, and bring me a tray of food—cold cuts and sourdough bread.

"It's not from a nice restaurant," you say. "But I hope it's okay for dinner."

I swallow a bite of bread and lean over to kiss you.

"I had my dinner," I whisper hoarsely. "It was delicious."

Medical Attention
SKYE BLACK

I woke up spread-eagled, stretched, helpless. I tried to move and nothing happened. As my vision cleared, I saw myself in the monitor facing the bed. I stared, disbelieving. My arms and legs were in full-length casts, toes to crotch, fingers to shoulders, all four limbs suspended with bolts through the sides of the casts, heavy traction weights holding me immobile. I had been forced into a giant X on the hospital bed, both my arms and legs cocked just slightly at a wide angle. My head was shaved and wrapped in thick white gauze and, under it, there was a white plastic brace that attached to shiny metal prongs inserted into the corners of my mouth. My belly was circled by a thick off-white plastic brace with shiny aluminum struts attaching to both my leg and arm casts. The brace went from my hips, just above my crotch, to my chest just beneath my breasts.

And there was nothing covering those parts of me. Not even a sheet. My breasts were bare, exposed on the big monitor facing me. My crotch, also bare, had been shaved smooth, even the tiny dusting of pubic hair I usually wear having been denied me.

The traction spread my legs very wide.

I saw the winking red eye of the surveillance camera, the camera providing me the perfect view of myself. The monitor alternated between a full-body view of me, spread-eagled and immobilized, a close-up of my bare pussy, a close-up of my tits, and a close-up of my distressed, gauze-shrouded face.

I had been painted with makeup. Far from the deathly pallor that should haunt an accident victim, I had been given rosy cheeks with blush, thick eyelashes with mascara, bright blue eyelids with eye shadow. And, most arresting of all, I had been given full, accentuated lips with an intensely red shade of lipstick.

The monitor showed me my whore's painted face, then my breasts, then my pussy, up close. Then it showed all of me again, all of me, helpless and stock-still spread-eagled in the hospital bed.

The hospital door opened. A nurse in a starched white uniform came in. But the uniform dress was just a little too short, too tight on her rounded hips, the top cut just a little too close on her full breasts. Her white lace bra was visible under the low-cut top, which had a button or two undone. She was wearing makeup, too—lots of it.

"I see our patient's awake," she said. "How are you feeling, Mrs. Rubin?"

I murmured a wordless groan.

The nurse *tsked*. "Poor girl, doesn't remember a thing. Well, I'll let the doctor answer all your questions. He'll be here in a moment; I've got to get you ready for him, or there'll be hell to pay. He can be so demanding. I would hate to get in trouble with him. Now, be a good girl and take your medication, won't you?"

The nurse produced a small paper cup of pills. "Do you have to use the restroom?" she asked.

I nodded, and she sighed. "All right, well, let's do that first," she said. She took a plastic urinal from a nearby table, positioned herself between my spread legs, and tucked it just under my crotch.

But before she pressed it there, she took a moment to slide her fingers up the inside of my shaved pussy. It felt exquisitely sensitive, almost painfully so. She teased my lips apart, perhaps under the pretext of making sure I wouldn't dribble. Whatever it was, I didn't ask her, because the touch sent shivers through my immobilized body.

"My, my," she said, slipping her thumb into my pussy and making me gasp suddenly as a surge of pleasure erupted into me. "The patient is producing excessive lubrication. Clearly she likes looking at herself in the monitor. Don't be ashamed; many of our patients get very turned on looking at themselves. And I do understand it, Mrs. Rubin; you certainly make a pretty picture. You like seeing your pussy all clean like that, Mrs. Rubin? We had to shave it. The doctor insisted on it. And those tits of yours look much better bare. It's a shame you don't show them more often."

The nurse tipped the urinal cup to my crotch and said, "All right, go ahead."

My face reddened until it was crimson at the horror of having to pee in front of the nurse. I held back, despite the fact that my bladder was stretched full to the point of agony.

"Don't you dare hold back," said the nurse. "I won't have you going later, and making a mess for me or the other nurses to clean up. Now go, you filthy girl, and don't hold back a drop."

With a sigh, I let my bladder go, a steady stream filling the urinal. When I was finished, the nurse dabbed me with a paper towel and emptied the cup into the nearby sink.

"Good girl," she said. "Now, to prep you."

She pulled out a pair of bolts that held the bed; I realized that I was not on a normal hospital bed, but a breakaway bed that folded under, turning it into more of a gynecological exam table. It had to be custom-built. As she folded the bottom half of the bed away, I was left hanging with my ass just barely on the edge of the table and my legs spread wide and thrust up into the air. My cunt was now even more exposed than before. The nurse took a position next to me and bent down, looking into my face and smiling. She was so close that I could smell her perfume, and the sweet scent of her breath.

Her hand traveled down my body and found my shaved pussy. She began to stroke me gently, rubbing my clit as my eyes went wider. My clit responded, growing harder as my pussy lubricated. Pleasure flowed into me and I resisted it as surely as I resisted the traction holding me still, but there was nothing I could do. Two fingers slid into me, telling the nurse just how wet she was making me. She drew firm circles around my clit with her wet fingers, and then drew back her hand and slapped my cunt.

I gasped; a strangled squeal came out of my mouth as she drew back and spanked my cunt again. She spanked harder, a third time, then a fourth, more rapidly, as I shuddered and moaned. Pleasure mingled with pain as she tortured my cunt.

"Clearly the patient likes it rough," she smiled as she paused in spanking my cunt. She then launched into it with new eagerness, slapping harder, faster, making my clit explode in sensation and making me mount toward orgasm. I fought off my climax even as it thundered toward me.

The doctor entered the room out of my field of vision; I couldn't even turn my head to see him. I lay there, displayed on the monitor, painted mouth spread wide open, body totally immobile, cunt being violently spanked as I was forced toward a climax, floating on cushions of sedated pleasure.

The nurse stopped. "The patient is prepped, Doctor."

"Start the recording."

"Yes, Doctor." The nurse produced a small tape recorder and held it out for the doctor to speak into as he came around between my legs. I tottered on the edge of orgasm, whimpering uncontrollably. I was so close I could feel it starting, my orgasm. Just a little bit would get me there.

The doctor's fingers slid into my pussy. I moaned, right on the edge. But he only gave me one smooth thrust, testing my wetness, and slid his hand up to test my clit. So close...but he didn't let me come.

"Patient presented with extreme vaginal lubrication," he said, businesslike, into the tape recorder. "And unusual swelling of the clitoris and nipples. Complete immobilization was recommended and performed."

As he spoke, the doctor unbuttoned his lab coat. I looked up at him through horny eyes, so turned on I couldn't even beg him for what I wanted.

"Vulvar assault by the attending nurse brought the patient

very close to orgasm, further indicating extreme arousal."

The nurse reached down and unzipped the doctor's pants.

"During examination, patient showed noticeable flushing of the chest, further distension of the nipples and a sexual response to the sight of her own lips painted like a whore's." The nurse's hand disappeared inside the doctor's pants and pulled out his cock, naked and half-hard. She began to stroke it and it swelled as he talked. "Doctor's recommendation is for vaginal intercourse followed by anal penetration."

The nurse guided the doctor's cockhead to my exposed pussy, and I moaned as he entered me. The nurse held out the recorder, capturing his grunts as he began to thrust into me. His hands rested on my casts, as if keeping my legs spread— though there was no way I could have closed them, held as they were by the traction cables. He pounded into me roughly, fucking me so hard it made the hospital bed groan and creak. It was only a moment before I came, gasping.

"Primary orgasm was achieved three minutes after penetration," the doctor said, glancing at his watch. "Buildup to secondary orgasm began immediately."

The doctor plunged deep into my cunt and fucked me as I came. The sliding thrusts of his cock brought me down from orgasm and I began to build toward a second one. As I did, I heard the snap of latex gloves and felt the nurse's gloved fingers prying open my cheeks even as the doctor kept thrusting into my cunt. Her fingers slid into my ass, slick with lube, and opened me up, first one finger, then two. More lube was added, and she forced a third finger into me.

"The patient is ready," said the nurse.

The doctor pulled his cock out of my pussy and let the

nurse position it at the entrance to my ass. My moans came even louder as he entered me again, this time forcing open my tight ass. I shuddered in the traction ropes and came again within moments. "Anal penetration produced a second orgasm in just over one minute. Oral semen to be administered now."

The doctor pulled out of my ass and took the tape recorder out of the nurse's hand. He came around the bed and positioned himself at my upper body. The nurse turned an unseen crank, lowering my head until my upper body was far enough below my hips to put my mouth within easy reach of the doctor's cock. Then she guided the doctor's cock to my mouth and began to stroke the shaft with her long, slim fingers as I opened wide, hungry for his come. The head hovered between my widespread lips, and the doctor groaned into the tape recorder as the first hot stream of come shot onto my tongue. I moaned and gulped it down, swallowing the next stream, and the next, overwhelmed by the pungent flavor of the doctor's come.

"Patient eagerly received administration of oral cumshot approximately fourteen minutes after initiation of vaginal intercourse. Condition of vaginal lubrication seems unchanged, but no further treatment recommended at this time."

The nurse tucked the doctor's cock back into his pants and buttoned up his lab coat. The doctor left without a word.

The nurse extended the lower half of the hospital bed again and unhitched the traction cables. She then pulled the Velcro straps on my hard breakway casts and unbuckled the brace on my stomach. I moaned softly as she unwound the gauze from around my head. Laying there naked, no longer restrained, I could feel the spasms in my pussy that spelled the afterglow of two intense orgasms.

The nurse wiped down my thighs, my pussy, and dabbed away the lube that oozed out of my ass. She bent down and kissed me on the lips, smearing my lipstick.

"Thanks for visiting the Citadel," she said. "We hope you return soon."

I was too tired, exhausted, and dopey with codeine to answer. I just smiled up at her and gripped her hand.

"Take your time getting dressed," said the nurse. "Your husband will be waiting in the lobby. I'll try to make him comfortable."

She winked at me, and I sighed. It had been way too expensive, this fantasy of ours—after all, there's only one professional dungeon in the state with a fully operational medical exam room, set up to provide traction.

It had been almost more than our budget could bear.

I looked up at the monitor, which still showed me, spread, naked, used. Glistening with sweat, painted like a tramp. I watched as it showed my pussy, tits, face. I felt my clit swelling. My hand slowly slid down my belly, still marked by the angry red impressions of the brace.

I touched my pussy, feeling it wet, hot and aching. I began to stroke my clit, feeling another orgasm surprise me as it began to pulse into being.

Expensive, yes. But oh so worth it.

I heard the hospital bed groaning and squeaking in protest as I came.

Dress Me Up

ERICA DUMAS

I love it when you dress me up. Well, you don't dress me up, exactly—though that's how I like to think of it. I put on the clothes, but you pick them out. When we play this way, you come over to my apartment and let yourself in using the key I gave you, never telling me what clothes you'll select for me. And they're always so much more revealing than I would have dared pick out for myself.

Tonight it's my tiniest white minidress, with a matching white lace thong, push-up bra, and garter belt. It's all laid out on the bed, with a handwritten note from you saying *Don't be late*. The stockings are white, too—seamed down the back to accentuate the curve of my legs. The white shoes you picked out for me have six-inch heels: fuck-me shoes. Fuck-me-*hard* shoes. Fuck-me-*till-I-scream* shoes.

And I know you will.

They're all mine, but I would never wear them all

together. The dress I probably wouldn't wear at all—it's much too naughty, too daring. I bought it with you in mind, knowing you would make me wear it. Just the way I want you to.

You set out my jewelry, too—a pearl and gold choker, matching earrings, matching bracelets. These aren't mine; they're new. The kind of gifts you'd give a prostitute. It turns me on to hold them, feel their weight in my hands. I don't worry about how you can afford all this; I know I'm worth it, because I'm your whore. And I know tonight I'll be the best whore in town.

I put it all on slowly after my long, luxurious bath, savoring the way the skimpy clothes reveal my body. I put on my makeup extra-thick, the sexy clothes inspiring me to paint myself like a slut. Then I do my hair the same way—big hair, porn-star hair. A whore's hair.

There's no purse and no watch—tonight I'm at your mercy. I know you'll take care of me.

You ring the buzzer at exactly seven, and I grab my jacket and head for the door. Then I stop and think, and put down my jacket—you didn't lay it out, so I won't wear it. I'm not to wear anything you didn't give me.

I hope it's not too cold tonight.

When you see me, I know you're pleased with the way I've filled out your selections. Your eyes rove over me as I approach the car. My breasts stretch the top of the minidress, and the push-up bra shows them to full advantage. It is a little chilly out, and I notice right away that my nipples are hardening under the dress, so much so that they're quite visible. My face reddens, but I don't move to cross my arms. I want you to see. I want everyone to see.

You lean over and kiss me, letting your hand rest on my belly and trail up a little to casually brush my tits. I shudder as you do; it sends a pulse of sensation from my breasts to my pussy. I shift uncomfortably on the seat as your lips curve in a smile; you can tell how turned on I am, and how the nervousness heightens my arousal.

"You look nice," you tell me.

It's all I need to hear. If you gushed over me, told me what a sexy slut I am, it would be too much. All I need is to know that I've satisfied you, that you're happy with the way I look. The fact that you've dressed me up like your tart is just the icing on the cake.

"Where are we having dinner?" I ask.

"Somewhere everyone can look at you," you tell me, and turn the heat on.

Somehow that excites me even more—the silent acknowledgment that you can tell how hard my nipples are, that you know it's not just the cold. My heart pounds as I sink into the luxurious heat blowing from the vents. You pull away from the curb.

People look at me as they pass by in cars or cross the street in front of us when we're stopped at lights. They can't see much, but they can see enough. They know I'm a slutty little bird. That's enough to make my pussy feel hot, to make my clit rub against the too-tight thong you've selected. The thong is entirely made of lace, see-through and a little rough, reminding me how hard my clit is. I know if I checked I'd find myself wet.

You take me downtown. You pull up outside the most expensive hotel in town, and the valets ogle me as they take the car keys.

I'm aware of all the eyes on me as we walk across the lobby. My nipples are still quite hard, with no hope of being any different until you've fucked me hard. You take me to the tower elevator and push the button. Businessmen look at me, trying to glance away so it doesn't look like they're looking. You have your arm around me and you pull me close, staring them down with a little smile on your face.

In the crowded elevator, you push the button for the top floor: *CAFE SKYE*. I lean close to you, half frightened that I'll feel a hand up my skirt—and half wanting to. The elevator empties out as we travel up ten floors, twenty, stopping every few floors as people disembark. Then I *do* feel a hand up my skirt. Yours—I think. I lean back onto it and feel your finger slipping between my cheeks, plucking the crotch of the thong out of the way. Easing between my barely-parted legs. Touching my wet pussy.

I have to stifle a gasp as your finger creeps forward to touch my swollen clit. It's your hand all right—no one can touch my clit like that. My knees almost buckle; my whole body feels like it's about to melt. You rub me as the elevator empties out, until there's only one man left. Then he leaves, one floor before the restaurant.

When the doors close, you grab me and push me against the wall. I moan as I sink into your grasp. You press your mouth to mine and your tongue invades me, pushing hard against mine. I can feel your cock hard in your pants, pressing against my belly. Even with the six-inch heels, I'm shorter than you. Your left hand cups one breast, your palm rubbing my nipples through the thin fabric, nudging it until it pops out of the bra cup and stretches the white dress, hidden from the world only by the thinnest of gossamer fabrics. Then you reach in and gently ease my breast out of the dress, making it press against the arm strap, tucking my bra cup underneath. Your other hand, now curved more fully under my ass, pushes firmly against my clit and then you ease your fingers back, fucking two of them into me.

I almost come right there.

The elevator dings and you turn away from me, leaving me panting and weak against you. I move my hand to tuck my breast back into my bra, into the dress, but you gently take my wrist and pull it away.

You tuck my breast in instead, always the protector—and always in control.

My face hot with excitement, I put my arms at my sides as we walk into the restaurant.

The maître d' eyes me, scandalized by my slutty dress. He opens his mouth like he's going to say something, but then he decides not to. As he looks through his reservation book to find your name, his eyes keep slipping up to my breasts. My nipples are showing plainly through the dress. Perhaps he thinks I'm unaware of how skimpy the dress is, that I'm not used to dressing in such a revealing fashion.

Perhaps he thinks I'm a dirty whore, showing off to any man who will look.

You hold out a twenty-dollar bill.

"Right in the middle of the restaurant, please," you say. "We're here to see and be seen."

"Evidently," he murmurs, and accepts the bill, tucking it into his tuxedo jacket.

He leads us over to our table in a section in the center

of the room on a raised dais where everyone can see me. As I pass through the room behind you, all the male diners, to a man, look at me. Their wives shoot me dirty looks. Every pair of eyes touching my hard nipples sends a wave of pleasure into my cunt. I know my thong is soaked by now. Dripping. You smile at me, glancing around to make sure everyone is looking. They're trying not to, but they can't help it. My knees feel weak as the maître d' holds out my chair. Perhaps it's an accident that his arm brushes one of my nipples as he hands me the menu. Either way, it sends an explosion of sensation from my nipple to my cunt. I can feel my clit throbbing hard in my soaked thong. It makes me even more aware that men are looking at my tits, looking at me, studying my exposed nipple. Wanting me, but hating me. A whore, showing off for everyone.

I don't notice much about the food or the service or the supposedly spectacular view. What I notice is you looking at me throughout dinner; undressing me with your eyes; taking off my tiny dress and my slutty underwear; using your gaze to tug my other breast out of my bra, out of the dress, to show off both my tits to everyone. I'm so wet I'm afraid I'll soak through the dress, leave a wet chair behind. In fact, I'm pretty sure I will.

But I also notice the patrons whispering, pointing at me. I notice the kitchen help, beautiful brown-skinned boys with wide shoulders, filling water glasses and pointing at me, bending close to mutter comments to each other while looking right at me. One busboy in particular fills my water glass every time I take a sip. He looks at me and smiles, his eyes filled with lust. And I notice our waiter, looking at me salaciously with mingled contempt and desire.

And I notice you leaning forward over the table, feeding

me chocolate cake for dessert, a tiny forkful at a time. Each bite makes me wish it was you in my mouth.

After you've paid the bill, you reach across the table and leave a hotel key card in a paper sleeve with a room number on it.

"I'm going to the room," you tell me. "Have a drink at the bar and meet me at the room. But don't come down for at least an hour. I'll be there all night, so take your time."

"You'll…you'll leave our tab open? I…I don't have any money," I say apologetically.

You shake your head. "No," you tell me. "I've already closed it out."

"Then…how can I get a drink?" My voice is quivering, half from arousal, half from fear. I'm terrified of what you have in store for me, but my clit is pulsing with anticipation. This humiliation is agony, but I swear if you don't fuck me soon I'm going to come spontaneously, without ever touching my clit.

You lean forward and smile, pointing with your finger. "See that man at the bar?" you ask me.

I glance over; there's a gray-haired man, perhaps sixty, dressed in an expensive suit. He's sitting alone, sipping whiskey from a highball glass. He's looking at me hungrily, not even caring that you've noticed him.

"Do you see him?" you ask me.

"Yes," I say, my eyes locked on the gray-haired man.

"You're going to get him to buy you a drink," you tell me. "And you're going to pay him back for it. Every time he offers you another drink, you'll accept it and finish it quickly. Within ten minutes. If he buys you one drink, you'll get him alone and give him a hand job. And let him come on your tits."

"Oh, God," I whimper. "You must be joking...."

"Not at all," you say. "I'm dead serious. If he buys you two drinks, you'll suck his cock and let him fuck you. And stroke him off onto your face when he's ready to go. Three drinks..."

You lean closer, smiling, looking into my horrified, humiliated face, knowing the effect your words are having on my aching cunt.

"Three drinks?" I whisper in a small, frightened voice.

"Three drinks, and he gets to fuck you in the ass," you tell me.

I shiver.

"What if he doesn't want to?" I ask.

"Come now," you say. "He's a man. All you have to do is ask him, and I'm sure he'll put his cock in whatever hole you offer."

"How...how?" is all I can say.

"You're a talented girl. You know about the birds and the bees."

"Where am I supposed to take him?"

"Perhaps he has a room," you tell me. "Or perhaps you can do him in the hallway, like any other whore. He looks like he's got money, darling. I hope you brought some lube."

I shake my head. "No, I didn't bring anything."

"Then I hope you're good and turned on by the time he puts it in your ass," you tell me. "I guess you didn't bring a condom either."

I shake my head again. "Nothing. You told me not to bring anything."

You chuckle. "I did, did I? Well then, no condom. I guess

you really should know about the birds and the bees by the time the evening is over. Men always prefer the feel of a naked pussy—or asshole. So I'm sure he'll appreciate it when you let him fuck you bare."

You get up from the table, bend over, and kiss me on the cheek.

"At least an hour, darling," you tell me. "But take your time. If he wants to fuck you all night, I'll be waiting. And as soon as he finishes with you, come to my room ready for more. I'm sure you'll just be getting warmed up."

You leave me there, panting, my face red. The busboys are eyeing me, particularly the one who has just appeared to fill my water glass. His arm brushes my nipple as he bends over, and I don't pull away. I'm too confused, too excited. I can smell his sharp sweat. I look over to the bar and see the man you've picked out for me. Thirty years older than me, if he's a day. He's leering at me openly.

Weakly, I smile at him.

I walk over on trembling legs and sit down next to him. He looks at me hungrily. Not knowing what to do with the key card clutched in my hand—of course I don't have any pockets—I lay it on the bar in front of me, making a mental note that under no circumstances can I let myself forget it.

The bartender appears in front of me, his face twisted in a look of disgust. He must be thinking I'm like any high-class hotel whore, working the restaurant.

"Can I get you something?" he sneers.

"I…I need a moment to decide," I say.

The bartender disappears and the man next to me leans close. "Hi," he says to me. "Here alone?"

I take a deep breath, barely able to speak. I can feel tears forming in my eyes. A little sob grabs my throat when I try to say something.

I cover up for it quickly, speaking in a tormented voice, plainly edging toward tears.

"I am now," I tell the man. "My boyfriend just broke up with me."

"Oh, baby, I'm sorry," he said. "What's your name?"

"Erica," I tell him.

"Erica, I'm Hal. Let me buy you a drink."

"I shouldn't," I say. "I shouldn't drink after a shock like that."

"Sure you should," Hal tells me, waving the bartender over. "Beautiful girl like you, first thing you need to do is have some fun. Get him back for being a careless bastard. I can't believe he'd let a girl like you go." He gestures at the bartender. "Mike, let's get this girl a whiskey sour. Whiskey sour, Erica?"

"That'd be fine," I say, my eyes glistening with tears of fright. That's one drink. I'm going to give him a hand job.

"And make it extra-strong," says Hal under his breath, leaning close to Mike the bartender, perhaps thinking he's speaking quietly enough that I can't hear. "She's having a rough night." His eyes lock in on my exposed nipple, and he licks his lips.

"One whiskey sour," says the bartender, leering at me contemptuously.

One drink. I'm going to stroke his cock. I'm going to jerk him off. I'm going to pump him until he comes on my tits. My clit throbs painfully against the bar stool.

The drink comes and I gulp it desperately while Hal tries to make small talk. He wants to know more details about the breakup.

"He...he wants to see other people," I say. "He...he says I can't...can't satisfy him."

"Oh, now, that's a shame. He must be crazy. Pretty girl like you, I'm sure you have a healthy libido. Want a refill on that?"

I want to say no. I want to refuse the drink, run to you, hide in your arms. But you've ordered me to accept, to take Hal's liquor and let him do what he wants to me. To let him get me drunk and fuck me with increasing intimacy depending on how drunk he gets me. I know I have to say yes. I know I have to let Hal buy me as many drinks as he wants, and for each drink, his cock will invade a new part of my body. This is the second drink. It means I'm going to suck his cock and let him fuck me. And when he's ready to come, I'm going to jerk him off on my face.

My voice quavers as I try to speak. I clear my throat. "Yes," I manage to croak, already feeling the heady effects of the whiskey mingling with the wine from dinner. "I'll have another."

Mike mixes another whiskey sour while Hal tells me he's single. I know he's lying, but I don't care. I know I can't refuse him. The least he's going to get, now, is my mouth, clamped around his cock. My face, presented to him for defilement. His come, shooting all over me. I can already feel hot streams hitting me. The humiliation makes me turn deep red, my body flushing hot. I can feel my cunt pulsing between my tightly closed thighs.

"Drink up, darling."

I try to make it last, but I can't. I'm so nervous every time I take a sip it turns into a gulp. By the time the ice rattles in the glass, I can feel I'm getting drunk. The whiskey is enveloping my head, taking me over. When I'm finished, Hal doesn't even ask. He just waves Mike over and orders another for me.

Three drinks. He can do whatever he wants to me—fuck my mouth, my pussy, my ass.

"Thank you," I say. "I feel like I'm taking advantage of you, letting you buy me all these drinks."

Hal chuckles. "Oh, I can afford it," he says. "And from the looks of it, you can too." His eyes rivet to my exposed nipple as he says it.

The whiskey sour goes quickly while Hal describes what a romantic he is. The right way to treat a woman. Make her feel special. I can smell the scent of Hal's body, the aroma of his sweat. I glance down at his crotch and see that his cock is halfway hard. He's leaning closer to me as he talks. His hand is on my thigh, up above the top of my stockings, past where the garters clip to the gossamer fabric. His fingers creep up under the hem of my dress. My flesh tingles as he touches me. I let my legs slip slightly open, and his fingers creep up still further—a planned invasion disguised as a casual, friendly gesture.

I'm going to spread my legs and feel his cock, naked, raw, latex-free, sliding into my pussy. I'm going to feel him hump into me, fuck me until he comes inside me. I'm going to go back down to your hotel room with Hal's come leaking out of my cunt. I find myself leaning against Hal, my hand grazing his thigh. When I shift slightly, I feel the press of his cock, half-hard against my palm. One hand creeps further up my dress, stroking my thighs. His other hand is on my arm, gripping me, steadying me from my drunken sway on the bar stool—or making sure I can't get away.

He thinks I don't see. He thinks I don't see him as he takes his hand from my thigh, reaches into his jacket pocket, turns away with a pill bottle in his hand. He tries to play it casual as he pops off the top, shakes two pills onto the bar, picks them up and washes them down with his straight bourbon, then tucks the bottle back into his jacket.

"Vitamins," he tells me. "Have to take them every day."

But I've seen it—seen the shape of the pills in his hand, just before he popped them. That telltale blue pill, diamond-shaped. He knows I'm going to let him fuck me.

He smiles, lifting his glass. "Here's a toast to you, Erica. The most beautiful girl I've ever met."

The fantasy requires that I be reluctant, but now I'm so turned on I couldn't stop myself even if I really did want to. I've let my hand drift up to Hal's crotch, let my fingers curve around the shaft of his cock through his pants. The pills have made him hard all the way—hard, and large. He's got quite a big cock, and I know where I'm going to take it.

The final marker has been passed. As I finish my drink, he puts his fingers gently on my face and turns me toward him. I part my lips. Hal kisses me, his tongue forcing its way whiskey-sweet into my mouth, his hand moving down to mine and pressing it hard against the shaft of his cock. His other hand, around my back, pulls me close and slides up to grip my hair. He holds me tight as he forces my hand against his cock. His lips come off of mine and I pant, feeling as if I'm on a merry-go-round. My cunt aches as I lean forward to press it against the bar stool. Hal is going to fuck me. He's going to fuck me in all three of my holes.

"See what you've done to me?" he whispers. "Let's go

somewhere, Erica. I think you'd like that, wouldn't you?"

I'm breathing hard, gasping for air.

All I can do is nod.

Hal tosses a twenty on the bar, stands me up. He steadies me with his arm around my shoulders, his hand gripping my wrist tightly. His suit jacket brushes my nipples through the thin dress. Everyone in the restaurant looks at us as he walks me toward the door.

Moving down the long hotel corridor, I lean against him, unable to stand on my own. I can feel the wetness of my pussy dripping down my thighs. I try to keep them pressed together, but I'm already tottering on my high heels.

"Do—do you have a room?" I ask.

"No," he says, "But I know a nice romantic stairwell. A whore like you doesn't rate an expensive hotel room, anyway. No wonder your boyfriend dumped you."

Hal opens a heavy fire door and shoves me through. I stumble down half a flight. Hal grabs my arm and shoves me to my knees. I feel my stockings ripping as Hal grips my hair and tangles his fingers in it. He's got his pants open in an instant and before I know it he's leaning back against the wall, dragging me forward and forcing my mouth down onto his cock.

A surge goes through me as I taste it. The second I feel his hard cock in my mouth, all I feel is the hunger for cock that led me here tonight in the first place.

"Oh, yeah," says Hal. "Your boyfriend dumped you because you were a little cocksucker. You're good at it, too. How many cocks did you suck while you were going out with him, anyway? Just a drink or two and you're down on your knees, Erica. You're cheaper than the cheapest whore. You would have sucked me if I hadn't bought you *any* drinks, wouldn't you?"

I don't even try to answer, since he already knows what I would say; all I can feel is Hal's cock pushing its way down my throat, his hand in my hair guiding me up and down. His cock is huge, long and thick, almost too thick for me to swallow. But I've had a lot of practice, and I manage to take his cock down my throat, my gag reflex ruined by all the alcohol. The stairwell spins around me as I bob up and down on his cock, moaning softly, feeling my cunt wet. *He's going to fuck me*, I think. *He's going to fuck me in my cunt.*

And then he's going to fuck me in the ass.

Hal pulls me off his cock, turns my head up toward him. I can feel the strings of drool running down my chin.

"You want my come down your throat, Erica?"

"Please…" I gasp, my mouth open wide, sticky spit glistening between my mouth and Hal's cock.

"You want it? You want to eat my come?"

"Please fuck me," I gasp. "Please…"

"You want me to fuck that sweet pussy of yours?" he growls.

"Fuck me…in…the…"

"What?"

I finally manage to choke it out. "Fuck me in the ass," I whimper, and tears fill my eyes. Hal chuckles and shoves me down onto my hands and knees. I stay there doggie-style while he reaches down and yanks my skirt up.

"You're still wearing your clothes," he tells me. "Underwear and all. Strip everything off."

My hands shaking, I begin to wriggle out of my dress. It

comes off over my head and I push it into a ball in the corner of the stairwell. Hal unhitches my bra and it falls forward, revealing my breasts.

"Panties, too," says Hal. "But not the stockings. Or the shoes."

The panties are under the garter belt; as I obediently begin to pull them down, Hal realizes this and I hear the click of his pocket knife. He slits the thin strings of my thong and pulls the soaked, ruined garment out from between my legs.

Still standing over me, he gets his hands between my thighs and forces my legs wide apart. His hand on my pussy makes me gasp, and he knows in an instant just how wet I am for his cock.

That's when I hear the fire door opening overhead, half a flight up. I look up and see the busboy—the one who couldn't stop refilling my water. He looks at me, shocked—not knowing what to think.

"Just what you need, Erica," says Hal. "Another cock to fill you. Get down here." He says something in Spanish, and I see the busboy smile as he comes down the stairs toward me.

Oh God. It's happening.

He unzips his pants and pulls out his cock as Hal takes his place behind me. Hal's cock nudges open my lips, making me shudder as he pushes his cock, still wet with my spittle, against my clit. I almost come right then, but I'm distracted by the feel of the busboy's hand tangled in my hair. He lifts my face onto his cock and forces my lips around the head.

I start to suck it, obediently accepting every inch of the shaft until it forces its way into my throat. Fucked wide by Hal's cock, my throat opens for the busboy, and he starts to fuck my face roughly as Hal positions his cock at my entrance.

Then Hal drives into me fiercely, quickly—not caring if he's going too fast. He shoves his cock in until the head strikes my cervix, and I utter a grunt deep in my throat. But the busboy's cock keeps me from screaming, or even moaning. Hal begins to fuck me.

As his cock slides into my aching pussy, I feel his thumb nuzzling between my cheeks. He pushes it in and I tense as he violates my asshole. But the busboy won't let me up; he's gripping my hair tight, forcing me up and down on his cock. Forcing me to suck him. Hal works his thumb deep into my ass and draws it around in big circles, opening me up for his cock. *He's going to fuck me in the ass*, I keep thinking, trying to prepare myself for the invasion of his cock. It's big, and I don't know if I can take it.

The terror rushes through me as Hal slides his cock out of my sopping pussy and presses it between my cheeks. He doesn't go slow, doesn't wait to see if I'm ready for him. He just shoves it into my ass, and a big strangled yelp bursts from my lungs, stopped dead by the thickness of the busboy's cock filling my throat.

There's a moment of pain as his cock violates my asshole; then the pleasure starts to flow through me. You've ruined me. You've planned all this to hurt me, to humiliate me. You know I come whenever you fuck my ass. You know I come easier from being fucked in the ass than from anything else.

You know I'm going to come on Hal's cock.

The busboy fucks faster into my throat, using my face. I open wide for him, feeling my orgasm thundering toward me as Hal uses my ass. I come just an instant before he does, and he knows—I can tell he knows—even though I can't make a peep, forced quiet by the busboy's cock. Once I've let myself go, feeling the pleasure explode through me, there's only a moment of soaring on my orgasm before Hal comes too, his hot come filling my ass, stinging it. And then the busboy pulls out, grabs my face, forces my mouth open wide with one hand and grabs my hand with the other. He wraps my fingers around his cock and I obediently start to stroke. "Stick out your tongue, bitch." When the first stream hits the back of my throat I moan and open wide for it; more streams follow, hot jism filling my mouth, splashing across my cheeks, covering my chin.

I slump forward on my hands and knees, my breath coming in huge panting sobs. Hal pulls out of my ass and zips up. The busboy also tucks his cock away.

"I don't think your boyfriend will want you back now," Hal says contemptuously as he mounts the stairs. The busboy follows him. Hal pauses outside the fire door. I look over my shoulder at him, still spread on hands and knees, my ass leaking come and my face covered with it, my pussy still aching from my intense orgasm.

"You forgot this in the bar," he says, and tosses the key card at me. It hits the landing with a snap. "Though I bet your boyfriend's already changed the lock."

Hal and the busboy disappear through the fire door, letting it slam behind them.

I pick myself up, limbs shaking, head still spinning from all the alcohol. I can't find my bra, and my panties are nothing but ruined, stripped fabric. I wriggle into my tiny dress, well aware that without a bra it shows my tits to anyone who will look. I don't even bother to wipe the come off my face, or try to dab it off my spread cheeks. I just let it run down the backs of my thighs as I sway down the stairs looking for the right floor. I can barely walk after all those drinks and the rough treatment Hal forced on me. I bend over and take off my high-heeled shoes, and walk down flight after flight wearing nothing on my feet but my shredded, ruined stockings, great holes ripped in the knees where I genuflected before first Hal's cock, then the busboy's.

I look like a well-used whore.

I finally make it to the right floor, stumble through the fire door. No one is in the hallway, thank God. I find the right hotel room and put the key in the door. The light flashes red at first, then red again, and I feel a wave of panic. You've abandoned me.

The third time, the light goes green and I push the door open, fall into the hotel room.

You catch me in your arms, pulling me into darkness. You carry me over to the bed, but before you can lay me down I'm on my knees again, feeling the plush hotel carpet against my now bare knees. You're wearing only an expensive complimentary bathrobe and I've got it open in an instant, your cock in my mouth, my lips gliding hungrily up and down the shaft as you caress the back of my head.

"It looks like Steve treated you right."

It was filled with surprises, this night. Not the general facts, but the specifics. The details tipped me off before we even got to the restaurant. The three lubricating suppositories you told me to put in my ass before we went out. The fact that "Hal," or Steve, as I knew him when we played together, had grayed his normally black hair and put on a suit. The fact that the restaurant you took me to was the one where Mark worked as a busboy, having earned the indulgence of his manager just enough to slip away for a quick scene in the stairwell.

It was risky, to be sure. Mark could have lost his job. Who knows; if someone had happened along at the wrong instant, they both might have been arrested for rape—though there would be little chance of my pressing charges, since it was all my idea. Since I begged for it, begged you to set this up, begged you to make sure everything went perfectly. And it did.

It was risky, but so worth it.

I tell you that with every stroke of my mouth on your cock, every little whimper I give as I suck you.

"Thank you, baby," I sigh, my lips sliding off your cock. "Thank you so much."

"Don't mention it," you tell me, and seize my head roughly, twisting my hair in your hand.

Full Body
SIMON TORRIO

After a long soak in the tub, I'm ready for a hand job. I climb out of the tub, towel off, and pass from the small hot tub area into the massage room. Even though there's a door between them, the massage room still stinks of chlorine; it also smells vaguely of male sweat and more than a hint of mildew. I stretch out on the massage table with its threadbare sheet, dark blue so the stains won't show. I pull the second sheet over my hard-on and flip the switch next to the table.

You come into the massage room a moment later. I look you up and down approvingly. You're wearing skintight red hot pants, very low cut, top button unbuttoned. Your almost see-through white halter shows off the curves of your large breasts, and the slight peaks of your nipples stretch the fabric. Your long legs are perched on gold high heels. The gold doesn't quite match your shoulder-length hair, a badly-bleached shade of yellow slightly messed up from the last client—I guess.

"Hi, I'm April," you tell me, smiling.

"Hi, April," I say, smiling at you as I let my eyes linger over your tits and the top button of your hot pants where the low waist shows off your hips. Your tattoo of stylized green and black ivy hovers around the top of the shorts, accenting the glint of your navel ring. I wonder if I'll find anything else pierced down below.

You purse your full, garishly red lips, making them as kissable as possible. "A rubdown is included in the price," you tell me, businesslike. "But if you'd like me to take off my top, it's another fifty dollars."

"How much for full service?" I ask.

"We don't do that here," you say, as if you've fielded the question a thousand times. "For me to take off my shorts, it's seventy-five, and to see me totally nude it's a hundred."

"And how much is it to fuck you?" I ask.

"That's not allowed," you say. "Would you like me as I am, topless, shorts off, or fully nude?"

"That depends," I say. "What are you wearing under those shorts?"

"Why don't you pay me the seventy-five, and you can decide if you want the shorts off after you see."

"What if I want to fuck you?"

"I don't do that," you say irritably.

I sigh in disappointment. "The money's on the table," I tell you. "That should be enough to let me fuck you."

"I told you," you say. "We don't do that here."

"Oral? I'd love to fuck that pretty mouth of yours," I tell you, staring hungrily.

"No, I don't do that, either."

"Then at least give me a hand job," I smile at you innocently. "That's not too much to ask, is it?"

"That's not allowed either," you tell me. "But if you'd like to finish yourself, that's all right."

"Take off your clothes," I tell you.

You prance over to the tip table, tottering in your tacky high heels. You pick up the wad of money and count the twenty-dollar bills.

"This is way too much," you say.

"I figured that'd be enough if I wanted to fuck you."

"I told you, I don't do that," you say. "But this'll get you fully nude. And full body."

"Full body?"

"I'll climb on top of you," you say. "Only while you're lying on your stomach."

"And a hand job?"

You look down, guiltily. Your eyes flicker up and linger for a moment on the bulge under the sheet, the hard-on I've had since before you walked in the room.

"Yeah," you say. "I can give you a release at the end."

"Sold," I tell you, and you roll the three hundred dollars up tight and put it in the pocket of your shorts. You come over to me and turn your back, leaning back to show me the tie of your white halter top.

"Will you untie me?" you ask.

I quickly curl my arm around you, move my hand up your belly and cup your breast, squeezing the nipple gently. It's very hard.

"I'd rather rip it off of you," I say.

"That's not allowed," you say, pulling away. You reach

behind your back and untie the halter. Stretched tight, it pops forward around your tits. As I watch, you unfasten the tie at the back of your neck and let the halter slip away from your breasts. They're big and round, gorgeous, with nipples that are much harder than when you walked in.

"Nice," I say. "Now the shorts."

You unbutton your fly and wriggle out of your shorts, sliding them down your long legs to show me a pair of perfect hips and a crotch covered only by a tiny, cheap red lace thong. You fold the halter and shorts together and place them on the table. You stand there for me to look at, and I smile.

"What are you waiting for?" I ask you. "Lose the thong."

You peel the thong away from your pussy, and I discover that you're shaved—smooth. You've got a ring in your clit and a heart-shaped tattoo just above your pussy, in the shaved patch. The name across it says *DADDY*. I can smell your cunt in the small room, musky and sweet. My cock pulses under the sheet.

"Roll over," you say, edging toward the table.

"I'd rather have you climb on top of me this way," I say, pulling down the sheet and revealing my hard-on.

"Uh-uh." You shake your head. "Roll over."

Grudgingly, I toss the top sheet on the floor and roll onto my stomach. My hard-on presses painfully against the padded massage table. You climb on my back and straddle me, your pussy wet against the small of my back. From the moment it touches me I feel the energy throbbing into my body, electric. I've got to fuck you if it's the last thing I do.

You drape your body over mine and start to brush your big tits down my back as you grind your hips against me, rubbing your pussy against the curve of my ass. I moan softly as you dry-fuck me and stroke your erect nipples over my shoulders. As you bend forward, drawing your breasts down my back, I feel your breath hot against the back of my neck. You move down and straddle the back of one thigh, your cunt rubbing against me. Your hands trace patterns down my sides and your breasts shudder back and forth on my skin. Your pussy rubs more firmly against the back of my thigh. I can feel the hard prick of the small ring in your clit. I can also feel your pussy getting wetter, sliding juicy up the back of my leg, leaving a cool trail of moisture. The last trick's lube leaking out of you—or a hooker getting turned on? The way your breathing changes—quicker, almost imperceptibly—could be an act, but the hardness of your nipples couldn't be. It's too warm in here to explain their firmness, but not warm enough to make either of us sweat, to explain the moisture between your legs. You press your lips to the back of my neck, trailing your tongue along it—but it's practiced, businesslike. You lift yourself onto your hands and knees above me, and I can feel the trickle of wetness you left on the back of my leg, close to my ass. You start to kiss your way down my back, your tongue barely touching me.

I do it fast—fast enough that you don't see it's happening until I've rolled almost all the way over. By that time I've dislodged you from above me; you've lost your balance and you would have fallen if my arm hadn't shot out and curved around your waist, catching you. When I pull you onto me, I've rolled over and your legs are spread around my cock, your wet pussy an inch away from it.

Your eyes are wide, your lips parted. You're breathing quickly.

"There's another two hundred in my wallet," I tell you. "Why don't you go get it?"

You shake your head. "It's not allowed." You start to squirm away, weakly.

My hands hold your hips, and I pull you down onto me, my cockhead nudging between your lips. Your muscles tense and you try to pull off of me, but your heart's not in it. You're propped on your elbows, your face close to mine. "Three hundred," I say, and kiss you on the lips. My tongue forces its way into your mouth and I feel your tongue stud. Your tongue stays limp, loose, slack, helpless as I savage it with mine. I lift my hips a little and the head of my cock presses moist with pre-come against your clit.

"Four hundred," I tell you, and reach around behind you to get hold of my cock, putting it in just the right position at the entrance to your cunt.

Your eyes go wide, looking into mine. I want you to nod, but you can't. You just look, breathing hard, not saying no, not saying yes.

"Go get the money," I tell you. "It's in my pants pocket."

You shake your head weakly. "After," you say, your voice hoarse. "We'll do it after."

I pull you down onto me, and you groan as my cock goes into you. Your pussy is dripping wet through, and it slides down so easily over my cock that I plunge all the way into you in an instant. I hold you there, grinding my hips up against you, feeling my pubic bone against your clit.

Then I kiss you again, harder this time, forcing my tongue against yours, deep, taking your mouth as I use your pussy.

Your hips start to move; you lift yourself up on my cock and slide back down, gasping as you do. You start to fuck me. I can feel the thick swelling of your pussy against the head of my cock, and you work yourself onto me more rhythmically as your pussy gets tighter, swelling with blood, filling with lust. You claw at the massage table, whimpering as you fuck yourself onto my cock. It isn't long before I feel your body go tense.

"I'm—going—to—"

You're not faking it, either—not unless you're very, very good. Your hips pump eagerly until your cunt begins to contract around my shaft, and then your whole naked body shudders. You stop thrusting and I take up the motion, pounding up into you, pumping deep into you with every circling motion of my hips. You come hard on my cock, trying hard to stifle your moan so the other clients in the nearby rooms won't hear—but there's little you can do to keep yourself from crying out. You moan so loud you hurt my ears.

When you're finished coming, your body is limp. I lift you up and slide out from under you, repositioning you on the massage table. You let me do whatever I want, lying there like a rag doll as I prop you up on just your knees, your arms hanging useless over the sides of the table and your face and tits pressed into the dark sheet. I spread your legs wider and enter you from behind, and you gasp as I do. I start to fuck you hard, pounding into you, your beautiful ass spread out under me. I lick my thumb and slide it between your cheeks, nuzzling your asshole. I hear a quick, surprised gasp, like you're going to say "No," but you don't. Instead, your gasp becomes a low moan as I work my spit-slick thumb into your ass. I slide it in deep, feeling my thumb against my cock as I fuck you faster.

Your hips are lifted high, your ass thrust up toward me, and you're barely moving at first. But as my cock slides into you more rapidly, you start to grind against me. You start to fuck me back, moaning even louder than when you came.

Your ass is so tight around my thumb, I can't resist it. I spy the bottle of massage oil next to the table, crusted and clouded like it's never been used. I snatch it up with my free hand and slide my thumb out enough to drizzle a stream of oil between your cheeks. Rubbing it in, I slide my thumb into you more easily, then add more oil.

"Wh—what are you doing?" you ask between moans.

"I'm fucking you in the ass," I say, easing my cock out of your pussy and moving it up to the tight bud of your rear opening.

"G—Greek's—" you gasp, unable to finish the sentence as I nuzzle my cockhead against the entrance to your ass. "Greek's—um—Greek costs—" You grope after the words, like you're desperately trying to think of an appropriate price, but you can't find one—and I know you've never done it before. I push my cockhead into your ass and it feels tighter than anything I've ever fucked. I go slow at first, listening to your little squeals as you feel your ass acclimating to the bulk of my cock. Slowly you relax and I slide my cock deeper, until you're wriggling against the table, fully impaled on my cock. And moaning.

I lean forward hard against your body, forcing your hips down and your legs wide. I start to fuck your ass and I feel the tickle of your fingers against my balls. I realize you've slipped your hands between your legs and you're urgently rubbing your clit. Your moans rise in volume as I pound into your asshole. Within minutes I feel you thrashing against me, your hand quickening. I take over, reaching under you and pushing my hand over yours, forcing you to rub your clit harder as I drive into your ass with new fury. When you come, your ass clenches so tight it almost forces me out, and I have to fuck you harder, almost violently shoving it into your ass to keep it sliding in as you come in great shuddering spasms. Then I come, too, as your climax intensifies and you start to lose it, shaking back and forth under me, lifting your ass to take deeper thrusts as I shoot my come deep inside you. When I'm finished, you lie there, panting with exhaustion.

I stretch and slide out of your ass, climbing off the table. I leave you there, ass upturned and opened wide, as I get dressed. You moan softly, eyes wide, staring at me but unseeing. Your hand is still pressed against your clit.

Before I leave, I take out my wallet and count out four bills.

"Four hundred dollars," I say, and leave it on the table. "Thanks for the massage."

I leave the room without kissing you good-bye.

Outside, I pass another couple and wink at them under the big sign that says *NO SEXUAL ACTIVITY*. The woman smiles at me; the guy looks away.

As I walk down the long line of doors, I can hear the occasional moan in the rooms beyond. I know this place is a poorly-kept call girl's secret; more outcalls happen here than in any hotel in town, if only because they rent by the hour and they don't offer full-body massages—thus eliminating the chance of unexpected competition after the fact.

That's why you and I picked this place; a friend of ours

who works as an escort tipped us off that it's a place where you can make as much noise as you want—and no one will bother you. But today I think you pushed your luck on even that rule, with your screaming climax as I fucked your ass. Normally it wouldn't matter, except I think we'll be coming back here a lot.

I leave a twenty for the towel girl and wait for you in the lobby. When you come out, wearing jeans and a T-shirt, you have that nervous glow about you that says "I just got laid." I wonder if I have the same look.

You smile at me and we head for the car.

Cocked and Loaded

THOMAS S. ROCHE

I usually don't speed, but this time it can't be helped. You hug my body as I hug the curves, leaning low into the seat. You keep your hand above my waist only because I've made you promise to do so—to transgress would be dangerous. But I can tell, this time in particular, that it's an effort for you.

I merge the Triumph onto the freeway, hitting sixty, seventy, seventy-five, and you grip me with your spread thighs tight against my hips. The wind whistles past us. You've unzipped your jacket, and even through the back of mine, I can feel them. Firm, insistent, unforgiving. And it's not because of the cold.

I can still feel our positions reversed, your body in my arms, your back against my front, me leaning down to line my eyes up with yours, smelling the scent of your hair and feeling your pigtails brush against my shoulders. I can still feel your ass against mine, pressing against my crotch, your tight jeans smooth and your round butt wriggling maybe a little more than it needs to. I can still hear you say "I can't," a little pathetic whimper designed, I suspect, to get me to do exactly what I'm doing: to curl my arms around you, put my hands on yours, and help you steady them. "You can," I tell you, and your body tenses as you pull the trigger.

The Magnum explodes in front of us, its four-inch barrel erupting in a flash of death, and you let out a yelp, a scream—and then a trembling giggle as I help you put down the gun, pointing downrange. You bring your hand to your mouth, gasping. A hole has appeared between the eyes of the shadowed target.

"I hit it," you say in a faint moan, as I put my arms around you and hug you. I realize, in an instant, that your nipples are so hard that they hurt my wrist as I brush by your breasts. Your ass is pushed back firmly against my crotch, my now hard cock resting centered in the furrow between your cheeks.

"Beginner's luck," I whisper, and you reach for the gun.

I can still feel it all as we pull into the driveway, stinking of cordite and flop sweat. Now I understand why you needed to fire a .44 Magnum for your first gun, why you begged me to leave the Glock at home, why you said you'd do anything if I'd keep the Sig .380 in the gun safe in the back of the closet. And I know why I agreed.

Because I remember, perhaps even more vividly than the first shot, how you glanced behind us, made sure the clerk wasn't watching through the filthy bulletproof glass; how you unfastened the top button of your incredibly low-slung jeans, took my cordite-stinking hand in yours, shoved it underneath.

No panties—I knew that, or I could have guessed it, because I've seen you in these jeans and I know even the skimpiest thong shows above your waistband. But tonight, for your virgin foray into squirting lead, you've got nothing at all under those tight low-rise jeans. Nothing but your pussy, smooth and shaved and—I find out as you force my finger into you—dripping. No, not dripping. Pouring. It's a wonder your jeans aren't soaked through. You ease my hand out of you, bring it to your face and lick my finger, breathing deeply, making love to the tip of my pussy-slick finger, inhaling its scent.

"Ever notice how pussy and gunpowder smell sort of the same?" you ask.

"Not until now," I say.

I understand it now—I understand a few things, maybe more than a few. Why, when you found out—after our first night together—that I was a cop, you searched all over the Net for interesting facts about women and guns, quoting them to me from obscure websites while I cleaned my service Beretta on the coffee table. Why you "happened" along schoolgirls-with-guns.com and giggled for hours with me over the ludicrously cheesy photos of scantily-clad pigtailed girls with assault rifles.

Why that was the night we fucked so hard we broke the bed, I was late to work and you called me at my desk the next day to masturbate on the phone for me while I sat uncomfortably amid the hubbub of the squad room. Why you started begging me to take you to the shooting range, show you how to shoot—not just any old gun, but the .44 Magnum my father left me.

Why, when you showed up at my place for the ride to the

range, you were wearing those low-rise jeans with the flowers down the sides, a skintight Britney Spears crop top too obscene for its namesake to ever get away with on national television, and your hair in pigtails. The guys at the gun shop couldn't take their eyes off you, their gazes of abject lust thicker than the smoke in the room as their eyes roved over your erect nipples showing through the top—but then, nobody fucks with a well-armed schoolgirl.

I shove you against the wall the second we're in the house, holding you hard with my whole body. I set down the gun case and rip off your jacket, exposing your firm breasts through the crop top. Your nipples are so hard they feel like rocks against my chest, and it's not from the ride. You're not wearing a bra.

"Will you give it to me?" you whisper into my ear as I devour you, my mouth biting and sucking at your neck, your shoulders, your cleavage. "Will you give me what I want, Officer?"

I step back, my cock throbbing in my pants.

"What's that?" I ask you.

"Oh," you say. "I think you know."

Wriggling out from under me, you pick up the gun case and saunter into the combination living room/bedroom. You set the gun case down on the bed. I watch as you kick off your Adidas and slowly unzip your incredibly tight pants. You have to squirm and struggle to slide out of them; I can see as you bend all the way over to take them over your ankles that your pussy really is smooth, smooth as silk—and that your jeans really are soaked. You stand up partway and look over your shoulder at me, your pigtails framing your gorgeous face and your smooth, round asscheeks framing your bare pussy.

Slowly, you crawl onto the bed, stretching out. You've still got the crop top on, maybe because you like the sense of innocence it imparts. I don't doubt it. But however innocent Britney may be, your tits with their hard nipples spell out that you're anything but. You cuddle up with the gun case and unzip it.

"Be careful with that," I tell you, and you smile coquettishly, as if daring me to stop you.

I stand watching, my cock hard in my jeans, my motorcycle boots planted firmly—I couldn't stop you if I wanted to.

You take the .44 Magnum out. It takes me a moment to realize you've switched the gun case—it's not the one I take to the shooting range, now. It's the one I use when I'm playing with you. This isn't the gun I shoot; it's the one I use to fuck you. It's identical to the gun I shoot with in every way—from the outside. But it's a stage gun, one that wouldn't even shoot a starter round if they made them in .44. The cylinders are filled, and there's no firing pin on the hammer. The barrel is solid, despite the fact that its opening looks black and dangerous like that of a real gun. If I hadn't removed the bright-orange cap that the barrel came with—that cap the law requires to make sure the cops don't shoot some B-movie actress by accident, thinking she's got a real gun—it wouldn't look real at all. But I did, and it does.

You lick your way down the four-inch stainless steel barrel. Spreading your legs, you ease the gun between them and, holding the gun upside down, nuzzle the muzzle of the gun between the shaved lips of your sex.

"Don't you need some lube?" I ask.

You shake your head, *no*.

The barrel disappears into your pussy, and you moan "Oh God, oh God, oh God." Usually when you're rubbing yourself to orgasm, you take it slow, warming up, getting yourself all hot. This time it's none of that—just slam, bam, thank you Ma'am. You shove the gun as deep as it will go and rub yourself as fast as you can. You come almost instantly, twisting and writhing on the bed.

When you come to a stop, you look up at me flirtatiously and lick your lips.

I want to touch my cock so bad, to climb up and slide it into you. But I have to watch—like one of your strip club patrons getting a lap dance, I can watch, smell, hunger—but not touch.

You spread your legs wide and set the gun between them on the bed. Your hands resting on your thighs, you look right at me.

"What do you say, Officer? Will you give a little girl what she really wants?"

I'm on you in an instant, the Sig coming out of my belt pouch before you can gasp. You know I pack, twenty-four/ seven—a sexy silver-finish Sig-Sauer .380 that you've always been fascinated with. But you never expected to have it shoved in your mouth. You never expected to suck it.

The fact that I've switched guns, too—grabbing my second stage gun, the automatic I like because its barrel is thicker and I can fuck you with both barrel and slide—hasn't escaped you. The Sig is just as safe as the .44, but you don't care. In our fantasy, it's a real gun—cocked and loaded.

My knee is between your legs, holding you down, as your eyes go wide. You're sucking on the barrel like it was my cock.

Your eyes are wide and I see excitement in them like I've never seen. "You like it, baby? You like tasting danger? You want to play on the edge?"

I see the effect my threat has on you. The terror heightened, your nipples become even more evident through the shirt.

"Reach for the Magnum," I tell you. "Fuck yourself."

I look down at the glittering revolver, wondering who owns you.

You pick up the gun, turn the barrel toward your pussy, ease it up to your sex.

"Pull the hammer back."

I hear the hammer clicking back, feel your body shivering with terror. "Put it in," I tell you, my cock so hard I can hardly stand it.

This time your cunt is tight, tight from the anticipation. The gun won't go in at first.

"You asked for it. Now take it."

Finally the barrel slides into your cunt, and you can't stop the spasms of your body as your back arches and you shiver back. Now I'm on top of you, my hand between your legs, holding both guns and shoving the .44 deeper into you. I've got the Sig out of your mouth and against your head now, dripping with saliva. You're sobbing. Sobbing because you're about to come, and even in these short months we've been together I've learned to recognize the sighs. I work the .44 around so the barrel is hitting your G-spot, and that's when your mouth goes wide, drool leaking out and soaking the front of your T-shirt, making your tits even more evident. I feel you grabbing for my belt, ripping open my pants as I fuck you. Both your hands wrap around my cock and it only takes a few quick, expert strokes before I know I'm going to come.

You, too. Maybe it's the feel of my hot jizz mingling with the gun oil, or maybe it's the click of the .44 inside you as I pull the trigger, the hammer falling on filled-in cylinders. Either way, we both explode and I come so hard I feel liquid shooting onto my chest, look down as it soaks through your drool-spattered top. Crying, you writhe under me as I feel the .44 twitching with the spasms of your body.

Gently, I ease the gun out. I toss it on the pillow next to you.

The fact that neither gun is real didn't do anything to lessen our excitement. Because that's who you are, whether you're begging me to fuck you with a .44 Magnum or tempting all the rednecks down at the gun shop. You're dangerous— you're a living, breathing, flirting, dripping edge scene. Whether you're jerking me off onto your tits or cuddled up in my arms, fake guns strewn across the bed.

Cocked and loaded, baby, that's you.

James Dean, One Thousand Bucks, and a Long Summer Night
Emilie Paris

We noticed him right away. The boy had a look that I've always found insanely attractive. Lean hard body. Dark denim jeans worn low down on his slim hips. Tight white T-shirt with the sleeves rolled up, the left one hiding a pack of cigarettes that I just guessed would be Marlboro Reds. He sported a cleverly designed facade that made me think nobody'd ever had the heart to tell him that the 1950s were over, James Dean was dead, and rebels didn't exist anymore, cause or no cause.

Here we were, on the Boulevard of Broken Dreams, in a city where fantasies are demolished daily, but for a moment, I thought my own personal fantasies had come true. Maybe rebels *weren't* dead, because tonight, James Dean was alive and well and standing on a street corner in Hollywood, and when Arthur slowed down the car as we cruised by, this particular modern reflection of James Dean put one foot up on the brick wall behind him, lowered his shades, and gave us a wink.

Us. Not me, specifically, not Arthur solely, but *us*.

"That's the one I want," I told my husband, sounding like a girl pointing to a diamond tennis bracelet in the window of an expensive jewelry store. "That one."

"You're sure, Charlie? We've only just started looking."

"Just turn the car around. Please."

Since Arthur had first suggested buying us a partner for the night, someone to fuck me while he watched, I couldn't get the idea out of my head. We'd discussed bringing a friend into our bedroom, but I'd ultimately vetoed the idea. I couldn't imagine asking Bryce, or Kevin, or Nathan, and then having to see any one of their faces around the table at a Christmas party, or poker night or Fourth of July barbecue, having to stand there with a hot dog in hand and talk about the weather while remembering I'd invited them into my bed.

No, it had to be a stranger. If we were going to do this—and I wanted so desperately to do this—we had to find a third party. Someone who had no ties to either one of us, but who might not mind tying one of us down if the evening progressed in that sort of style....

Now that I'd seen this handsome rebel, waiting for us as if positioned by a casting director, I didn't want anyone else, couldn't imagine going even another block in what would undoubtedly be the wrong direction.

Without another word, Arthur pulled an illegal U-turn and swung the car around. The boy eyed us from his post, but he didn't approach the sidewalk until Arthur rolled the window down on my side. Only then did Dean amble to the car, bending down to look through the window at us.

Were we cops?

Were we dangerous?

I saw the knowing expression in his dark green eyes as he took in the situation. Quite obviously, we were an upper-middle-class couple out for a thrill on a Thursday night. There was redheaded Arthur, in his khakis and denim shirt, his hair carefully cut, his body primed from hours working with a personal trainer. He looked precisely like what he was—a Hollywood executive, someone who never, ever got his hands dirty. This boy on the corner was something else entirely. I could imagine him covered in grease, his hands filthy, his body soaked with sweat. Even young, he looked more like a man than my husband was. As soon as I thought that, I felt guilty.

The boy cocked his head and then looked at me, and I saw curiosity in his expression. I understood from reading exposés in *L.A. Weekly* that boys like this were mostly employed as party favors for other boys—or men, businessmen who had married themselves off to their appropriate sweethearts, but yearned for something else entirely late at night. That might have explained why Arthur was in the car; but what was I doing there?

Simple enough to answer: waiting to be fucked.

"How much?" Arthur asked.

"First time, eh?" the boy responded, answering a question with a question.

"Don't talk money," I hissed to my husband. "Not yet. Not here." To the handsome blond youth, I said, "Would you like to get a drink with us?"

"A drink," he repeated, and he gave me the look now, and I felt his eyes roaming over my white halter top, staring

244

at the cleavage spilling over the cups. I'd chosen my outfit so carefully, looking through all of my adult attire and rethinking my college days. I'd finally found this white eyelet halter tucked into a drawer and I'd paired it with worn Levis and ankle boots. My long dark hair was loose over my shoulders, brushed until it shone with a glossy light. I was going for hip without trying too hard, but I realized when the boy's eyes stayed locked on my breasts, that he didn't care about the clothes or carefully crafted appearance at all. He liked the skin spilling through. He was trained to like that.

I watched him reach for the handle on the back door, and saw Arthur shift to release the button opening the automatic locks. Then he was there, behind us, and the positioning felt all wrong with the two of us up front and our prize all by himself in the backseat.

"Don't drive," I told my husband. "Not yet."

Before Arthur could say a word, I opened the door, slid out, and got into the back with the boy, who I could only think of as Dean.

"Now," I said, and Arthur pulled away from the curb as I curled myself up and stared at our new playmate. "You don't want to talk money," I said, "because you don't want to say anything that would get you into trouble if we were police officers."

He said, "Can I smoke in here?" and I watched Arthur's eyebrows go up in the rearview mirror, while I said, "Sure. No problem."

He extracted his pack from the sleeve—Marlboro Reds, as I'd guessed—and he lit his cigarette slowly, and then he relaxed against the plush leather and looked at me. "You said a drink."

"At our house."

"A few drinks, then."

"All night."

"Paid companionship," he said, blowing smoke out the window. "Lonely, you need company—"

"I have him," I said.

"You both need someone else. Someone to break the ice."

We'd been together eleven years, me and Arthur. Our ice had melted long ago.

"One thousand dollars," Dean said softly. "For the night."

Arthur handed his expensive leather wallet over the back of the seat, and I pulled out ten crisp hundreds. After that, Dean became much warmer. He pulled my legs over his and began to stroke his fingers up and down the faded denim. "Do you have ideas," he said, "or do you want me to play by my own script?"

In Hollywood, everyone has movie vernacular. Even street whores.

"I have a script," I told him, smiling.

He waited, his eyes on me.

"My driver doesn't care what we do back here. Does that make sense?"

"Your driver," he repeated, and I saw him glance toward Arthur again, and then he tossed his cigarette out the window, slid me down on the seat and started to kiss me, my shoulders, my neck, my exposed cleavage, while Arthur drove us up into the Hollywood Hills. *My driver*, as if I were some starlet, giving her limo driver a thrill. I could feel Arthur listening to us, listening to our skin on skin, as Dean undressed me, pulling my halter off and leaving me half-naked in the car seat. His warm, strong hands were all over me, and I closed my eyes and thought that this was the first time another man had touched me since my wedding day—since six months prior to my wedding day. The first time my breasts had been caressed by someone other than my husband in over eleven years. I wanted to tell this boy that I'd had such a body. I know I look good now, but thirty-three can't compare to twenty-two, no matter what exercises you do, Pilates or power yoga or anything. I wanted to tell him that I was so fucking hot when Arthur met me, he actually had to jerk off at home before our dates so that he could keep from coming too soon when we had sex. He dreamt about the taste of my pussy, and he fell asleep sometimes with his head between my legs, tongue on my clit. He couldn't get enough.

But Dean didn't need to know any of that. All he needed to know was that he had our thousand dollars in his pocket, and he had my naked breasts to lick, and when I said, "Bite them. Come on, boy. Bite them for me," he did without question. I could almost feel Arthur getting harder in the front seat. I could almost sense his erection straining against his pressed khaki pants, and that thought made me so wet, that I reached down and cupped my hand against the fly of my young playmate. He was hard, but not that hard.

"Do you like girls?" I asked.

"I like you," he insisted, his voice husky.

"But do you like girls?"

His mouth moved back and forth, between my breasts, and I said, "Doesn't matter. You can tell me. Doesn't matter—"

"I like everything."

"But would you rather be with a man?"

His green eyes shone at me like emeralds in the night, and I knew. That's what you get for picking the prettiest one in the litter. "Drive us home," I told Arthur.

"Come on, baby," my husband said softly from the front seat, and I knew he was reminding me of our plans, our careful plans. Fuck in the car, so he could watch, then drop the hooker off again, and make our safe way home. No strings. No mess. Nothing to challenge our happy life.

"Get us home," I said, and I felt the shift in power as Arthur followed my command. I cradled Dean against my breasts, and I stroked his soft blonde hair, the pretty boy, and I crooned to him, "So handsome, such a good boy, when we get home, I'll let you fuck my husband." He shuddered when I said that, and it was as if he and Arthur were already connected. I could see it in my head. This young stud, with his flat stomach, and his tight abs, bending my husband over the bed, spreading Art's cheeks, and sliding inside. My pussy spasmed at the thought, and I wondered where I'd end up in all this. Somewhere messy, I guessed. And sticky. And satisfied.

Arthur said, "What are you doing, Charlie, what do you think—"

"Just drive," I said, and I could feel Dean against me, his mouth sucking on my tits so hard, and I drove my fingers through his thick hair, and I murmured to him, "Bite them. Come on. Harder. That's the boy—"

I don't know how it changed like that. First, Arthur was giving me a gift. Getting me a hot young pup to fuck in the backseat while he watched via the rearview mirror. Someone he could catch a glimpse of. A situation that would let him listen in, as the ultimate voyeur. He was going to hear our moans and sighs and then drop Mr. Stranger off on the corner again. That was going to be that. Fantasy fuel for years to come. Instead, I took the role of director, and when Arthur pulled into our driveway, I grabbed both of my men by the hands and led them after me into the house.

"That's my husband," I said to the boy, pouring each one of us a stiff drink. "He hasn't done this before."

"Come on, Charlie," Arthur said again, his dark blue eyes wide. He rubbed his hand over his ginger-colored goatee in that nervous habit of his, and I just grinned, feeling the foxy smile on my face, and said, "You haven't, have you?"

"Charlie—"

"He hasn't," I said, "and he made this big deal about how it had always been his fantasy to see me fuck another guy. That he wanted to listen and surreptitiously watch. But the only real part of that fantasy was the other guy part, wasn't it, Arthur?" Things were so clear in my head now.

"Charlie—"

Dean watched us, his green eyes flickering as he looked from Arthur to me to my husband again. He was easygoing, but wary at the same time. Wouldn't he have to be? What was going to happen to him? Was this all one big setup?

"Look," I said, "I want to do this right. Let's all go back to the bedroom, and let's just relax."

Arthur, his hand running over his goatee, started again, "Char—"

I said, "We all know my name's Charlie by now. So let's just go back there and see what happens." My husband didn't know what to do. I could see it in his eyes. He wanted to follow my lead, but he couldn't handle the fact that after eleven years, I actually had taken the lead.

"Now," I said, and the power in my voice made Arthur move. Dean followed right after him, and I trailed the boys, entering the room and opening the closet to get out our big bottle of lube. I had Dean strip out of his clothes and while my husband watched, I oiled that boy's cock up until it shone.

"See, Arthur?" I said, "I'm getting it all nice and ready for you."

"Jesus, Charlie."

"And you know where it's going—"

For the first time of the evening, I got the gratification that I was on to something, because Arthur said, "But, you know, Charlie. Not without a condom—"

I could have laughed. Was that all he was worried about? The solution was inches away. I reached for the box of condoms in the top drawer of my nightstand and I handed one over to Dean. He put it on like a pro, of course. Then I motioned for Arthur, and my hired hand and I watched my husband undress, slowly, half-scared, kicking out of his shoes and slacks and casual shirt, then standing, unsure, at the foot of the bed.

"You know men, don't you?" I asked the boy.

"Yeah—"

"So help him out."

Dean reached for my husband and spread him on the mattress, and he started to rub Arthur's shoulders and his back, making my man sigh and moan. And then he motioned for me to hand over the lube, and I did, getting closer, close enough to watch this paid-by-the-night prostitute grease up my husband's asshole with a healthy supply of lube.

"Charlie—" Arthur moaned, and I knew what he was going to say somehow.

"No fucking way," I told him. "I'm not leaving." That was the deal. Arthur had bought me a present, and his only stipulation was that he got to watch. Well, the same fucking rules applied for me, as well. But Arthur didn't want to play by those rules anymore.

His face was bright red. "You can't watch." I could hear the catch in his voice, the begging. "You can't."

"Oh yes," I told him. "I'm going to watch every stroke, Arthur. I'm going to watch this boy fuck you senseless."

Dean grinned when I said that, as if I'd given him an unexpected compliment, and he moved behind my husband and parted his asscheeks wide and he pressed the head of his thick, hard cock at Arthur's asshole. "You ever done it like this?" he said softly. He'd spoken so rarely this evening that each time he said a word, I learned his voice anew.

"Yeah—" Arthur started.

"Fucking me doesn't count," I said.

"Well, yeah—" Arthur repeated, and now my eyebrows were the ones to go up. "You know," Arthur choked out. "Way back when. Before you, baby."

Dean looked at me, and I saw that hard quality in his face despite his youth, that tenderness all eaten up by being on the streets at a young age. I saw that we didn't surprise him, not in the least. That this was no big deal for him. But it was for me. Arthur had been ass-fucked before, and I'd had no idea.

"Go on," I told the boy. "Do it."

251

And as I watched him mount my husband, I poured another handful of that lube in my palm, and I greased myself up, my fingers sliding inside my pussy, deep in there, desperate to watch as Arthur had his not-so-virgin asshole reamed fiercely. It was clear Dean did know what he was doing. He held Arthur's cheeks firmly apart, and he slid in the head of his cock, and Arthur made a low, hard moan deep in his throat. Then Dean slid in a little deeper, and I thought Arthur was going to explode on the spot, but the boy had other ideas. He seemed interested in earning his money now that I'd given him the prospect of fucking a man instead of me. He worked slowly, and he talked softly to Arthur with each thrust, crooning and encouraging.

"Look at me," I said, and Arthur turned his face toward me. "Don't stop," I said to Dean. "Don't stop."

My fingers pressed so hard against my clit, and I drove my middle finger over and over into my pussy while I watched Dean fuck my husband. Dean rocked back and forth, moving back on his heels and then gripping Arthur by the hips and forcing him to find the right rhythm. Arthur groaned with each thrust, making noises that sounded so different from the ones he makes when we fuck. Seeing him on the bottom, being taken instead of doing the taking, changed my whole worldview. The room seemed to shimmer with the white-hot sexual heat of the three of us, with me the voyeur and the two men on the bed the stars. Arthur seemed to want to tell me something with his expression, but then his eyes went cloudy and I knew he was going to come.

I thought about our best-laid plans, the ones we'd discussed over dinner at a Beverly Hills bistro before cruising the strip. Meet someone. Use protection. Do it all in the car. Return home safe and sound. Those plans had sounded fine at the time, but now somehow we were here in our master bedroom, on our own bed, and nothing really would ever be the same again.

And I was glad. I didn't want things to be the same. I was tired of sameness and ready for a change. Maybe that's what I'd wanted this whole time. Maybe I hadn't needed a hot young stud to fuck—maybe what had really needed a fucking ride was my life.

So some fantasies *can* come true.

It can happen to you.

And all you need is James Dean. One thousand bucks. And a long, long, hot summer night.

About the Authors

Living and working in Hampshire, England, **J. HADLEIGH ALEX** is keen to explore fiction that breaches boundaries and tells stories that ease taboos, and to write without limitation or fear. J's first novel—a fast-paced, sexy science fiction thriller—is currently in search of a publisher.

FELIX D'ANGELO'S writing will appear in the anthology *MASTER* and recently appeared in *Sweet Life 2*. Also a photographer, he has been working on a series of erotic female nudes.

SKYE BLACK'S darker erotic work has appeared on the websites Necromantic.com and Noirotica.net as well as several Usenet newsgroups.

M. CHRISTIAN'S work can be seen in *Best American Erotica*, *Best Gay Erotica*, *Best Lesbian Erotica*, *Best Transgendered Erotica*, *Best Bondage Erotica*, *Best Fetish Erotica*, *Friction*, and over 150 other anthologies, magazines, and websites. He's the editor of over a dozen anthologies, including *Best S/M Erotica*,

Love Under Foot (with Greg Wharton), *Bad Boys* (with Paul Willis), *The Burning Pen*, and *Guilty Pleasures*. He's the author of four collections: the Lambda-nominated *Dirty Words* (gay erotica), *Speaking Parts* (lesbian erotica), *Filthy* (more gay erotica), and *The Bachelor Machine* (science fiction erotica). For more information, check out www.mchristian.com.

ELIZABETH COLVIN is a journalist and sex educator with a very dirty mind. She loves introducing new men to the joys of strap-on sex.

DEXTER CUNNINGHAM has been writing porn for twenty years. His stories of extreme male submission and sexual punishment appeared in the fetish magazine *Nugget* in the early 1990s. Since then he has shared his exceedingly deviant stories with his exceedingly deviant female lovers.

DANTE DAVIDSON is the pseudonym of a professor and screenwriter who teaches in Santa Barbara, California. His short stories have appeared in *Bondage*; *Naughty Stories from A to Z* volumes *1*, *2*, and *3*; *Sweet Life 1* and *2*; *Naughty Fairy Tales from A to Z*; *Best Bondage Erotica*; and on the website www.goodvibes.com. He is the coauthor of the best-selling collection of short fiction *Bondage on a Budget* and *Secrets for Great Sex After Fifty* (which he wrote at age twenty-eight).

SARA DEMUCI has written for the anthologies *MASTER* and *slave*, edited by N. T. Morley, as well as *Down & Dirty*, edited by Alison Tyler.

ERICA DUMAS has written for *Best Bisexual Women's Erotica*, *Naughty Stories from A to Z*, Noirotica.net, and the *Sweet Life* series.

BRYN HANIVER loves the ocean and writes from islands and peninsulas on both sides of North America—with occasional stints in the Caribbean. Previous anthology credits include *Delicate Friction* and *A Taste of Midnight*.

P. S. HAVEN was raised on *Star Wars*, comic books and his dad's *Playboy* collection, all of which he still enjoys. His work has previously appeared at www.cleansheets.com and www.peacockblue.com. He peddles his smut from North Carolina, where he lives with his lovely young bride and fights a never-ending battle for truth and justice from deep within the Bible Belt.

Fast becoming a one-person Stratemeyer Syndicate, **PEARL JONES** writes under a plethora of pen names, and will try any kink or genre at least once, if promised caffeine and/or designer shoes. Her work may be found in *Prometheus* and various online venues. She publishes dark fantasy, paranormal romance and horror under another name, and (gasp) ghostwrites romance and genre fiction, from which the sex scenes are always cut before the books reach print.

ISABELLE NATHE has written for anthologies including *Come Quickly for Girls on the Go* (Rosebud), *A Century of Lesbian Erotica* (Masquerade), and *Naughty Stories from A to Z*, volumes 1 and 2 (Pretty Things Press). Her work has appeared also on the website www.goodvibes.com.

EMILIE PARIS is a writer and editor. Her first novel *Valentine* (Blue Moon) is available on audiotape from Passion Press. She abridged the seventeenth-century novel *The Carnal Prayer Mat* for Passion Press. The audiotape won a *Publishers Weekly* best audio award in the "Sexcapades" category. Her short stories have also appeared in *Naughty Stories from A to Z,* volumes *1, 2,* and *3; Juicy Erotica* (Pretty Things Press); *Sweet Life 1* and *2* (Cleis); and on the website www.goodvibes.com.

AYRE RILEY has written for *Down & Dirty* (Pretty Things Press) and *slave* (Venus). She would like people to know that her name is pronounced like "air," not like "ay-ree."

THOMAS ROCHE has written more than 300 published short stories and 350 published articles for a wide array of anthologies, newspapers, print magazines, and websites. His work has appeared in the *Best American Erotica* series, the *Mammoth Book of Erotica* series, the *Best New Erotica* series, and the *Best Gay Erotica* series, among many other anthologies. He is also the editor of the *Noirotica* series of erotic crime-noir anthologies and can be found online at www.skidroche.com.

ERIN SANDERS enjoys writing about her sensual explorations almost as much as engaging in them. Her work has previously appeared in *Master/slave*, edited by N.T. Morley (Venus Book Club). She lives in Southern California with a man she calls "Master"—even when they're not in the bedroom.

DONNA GEORGE STOREY lives in northern California with her husband and two sons. Her fiction has appeared in *Clean*

Sheets, In Posse Review, Rain Crow, and *Grunt and Groan: The New Fiction Anthology of Work and Sex.*

Newly transplanted to Southern California, D.C. native **SIMON TORRIO** has written for the anthologies *MASTER* and *Sweet Life 2*. He is currently at work on a detective novel.

ALISON TYLER has been writing erotica for more than a decade. She is the author of eighteen sexy novels, including *Learning to Love It, Strictly Confidential, Sweet Thing, Sticky Fingers,* and *Something About Workmen* (all published by Black Lace Books). Her short stories have appeared in *Sweet Life 1* and *2, Wicked Words 4, 5, 6* and *8, Best Women's Erotica 2002* and *2003, Guilty Pleasures,* and *Playgirl* magazine. She is the editor of *Best Bondage Erotica* and *Heat Wave* (both from Cleis Press). Ms. Tyler is the executive editor of Pretty Things Press (www.p rettythingspress.com).

SASKIA WALKER is English and lives the life of a benevolent shrew on the windswept landscape of the Yorkshire moors. Saskia has a BA in Art History, a Masters degree in Literature, and writes across several genres. Creative writing has always been part of her life but has become more important as time has passed, drawing her away from all manner of bizarre careers. Her partner, Mark, is just as naughty and eccentric as she is, but somehow manages to keep her sane and grounded when fiction threatens to take over. Visitors are welcomed at www.saskiawalker.co.uk.

OSCAR WILLIAMS lives in the Central Valley of California with his wife and their dogs. His work has appeared in the anthology *MASTER*. His current projects include an erotic novelette about circus clowns and a screenplay about hot air ballooning.

About the Editor

VIOLET BLUE is senior copywriter at Good Vibrations where she writes book and video reviews, which has her watching an awful lot of porn and reading virtually everything imaginable written about sex. She is a sex columnist and a sex educator, and was the founding editor of *Good Vibrations* magazine. She is the editor of *Sweet Life* and *Sweet Life 2,* and the author of four books, *The Ultimate Guide to Sexual Fantasy, The Ultimate Guide to Cunnilingus, The Ultimate Guide to Fellatio,* and *The Ultimate Guide to Adult Videos*. When not thinking about, writing about, or having sex, she spends her time turning a wrench in the world of mechanical art and robotics as a member of Survival Research Laboratories. Or sipping delicious inebriants from the belly button of a squirming lover. Visit her website, www.tinynibbles.com.